STAMPED: Excess Baggage

STAMPED:
Excess Baggage
Tale of an Illegal Immigrant

Alan McDonald

iUniverse, Inc.

New York   Bloomington

Stamped: Excess Baggage
Tale of an Illegal Immigrant

iUniverse books may be ordered through booksellers or by contacting:

iUniverse
1663 Liberty Drive
Bloomington, IN 47403
www.iuniverse.com
1-800-Authors (1-800-288-4677)

ISBN: 978-1-4502-3676-8 (sc)
ISBN: 978-1-4502-3677-5 (ebk)

Library of Congress Control Number: 2010908427

Printed in the United States of America

iUniverse rev. date: 06/11/2010

*A*s I am sitting in a recliner, staring out at the lights of the city, I ponder about the events that have shaped my life. I am sitting in the dark again, reflecting on my life as I have done for so many times over the years......... Sitting in the dark, thinking about that darkness, thinking about the darkness in that mine tunnel when I was five years old. That total absence of light when Norm and his partner left me there. They handed me a carbide lamp and said "Stay here, Alan. We will be back in a few minutes." They had no sooner disappeared down the portal and my lamp went out. My first thought had been to rekindle the lamp, but I was only five years old and had no idea how to do it. Many years later I discovered that my hand was too small to cover the reflector to trap the gas from the carbide, much less move the striker. Unless you have experienced it, you cannot relate to the darkness in a mine tunnel. You cannot see your hand in front of your face until it touches you.

I sat there in the darkness of that mine with my imagination running wild. My first fear was of snakes. Could they see me in the dark or could they just sense that I was there? I was certain that any snake's primary goal in life was to bite ME. I was terrified that at any moment I would feel their fangs sink into my flesh, after which I would die some horrible agonizing death. From that day forward, or more accurately, should I say, total darkness forward, I was never to be afraid of the dark again. I instinctively knew the darkness was my friend and I was a survivor. In essence, this was the beginning of the end of my childhood, but future happenings would seal *the fate of any remnant of the child in me. It is in that survivor mode that I want to take you back to the past...back to the time when my story really began...back to my ancestry and the cheese factory story...back to the symbol, in my mind's eye, of good and evil.*

I know where it all began; I know all the highs and lows. I have heard the whole story dating back to the early years even before my grandfather started the cheese factory. My grandfather's dream for the future was that the family would achieve a measure of success, a place where they would not have to work as hard as he had in his early years. I always listened intently when stories were told about Grandpa George and Grandmum Winifred. I didn't care how many times I heard the stories; I would listen to them again and again, until I could quote them verbatim. I believe that these stories gave me some sense of family...some sense of belonging and roots.

I look out into the night sky filled with stars and try to imagine what George and Winifred had thought about as they looked up in the sky. It doesn't seem possible that the same sky was everywhere in space and time. Winifred's stars happily blinking down on the sheep of her own farm

in Scotland... why would it not be the same ones that she and George saw together as they raised their family and built their dreams in Australia? George and Winifred were young and as much in love as was possible for any young couple regardless of the era or their status in life.

Chapter 1

D awn warmed the dark night skies as these British shepherds
called their flocks to the water's edge and onto the last ship
slated for the colony in Australia. Winifred carried everything they
were allowed to take with them in two large satchels. Her walk was
slow and labored as she tried to balance herself between the heavy bags.
It didn't help that she was wearing three layers of clothing. Clothing
that wouldn't fit into the bags had to be worn or left behind. They were
emigrating from Scotland Australia at the tail end of the ethnic clearing
that had occurred in Scotland. The British decided that they needed
more land for their sheep and the people had to go.

Sweat trickled down between Winnie's shoulder blades and had
begun to pool around the waist of her everyday shift. "No doubt it will
be soaking through tae outside soon enough," she half-muttered under
her breath. "Can you go on, Winifred?" her mother asked. "Perhaps
we should rest a few moments. We have two hours before the ship is
supposed to sail."

"I'm still able tae go on, Mother. I would like to hae everything
settled in our berth and be back up on deck before we sail." Carefully
picking a path through the street was made infinitely more difficult
with her mother hanging on to her left elbow and banging into the
heavy bag in her left arm at every step. Winifred gripped tighter as
they turned the corner. Her head snapped up and they did have to stop.

Mother crashed into the bag and out it flew, into the street ahead of them. "Oh my God!" The curse was out of her mouth before she or her mother could stop it. The hordes of people reminded her of the salmon run. In the spring of the year, Winifred loved to go to the streams and watch the salmon.

She loved watching the salmon, covered in foam, as they arched their way upwards, a wide, writhing mass of silver and black with a few bright patches of color. She always felt sorry for the salmon caught during the spawning, even though she could not allow her feelings to interfere with the family's food source. She quickly yanked free of her mother's grip and lunged for the bag before it could be carried away in the surge of people - people who were her friends and neighbors – all moving toward the dock and the ship that would take them to the other side of the world.

Mildred said, "We'll have tae join the queue, Winifred. I see Mrs. Douglas and her children coming just now. We'll walk the rest of the way with them."

"Yes, Mum." What more could she say? She leaned down to pick up both bags and wait for her mother's death grip once again on her elbow.

It looked like a bizarre funeral procession moving through Dundee. Most of the women wore their "Sunday Best" as an outside layer of clothing. The winter gray dresses hung somewhere above the boot tops. Showing so much leg in public wasn't proper, but was overlooked even by Winifred's prudent mother given the circumstances. The few men leaving on this last voyage wore the kilts and tartans of their respective clans proudly, but the look on their faces was a mixture of defiance and resignation. Dark bonnets and hats bobbed together as the crowd pressed tighter to pass through the last bit of street and out onto the quay. Even the water in the Firth of Tay looked dark and cold today; whereas, before this, it had seemed to Winifred that the firth was full of life. It had somehow appeared warm with the life it carried to and from the great, cold North Sea. Winifred's heart was thudding and her sweat mixed with the salt from the sea that misted over them as they neared the edge of the land that had been their home. She felt the slight tremble and slowed a bit as her mother stepped off the curb with her to join the Douglas family and the others who were moving, like the salmon, up the street. Winifred dared glance at her mother and saw her chin go up and her shoulders square resolutely. She could see the grim determination in her mother's face mirrored in the faces of those around them. Mother had made up her mind that this way was the only way; the best possible solution to a horrific problem foisted on them by the British.

At only five feet two inches tall, Winifred couldn't tell how close they were to the end of the road. Elbows and shoulders padded with extra layers of wool and tweed jostled and pushed them in the direction of the docks. Winnie couldn't have stopped now even if she wanted to. A melody swirled over their heads, drawing them closer. The crowd loosened and spread out as they spilled out over the cobblestones onto the wider expanse of the docks. Mother was actually humming quietly as they found a small space to stop and set the luggage down. For the first time since they had left the boundaries of their land, Winnie was able to draw a breath and look around her. She was surprised to see such a large military presence. The British soldiers had recruited some obviously unwilling volunteers from the local police force to make sure the ship set sail smoothly. This was the Brit's show; they had paid the passage for the entire boatload of Scots; and, with this last group, the process for loading and stowing was accomplished nearly by rote.

The band was set up in front of Old Malcolm's Fish Shoppe windows. A smile crept over Winnie's face, momentarily creasing her work-reddened cheeks as she noted with great satisfaction that the British section of the band had been seated squarely on top of the grate into which Old Malcolm threw out the guts and rejects from the day's catch. Try as they might, those dastardly Brits could not hold their breath and play at the same time. While they gasped, Winnie's kinsmen took every opportunity to play yet another traditional Highland air in an attempt to make the impending departure a true "Bon Voyage". The only common threads among the band members were the black coarse ones that held the brass buttons on their uniforms.

The British soldiers in the band, as well as those other Brits striding around trying to look important, were all of one mind and that was clear, "Get the bloody Scots the hell out of here as quickly as possible." Winifred and her mother were propelled forward as the band struck up a rousing march.

British soldiers started to usher a new wave of landed passengers towards the gangplank where their names were checked and they became the responsibility of the soldiers aboard ship. Of course, the size of the crew had been greatly augmented for this historic voyage. The Crown spared little expense for implementing their "Great Plan". The poor Scots who had "agreed" to leave their land were herded together like the very sheep that would replace them on their land. Winifred remained silent, with her head down and her tongue clenched firmly between her teeth, allowing her mother to speak in their behalf to the soldier stationed at the bottom of the gangway.

"Winifred Gunn and Mildred Gunn? You are to bunk together in steerage with the other women and children. Please stow your valises under the bunks as soon as possible. One of the men should be there to lash everything down for the voyage before we ship out or shortly thereafter. Please ensure all personal items needed during the voyage are on top so that you can reach them without untying the lashings. We would hate to have to take any of the sailors away from more important duties in order to take care of ladies' personal requests. Please take these numbers with you as you board and you will be directed to your berth. Next!" He said as he stamped their paper and without looking up, holding them out toward Mildred.

Winifred hefted the bags again and waited for mother's fingers to dig into her upper arm. She was sure to have five permanent indentations in her arm before the journey's end.

"Can you make it, Mum, or should I take the luggage up and come back for you?"

"Don't worry about me, lass. I will be right here beside you this entire voyage. Our dreams for your future are finally going to come true." With her boot heels clicking a slow but recognizable version of their own clan's traditional reel, Mildred lifted her skirts another brazen half-inch and danced on to the deck. Winifred dutifully started to follow behind her mother. This time, the sigh that echoed through her small frame was as much from fatigue as it was from an overwhelming sense of loss and what she thought was to come. When she began the steep climb, she realized where she was and what it meant to her. The last of her sigh became a deep shudder of uneasiness.

The ship itself was the largest Winifred had ever seen. Ships rarely entered her consciousness as she worked the fields and livestock on her family's land. The highest deck was the bridge amidships; it loomed above them and made Winnie feel even smaller than she was. The bridge was seven decks above the water line, but it appeared to go on forever. Behind the bridge one deck below was the stack that went inside the vessel to the coal-fired boiler sending black smoke into the clear cold blue sky. The mast with its jumble of cables controlled the large loading derricks. Just ahead of the mast lay the forecastle where some of the crew was stationed along with the anchor and chain. The machine shop was also located here; its services vital to the ship because, at sea, there are no repair stations. Located behind the bridge, with direct access to the wheelhouse, lay the Captain's Quarters. One deck down and behind the Captain's Quarters was the galley...a popular spot for everyone. As her eyes moved over the ship's vast structure, she could only guess where her quarters would be located in the huge mass of steel, smoke, and cables. Behind the galley, the decks seemed to drop straight down to another deck with a large square hole in the middle. This was the aft deck and the aft cargo bay, which had been transformed into sleeping quarters for the men on this voyage. Beyond the cargo bay was the same configuration... mast and derricks, and the aft castle with the alternate steering station, from which the name steerage is derived. Below the steering station, two decks below were the steerage accommodations, if you could call them that. It was a large room with multiple bunks, stacked three high, with barely room for a body to squeeze between the straps that held each bunk that sagged in the middle. Winifred looked over her shoulder and back to the Dundee she had known all of her life. Her countrymen had moved to the water's edge to play every song they knew in the short time remaining before the final whistle sounded for departure.

"Please hurry, Mum. I want tae set these things down and get back tae the rail before we sail. I need tae see our land for as long as possible so I can carry it in my mind forever." Heads down, they moved as quickly as their "land legs" could carry them toward their berth.

"Wait Mother, I'll go ahead of you down the ladder." That would be the end, wouldn't it? To come this far and see her mother pitch down the hole into the bowels of the ship and break her neck before they even left the harbor. "I'll just take the bags down and come back up for you. Please, please, wait right here for me, I beg you." Her face, set with dogged determination, shone through the salty mist of sea and perspiration as Winifred stuffed the bags into the mouth of what looked like a bottomless pit and struggled to hold the ladder at the same time. With each labored step, she fought to keep her grip on their possessions and the ladder. She concentrated on the rungs in front of her face, not daring to look away for even a second to catch a glimpse of what would become their home away from home for the time at sea.

After what seemed to be an eternity, she reached the bottom. Gratefully, she leaned her forehead against the splintered ladder and breathed in the stale air of the below-decks. She still had the luggage in her hands and awkwardly turned around to survey her berth. Dim light from the few oil lamps that swung from the rafters cast eerie shadows about the women's area. Already a few of the women had set up housekeeping to make use of the time before the ship sailed. Fresh herbs, flowers, and grasses were hanging from the walls and bunks were tied with gaily-colored ribbons. Bunks had been made up with clean bright quilts and crisp muslin sheets. The stagnant air below-decks was faintly flavored with the perfume of clean Scottish sunshine and wildflowers.

"Winifred!" Her mother's muffled cry came from the darkness above.

"I'm on my way back up tae you, Mum. Give me but a moment to set down our things." For only the third time since dawn, Winifred released her grip on their worldly possessions. She moved the bags to the right side of the ladder.

"Now which is it? Starboard or Port? They cannae say gee and haw like everybody else and make it easy, could they?" she thought as the rustling of petticoats above sent Winifred scurrying back up the ladder to her mother.

"Wait for me, please, Mum. I'll nae see you dropping down into this hole like a stupid sheep who knows nae better."

Winifred reached her mother in time to direct one small boot onto the next rung. This had been a long and tiresome day for everyone, no matter how stouthearted or determined they might appear on the surface. Together, they slowly descended to the bottom. Winifred watched her mother's face as she scanned the room.

Mother's eyes narrowed, her mouth tightened, and one hand fluttered toward her chest before she was able to gain her composure.

"Well lass, I guess we'll claim these empty bunks here for our own. Come along now, so we can tidy up before we're away." Mother quickly unpinned her hat and laid it on her new "bed". She spun around to take one of the bags from Winifred. "Our sheets and quilts would add their own comforting scent of home and would mix well with the others."

"Cannae you unbutton my dress as soon as I've got my coat off? I want tae take at least two of these dresses off and put them away with our other things." Winifred's fingers trembled with fatigue as she unbuttoned her own coat and unpinned her hat. She lay the coat and hat on the bed so that she could put them right back on again, after peeling off several layers of woolen clothing that was stifling her in the closeness of their berth.

"Is it nae a comfort tae know that we will be taking a part of the land with us tae our new home, Winifred?"

"Yes, Mum. It was four years ago now that we sheared the sheep, carded the wool and spun it for this dress. I must admit I really like the packets of dye we purchased for this cloth. There are such pretty shades of color in the store that we cannae get by boiling our own. I wonder if they use wool in Australia. From what we've heard, there's verra little call for heavy woolens. Tell me again about what you heard from Mrs. Douglas' niece. I cannae imagine any temperature where you'd only wear light cotton every day. Did Mrs. Douglas' niece really say that she had put all of her best dresses into mothballs?" For the next half an hour, Mother slowly and carefully repeated what Mrs. Douglas had read to her from her niece's letters. She had described a land that was scorching hot, filled with dust and flies, and vast empty spaces. Winifred and her mother worked quickly to get everything shipshape so they could get back up topside to wave at the family and friends who were left behind. Winifred was trying not to think about the beautiful little house, the sheep and the rolling green hills that had been her only home. She had steeled herself to avoid any tears. They had been given no real choice, the "Clearing" was happening whether they liked it or not. Before you could barely blink an eye, here they were buttoning their coats back up and pinning on their hats before climbing the ladder up to the rail for a long, last farewell. Winifred climbed behind her mother again. She prayed she would not have to break her mother's fall. "Be careful now, Mum. You're nae yet used to the motion of the ship. We'll huv tae practice our walking a bit tae get comfortable." In her mind Winifred saw spring lambs, their legs a wobble trying to navigate some of the rocky hillsides for the first time. "Baaaaa," she said, under her breath.

"What was that, darling?"

"Nothing, Mum. We're almost there. Just a couple more steps." The feel of sea air on their faces was as delicious and cool as a field fresh with morning dew even after the short time below. They had to shield their eyes with their hands a moment to allow their eyes to become accustomed to the daylight again. Bells and whistles sounded and men were rushing and hollering for everyone to either get to the rail and stay there or go below. The King's sailors had no time for these Scotsmen and women. They felt it far beneath them, indeed, to have to be civil to a group of people who had been decreed by the King himself as less worthy than sheep. Winifred was a young woman, barely eighteen. In all of her young life, she had never felt like this before. There were a few young "ladies" in town who were taught to have the "vapours" should they ever fear feeling anything unpleasant. "I should be havin' a lie-down right now," thought Winnie. She couldn't begin to define the overwhelming emotions churning from her head down into her stomach. With both hands she grabbed on to the brass rail and held on for dear life. She had to close her eyes for a moment and swallow down the familiar, sweet tea they had drunk for the last time in their little home that morning. The familiar taste turned bitter and she swallowed again. She opened her eyes and straightened her spine. "I will survive. I dinnae ken what our future holds, but I cannae fear what I do nae yet know. We will work each day as it comes tae us and we will live our good lives." Winnie didn't realize she had spoken aloud until her mother's hand gripped hers on the rail. With tears in her eyes, she echoed her daughter's words. "We will live our good lives."

Chapter 2

Mother and daughter stood together as the lives they had known forever faded away. Australia seemed so far away but they could sense it drawing them away from their own good Scotland. Most of their friends and neighbors seemed to be of a similar mind. Men, women, and children milled about the deck in small clusters. No one wanted to leave the rail before his beloved land was out of sight. Of course, there were also those who couldn't leave the rail. The aft portion of the deck was dotted with those miserable souls who were not having an easy acclimation to the rolling motion of the boat at sea. A few of the indisposed had loved ones near who tried to shield their pale, embarrassed faces from the others. There were others who had to suffer this shame on their own.

Winifred and Mildred were not ones to have idle hands.

Mildred said, "Roll up your sleeves, darlin'. I'll go below for some water and rags. We can be of some help to these poor unfortunates." Obviously, Mildred wasn't going to allow the strange movement of the ship to affect her in any way when there was work to be done. Winifred scanned the wretched forms doubled up over the ship's side. She spied one young man who tried so hard not to appear seasick. He would stand up straight, his back rigid with pride, only to crumple in another violent spasm of nausea. Winifred had decided to make her way to his side when her mother put the same morning's death grip on her arm. She winced in pain as her mother steered her to the side of a young and miserable pregnant woman and her equally young and miserable husband. "Elizabeth!" They both croaked as three children, who were clearly unaffected by the ship's motion, scampered by them. They were running pell-mell up and down the length of the deck, while the poor couple could only attempt to comfort each other. Mildred had already made up her mind that she and her daughter would be the angels of mercy sent by God himself to rescue and comfort all. With just one sharp look from her, all three of the children came to a halt in front of her, mouths agape and eyes wide with the terror of children who know they are about to be scolded. Even though Elizabeth was only nine, she pushed her older and younger brother behind her before attempting a shy smile for Mildred and Winifred. Then she rattled off an explanation without even taking a breath. "We haven't even fallen off the boat yet, so you see we're just fine and don't trouble yourself to think up a punishment because we didn't do a thing yet, thank you very much, mum." Winifred had to turn away before she laughed aloud. Elizabeth's parents groaned, in unison, and tried to beg forgiveness for the impertinence. Mildred waved them quiet. She knelt down to minister to the stricken parents and motioned to the three children. "I'm verra glad you hae nae fallen overboard. T'would be a shame tae have tae leave you way out in the ocean all by yourselves to swim with the fishes. Even though the fishes swim in schools, they aren't too smart about human children and perhaps you would get hurt. I do know you can see your parents are nae feeling well and they dinnae need tae worry about the likes of you falling off the ship. We need to think about what you can do to ease their minds while my Winnie and I try to make them feel better." Silence greeted her. All three heads turned toward Winnie to see if she had anything to add. Winnie sat on the deck and reached for one of the ribbons tied on Elizabeth's pigtails. "What do you do when you're at home? Do you have sheep on your farm?"

"I'm Thomas, I'm three, and I dinnae huv sheep nae more. All our sheeps and our farm went tae the Englishes. They made us go on this big boat but I wanted to, anyway. I know we'll find new sheeps on our new farm in 'Tralia. My Daddy knows how tae get the best sheeps."

"And we'll get a new dog when we get there, too." Michael piped up.

"Oh, Michael!" Slowly his father reached for Michael to draw him closer. Michael shrugged away from him. With soulful eyes, Michael was trying to keep a stiff upper lip. He was ten years old, early a man, anybody knows that. Losing an old sheep dog wasn't going to make him cry like a baby.

Winnie could feel the tears rising to her own eyes as she ruffled the brave little boy's hair. She took the hair ribbon and looped it around Thomas' wrist. "We cannae brand you as we do the sheep at home, so we'll use this ribbon tae show that Thomas is the sheep. Michael, you'll need tae show us what a good herding dog can do. Elizabeth will be the shepherdess. Our past is yesterday now, and our future is today and tomorrow. We'll need tae use what we've learned tae survive in the future. Michael, you know how it's done. Now get along with you, but stay near so we can see you. You'll need tae work together tae make a good show of it. As soon as you've gone down and back once, we'll change our jobs around again." With a chorus of bleats and barks, the trio scampered off, past smiling adults who had stopped to listen.

Mildred wrung out a rag and smoothed it over the pregnant woman's forehead. "Now, dinnae you worry; they'll be fine. My Winifred will look after them until you're feeling better."

Winifred knew better than to argue with her mother. She looked for the children and saw them herding happily in the sunshine. The cuts that the Michael dog made were quite skillful, even though the shepherdess didn't always order them and the Thomas sheep didn't always follow them.

As Winifred's gaze traveled back along the deck, her heart skipped a beat. Huge, brown eyes, with as mournful an expression as any dog's, followed her path from the rail. A nervous glance at her mother tending to the sick allowed Winnie a second of freedom to return the gaze of the young man her mother had skillfully steered her away from earlier. Winifred was not easily swayed by emotion; life was something that existed because nature dictates what will happen next. She couldn't allow emotion to cloud her judgment, to overrule the simple necessity of what had to, by nature's dictate, happen next. One look was all it took to completely change Winifred's life forever. The future was not going to merely happen with her blindly following on. This young man would mold Winifred's future of her life, love and all of her being. She averted her eyes for a moment while he slumped over the rail for perhaps the millionth time.

George, the young man who attracted Winnie's attention, wasn't much of a seaman and spent most of his time hanging on the rail. After the fourth day at sea, it appeared he would not make the crossing in any comfort. He was at his usual spot on the port side rail, when he first heard an angel. He was not certain, but he decided that the voice must belong to his guardian angel.

"Do you nae feel well?" the angel asked. She was standing behind him and he was afraid to turn to see who had asked the question for fear of vomiting on the deck and whoever was there. "I ken an old remedy that would give you a better time of it. If you want, I will go and fetch it from my bag in steerage."

All George could do was nod his head to let her know that he needed the remedy more than anything he could imagine. He didn't know how long she was gone because he wasn't able to leave the rail to see if she had gone or not. "Drink this and you will feel much better," said the angel's voice. George could hardly hold up his head, but he managed to drink some of the remedy. It tasted as though it had been concocted out of the foulest-smelling, unmentionable, sheep-pasture leftovers. First he was sick and now he was poisoned...He couldn't believe he was going to survive this ordeal. It took about ten minutes for the remedy to work; possibly the worst ten minutes of his life. Then he began to feel a little better and, as time went on, he actually began to feel good. He barely remembered how wonderful "plain old good" felt.

With one passing glance over her shoulder to the children and her mother, Winifred firmly turned toward the person who she knew would command her future. "I'm Winifred. Very pleased to make your acquaintance."

"I'm George and I am forever in your debt. I believe that I owe you my life in return for the kindness you hae shown me." He laid his hand at the small of her back and drew her to his side. Winifred instinctively knew she would be happy to spend the rest of her life right there. Her thoughts raced and she felt dizzy and weak. She leaned on the rail to steady herself.

A rush of wind past her ear startled her and the angry little fist that narrowly missed her ear connected with George's left temple. As weak as he was, that was all it took to send him crashing to the deck. George and Winifred saw the white-hot rage of a mother protecting her only daughter.

Mildred's fist was inches above poor George's face as she delivered her message. "My daughter has a life planned for her when we arrive. You'll nae interfere with me, neither with those plans, nor with her ever again. I hope you understand these words as this is the only time I expect tae ever have tae say them!"

Elizabeth, Michael, and Thomas stopped in their tracks and watched as Winifred was dragged away by her ear and over to the ladder. George, still sprawled on the deck, could only stare after them. The three children made silent but solemn oaths not to ever cross Mildred. Winifred went along with her mother merely to avoid causing a scene. Her heart had already sent a message to her brain and nothing her mother could do or say would change that. Even after the initial dust-up and, in spite of Mildred's rather graphic warning, George and Winifred were never too far from each other for the rest of the trip. True to form, Winifred's mother would always be within shouting distance of them. "Winnie, you ken that when we get tae the colonies, your promised will be there waiting and you will huv tae tell your seasick patient good-bye."

"I dinnae think so, Mum; you are verra aware I never cared for this arrangement you set. If I marry George before we arrive, my supposed promised, Jack is it? will have to find another bride from this lot on board."

"Jack will nae hear anything of what you are saying. We can wait until we get tae Sydney and your new husband, Jack, will work something out."

"I dinnae want tae work anything out with Jack. He does'na have any title to me; I dinnae agree tae this arrangement you and his mother made." Winifred stormed out of the barracks-like quarters of steerage and went to find George. He spent most of his time, when not with Winifred, on deck. He needed the fresh air to maintain his road to recovery. The first days of the voyage had rendered him to a mere shadow of himself. He had lost substantial weight and he appeared to be mostly skin stretched over a six-foot skeleton. He had gained some of his weight and was beginning to gain strength, but still had to remain on deck where the wind would cool and aerate his body.

For the most part, men were billeted on deck, while the women were quartered in steerage. The majority of the ships used to transport immigrants were old cargo vessels not built with passenger accommodations in mind.

"George, I huv an idea."

"What is it?"

"You love me, dinnae you?" Now, what was George to say? Of course he did, with all his heart. George had never known anyone like her and couldn't even imagine life without her.

"Well, you do! Didnae you?" Winnie stamped her little foot and stood with her hands firmly placed on her narrow waist staring up into his blank face.

"Yes, of course I do! I could nae love anyone else or even think of being with anyone else."

"George, I huv something tae tell you. Please didnae say anything until I have finished." Winifred began her story to George, from the point where she had lived most of her young life, just outside of Edinburgh.

She explained that she was a farm girl and knew about sheep and the farming skills needed in the colonies. She had been promised to a Jack Carrigan by her mother and was on her way to marry him against her will. She didn't know this Jack Carrigan and had only seen a picture of him. She felt no financial obligation to him, because the British were paying for her passage, just like all the others on board. Jack was doing well in the colonies, mainly because he was a "Brit" and had an advantage over the Scots who were sent to the Colonies. Some of the Scots and the Irish were sent to the colonies in America; while still others were sent to the colonies in Australia. The Brits in the colonies had some say about where they were sent. Jack had first seen Winifred in a photo that his brother had shown him when he was last in Edinburgh. Jack immediately fell in love with the girl in the photo and wanted her for his bride. She was not yet aware of the possessiveness that dominated Jack's being. So she said, "I dinnae love Jack Carrigan! I love you and I want tae marry you."

This was all George needed to hear; he had agonized for days about how he was going to ask her that very same question. "Winnie, t'would make me the happiest man in the world. I believe the captain could marry us, but we huv tae see him today! I heard others say that we will be docking tomorrow evening."

"Oh, George, that would be wonderful! We could start a new life in…Oh, I dinnae even ken where you are scheduled to go."

"Kyabrum," George said in an uncertain manner.

Winifred couldn't believe what she heard. That was where she was slated to go, but that was also where Jack was.

"Kyabram! I hae a job at a sheep station, but I hope tae start my own business someday…a cheese factory," George stated more firmly this time.

Winifred had never looked much beyond the physical bodies of the sheep she tended. They were raised for wool or for food. Not many of the sheep in her area were used primarily for dairy products. The added expense in fodder alone kept most of them away from milking. They had milk and made butter and cheese from the few ewes they kept close to the house. Winnie had never entertained the thought of cheese on such a grand scale.

As they walked, George explained the second part of his dream to her. He told her of the cattle that were in Australia and his dream to acquire land after he served his commitment to his sponsor. Land was inexpensive. The Crown wanted more farms and stations to be developed for the tax revenue they would generate. This policy made obtaining land after completing the commitment relatively easy. The low price of land would give him more toward the purchase of the cattle for the milk to produce the cheese. "Mind you, I'll huv tae work verra hard for quite a while to save the seed money for my place. I hope tae find someone I can trust tae partner with before I'm too old tae work it well."

"You keep talking about the cheese factory as the 'second' part of your dream. Hae you told me the first part yet? I'm sure I would hae remembered."

They turned down a narrow hallway and George stopped, turning Winnie to him. The smile that lit up his face alarmed her. Had he been drinking before they met on deck this evening? "You are the first and most important part of my dream. I could'na hae imagined I would be as lucky tae huv the love of such a one as you." He held her close and kissed her with the tenderness and love that she would carry with her for the rest of her life and beyond.

They found the First Mate and requested an interview with the Captain. The First Mate knew what the interview was about for he had watched them together for the entire voyage and was certain why they wanted to see the Captain. He stepped past them and knocked at the Captain's door.

"Come in," boomed a loud voice. The door swung open, exposing a large man with a red face that had weathered many years at sea. He was dressed in a double-breasted, blue captain's coat with cream-colored pants and black shoes.

"So you think you want to be married. Do you understand all the responsibilities of that undertaking?"

"Yes, sir, we do," answered George. He was somewhat intimidated by the forceful Captain.

Winifred knew everything would be fine when the Captain smiled and asked, "Do you have a ring?"

"Uh, uh, no! We don't," George and Winifred stuttered in unison.

"Well, maybe this will do until you have one," he answered as he pulled a small gold band from his own right hand. They later learned that it was the Captain's own departed wife's ring and he had been saving it for an occasion such as this. "Do you have a witness? No matter! Mister Hardy will be more than happy to be a witness, won't you?"

"Yes, Sir! It would be my pleasure," answered the First Mate. He had kept the Captain informed of the progress of the shipboard romance.

"Now, young lady, you realize that once I marry you to this scruffy chap, there's no turning back?"

"Oh, yes, I do!" Winnie exclaimed and the thought that she was semi-promised to another man didn't enter her mind. Truth be told, she didn't think twice about whether her mother would be disappointed to miss the wedding. This ceremony was for them alone. If her mother wanted another to celebrate with friends, she could plan for it after they arrived. The gold band slipped onto Winifred's finger as though it had been made especially for her. It wasn't until Captain had pronounced them man and wife that she felt the first little twinge of fear. She wasn't afraid of George, even though they had known each other such a short period of time. They knew each other well enough to know they were destined to share a long and happy life together.

No, the little twinge she felt was fear of Jack Carrigan. She didn't know him, but from what she had heard, he was accustomed to having his own way. Her arrival in Sydney as another man's wife was not something that would make Jack Carrigan happy. That fear vanished when George took her face in his hands and kissed his bride. Tears of absolute joy sprang from her eyes and George kissed the tears away. He kissed her salty lashes, her soft cheeks, and her pink lips!

"Ahem! I realize a man and his wife need a bit of privacy," the Captain interrupted. Blushing, Winnie stepped back from her new husband. George wouldn't let go of her trembling hands and, after a tiny tug; she listened expectantly to what the Captain had to say. The Captain crushed them both to his huge chest in a fatherly hug, brass buttons and all. "I can't offer you the privacy of a stateroom, but Mister Hardy can tell you about some quiet spots on the ship that I'm not supposed to know about." He hugged them close once more and added, "May you come to know the kind of love my wife and I had. That is the most sincere blessing I can give you." He let them go and straightened his tunic. Winifred feared for a moment that he would pat them both on the head and offer them a sweet. "Good luck to you both, tonight and always," he laughed, as Mister Hardy opened the door for them. George swept her up into his arms and followed Mister Hardy down the quiet hallway.

"Pinch me, George," Winnie whispered.

"What are you talking about?" George was startled.

"If this is nothing but a dream, I huv tae know now".

With delicate, new-husband courage, he gave her the pinch she had asked for, but on her bottom. She stifled her giggles in his neck as they continued after the First Mate. True to his nature, he pretended not to hear whatever 'unofficial' monkey business was going on. He was eager to display his handiwork. Already warning the crew that this special spot would be off-limits for the evening, they would have to find another place to steal an on-duty catnap. He led them to a cozy nest he had prepared under the stacks amidships. A pallet made up with one of his grandmother's quilts was hidden in the darkened crawl space. They carried no flowers aboard ship, so he had pinched a few sprigs of mint, chamomile, and other dried herbs from the galley. The cook had also contributed a flask of sherry for the occasion. Winifred bowed her head, trying to thank him for all he had done. The blushing color was creeping up to her face again. George set her down, but didn't let go of her as he shook hands with their benefactor.

"No thanks are needed. Just doing my job." He saluted and was gone before they could say anything else.

"I know this cannae be what you expected for a bridal bed but..."

"Sssh! As long as my husband approves, I shan't complain." It was suddenly too much for her and she collapsed into a fit of giggles again.

She had engaged in the normal girlish flirting and banter with the boys back home, but never thought of the actual wedding night. Even farm girls have trouble equating the activities of the animals on the farm to the human mating process. The combination of herbs emitted a pungent aroma so that the smell of fish, brine, and oil were hardly noticeable. At least, Winifred didn't notice. Everything was warm and wonderful and made perfect by the fact that she was with the man she truly loved. The rocking movement of the ship didn't seem to bother George in the least as he began kissing his wife's hair, her cheek, and her neck down to where the sea of buttons began at her throat. Winifred spied the tiniest glint of gold in the dim light as she helped her husband to unbutton her dress. She was amazed at the energy and resolve that one plain gold band had already given her. As she finished with the last button, she looked up to realize George was almost unclothed himself. In the dim light, she wasn't embarrassed to see him or to have him see her. They were nothing more than shadows, creating a new dance born of passion and trust. Winifred felt her own heart beating and when George pulled her to him in his best imitation of the Captain's manly embrace, she could feel his heart beating in time with hers. The heat from his chest as it crushed into her naked breasts astonished her. Her mind began to reel as she intertwined each part of her body with that of her husband. Her mother hadn't tried to explain the love act when she asked. Wisely, she had told Winifred that when she experienced it for herself, she would find her own definition. George's hand returned again to the small of her back as he pulled her to him. Winifred couldn't tell where the throbbing of the ship's engines ended and their own passion began.

She felt the muscles in his shoulders and then slid her hands down his back. This time it was she who placed both hands on the small of his back and pulled him to her. George whispered to her, but she didn't try to discern the words. She understood the meaning of love as his body described it to her. Every unintelligible whisper, every time his lips brushed her body, every caress gave Winifred a deeper understanding of true love. The rhythm of the ship played a kind of harmony to their movements, culminating in a breathtaking finale.

George and Winifred spent the night on deck in the warm embrace of the Indian Ocean and each other, speaking the language that only two people in love can understand... their amazing love, their hopes and dreams, and their plans for the future, all went unsaid, but understood. Winifred took the ring from her finger and tied a ribbon to fashion a necklace, not wanting to show her marriage until the time of her choosing. George watched and said nothing for he trusted she would explain if he asked, but thought better not too.

Chapter 3

Sydney Harbor was a bustling seaport and the docking process lasted longer than anyone expected. Clearing customs seemed to take forever and the fact that George and Winifred had been married did not make the clearance process any easier. The customs official did not seem to care about his job and he especially didn't care for the Scots. It was evident that he felt Australia would be better off if immigration was limited to the Brits; this was the feeling shared by most Brits who were appalled by the whole "clearing" concept. George and Winnie were finally able to breathe sighs of relief when they made it through the ordeal. Winifred's mother had paid no attention to the reason for the delay; she was worried sick because Jack had not arrived. She still was of a mind that Winifred would give up her crazy notion about George. Of course, she lacked the knowledge that they had married. Then she discovered that Jack was not coming, but had sent a subordinate to meet up with them instead. George and Winifred still didn't say anything about the change to their status to her mother and they boarded different coaches for the five-day trip to Kyabram. Winifred wanted to keep their secret until they arrived in Kyabram. She thought it would be better to face Mildred and Jack after she saw how George's sponsor reacted to the change in his status. George didn't want to wait. He felt it would be better to confront them at once, but he conceded to her wishes.

Jack and Mildred were to be kept in the dark about the marriage; not that it mattered, as Jack had already secretly married a local girl. They did not know that Jack's plan was to have two women for himself. They did not know that Jack believed that he would be able to keep the two households separate, one in Stanhope and one in Kyabram. The five-mile distance between the two towns was adequate because travel for women in those days was limited within a small radius to the town where they lived. Jack was in for the surprise of his life and would never forgive Winifred for what he was about to find out.

George's coach, nothing more than a converted freight wagon with a tarp stretched over wooden bows and benches placed in the bed for seating, arrived several hours before Winifred's. The country surrounding the road seemed stark and alien from home. In comparison, Scotland's trees and meadows looked as though tended by gardeners; this was wild country. Some of the trees had gray peeling bark, lending them a ghostly look. In this inhospitable land, they were called ghost gums. They learned later that the aborigines believed that the ghosts of men who had died violent deaths and were unable to rest inhabited the trees.

Winnie was viewing the landscape with great interest... at the clumps of bushes; here and there, feathery wattle bloomed; she could smell its fragrance. Ever after when Winnie smelled that unusual haunting perfume, she was reminded of that drive. There was a strange grandeur about the landscape that appealed to her in some elemental way. But, there was a sameness about it that made her want to pick out landmarks as reference points, just in case one got lost.

There was a large contingent waiting for the travelers from Scotland to make their appearance. They eagerly watched for the arrival of old friends and relatives and were curious about the new workmen like George, although he had no friends or relatives to greet him. He would make his own way to the station where he was to work. Jack was waiting for Winifred with no idea that George and Winifred were married.

He greeted George in a friendly manner along with the other arrivals.

George realized the moment Jack introduced himself, he was the Jack Winnie had told him about. George felt a little uneasy shaking the hand of the man he had helped Winnie betray, even though he felt that there was no betrayal because it had been an arrangement that Winnie had no part. He looked at this man standing before him, with eyes that seemed to look beyond their conversation, hair black as the coal used to fire the ship boiler, and slicked back passing over his small ears and down the back of his narrow neck. He stood taller than he really was as if the puff up beyond his size to intimidate anyone around or before him. There was something very sinister about him, he always appeared to have an alternative reason for every thing he said or did.

After the men had exchanged greeting, Jack discovered though the station clerk the other coach, containing Winifred and Mildred, had a wheel problem and would not arrive until the next day.

George needed a place to stay until he could get out to the station to work as a sheep Shearer.

"Why don't you stay at the rooming house, as my treat, because I'm sure you're low on funds and you can pay me back when you can," Jack suggested. He knew that in the future George would need supplies and he thought it would be good business for George to shop at his store, rather than with his competitor. George reluctantly accepted, but he thought it would raise some concern from Jack if he refused, and so the two men decided to meet later for a drink at the local pub. George went to the rooming house with the invitation in hand, wondering what would take place when Winnie and Mildred arrived the next day. He thought about what they would talk about that evening and if he would be able to keep the secret, and if he would be able to find out what kind of man Jack really was.

When they met that night and began drinking at the pub, Jack proceeded to gather as much information about George and the others coming from the old country. He formed and placed his words with caution as not to alert George to his intension. George, too, was acquiring knowledge about Jack. He found that Jack had been in Australia for five

years and, due in large measure to his status as a Brit, he had gained
a prominent position in the community. He owned a mercantile store
and a livery stable, as well as some acreage in Stanhope. George didn't
realize he was also being plied for more information on the others and
thought Jack was just lonely for news from the old country. They drank
and talked long into the night and seemed on friendly terms. It became
late and George felt as he was losing his ability to conceal the one thing
he could not disclose, so he said, stumbling over his words. "I should be
getting on, because I will be going to the job in the morning and will
need to be rested and sober to start."

"I should be off too, because tomorrow the other coach will be in
and I've to meet someone," said Jack.

"Then, it's goodnight, Jack. I will see you tomorrow, because I
have to be back to meet my new bride when the coach arrives." George
managed to reply.

"I hope she is pretty as mine," mumbled Jack as he reeled out the
door on his way to the apartment he had constructed over his store.

George was up very early and walked the five miles out to the Station
House where he met Jacob Mallory, his new boss and sponsor. Jacob was
a small, thin man with bright red, wavy hair that shone in the sun as
though it were wet. His size was not a disadvantage for him because he
was strong and wiry about forty years old, and his face looked like leather
baked in the Australian sun for most of his forty years. He had come to
Australia when he was very young with his parents and worked with them
to build the Station. His family came from the south of England and had
linage too the Franks related to William the Conqueror.

"G'day, mate! And who might you be?" asked Jacob in a loud, high-
pitched voice.

"George McLean from Dundee. And who might you be?"

"I'm the bloody owner of this sheep station and I would guess you
would be the bloke I sponsored and who will be working for me for the
next two years to pay for the sponsorship," he said with a laugh, as they
shook hands in an immediate familiarity.

It seemed the Aussies respected men with George's apparent spunk and they felt that men who possessed that spunk would be good workers and honest, reliable men.

"Mister Mallory, I have some news for you that you might not appreciate; but here goes...on board ship I met a girl and we were wed. I know it's not covered in the contract we signed, but would it be possible to have her here with me?"

"So, you broke the bloody contract already, have you? I should have known a Scotsman couldn't be trusted."

George was dejected by Jacob's response. "You know you'd have to be in a larger place than we had agreed on; but, that's all right, my lad. I am the same; I could not be without me girl Jannis," Jacob said, with his eyes shining in approval. "When will she be here?"

"I'm told that since they had trouble on the road that it should be about noon," George said.

"Good, then we'll all go to meet her coach."

"I'm sorry, Mr. Mallory; but there's one other item."

"What now?"

"She has a mother."

"That's no problem! Can she cook? We just lost our cook to that scoundrel, Jack Carrigan."

"Jack! I met him last night and he seemed like a pleasant chap" said George, not wanting to show his true assessment of his encounter with Jack.

"You best watch him," cautioned Jacob.

This was George's second inkling that Jack might be less than he seemed. He took this warning deep within his subconscious, to have a better idea of what he was to be up against when Jack found that his intended was now George's wife. Jacob, Jannis, and George loaded into the wagon, hoping to be there before the coach arrived.

People were gathered at the hotel where the coaches stopped, waiting for the next arrival. Jacob stepped down and helped Jannis down; George jumped down and headed toward the hotel where everyone had gathered to greet the travelers. Someone shouted "Here it comes!" Everyone looked down the street to see the coach lumbering along. The coach still had a wobbly wheel; but, by some miracle, they had made the remainder of the trip.

Winifred was waving to George, but Jack thought she was waving to him. Mildred had found out about Winifred's marriage the night before, so she was certainly not happy. She thought it would be better for them both if Winifred married a man of stature, rather than a man who would work for two years before he could begin to gain the stature that Mildred wanted for her daughter.

The coach pulled up and both Jack and George went straight to Winifred. They were shoulder to shoulder when Winifred reached for George. Jack could not believe what was happening. "What are you doing? I sent for you and now you are with this man?"

"Jack, there was an arrangement between you and my mother, not me; the Crown paid for this trip, and we owe you nothing."

"I don't care! You belong to me and that's all there is to it!" Jack reached for her and felt George's hand on his arm. In the next instant, he was on the ground watching George, Winifred, and Mildred walk away.

"Look out George," Jacob yelled. Jack was running toward George with a knife in his hand. George turned just in the nick of time, catching the blade in his shoulder. Two other men grabbed Jack and held him. The constable appeared on the scene just as it was ending.

"What's going on here?" he asked.

"Nothing," responded George, hiding his small wound. The leather jacket he was wearing impeded most of the thrust and the constable didn't notice the small wound. They later discovered that the constable had witnessed the whole thing but would not have interfered because he owed Jack money. When the constable left, Jack turned to George, scornfully and said "I won't forget this! One day I will have revenge!"

"Don't threaten me with your revenge. I will not be intimidated by you or anyone like you!" George responded, heatedly.

"I would watch myself, immigrant, if I were you! You know it's my people, the British, who are in charge of this new land; and, just as in Great Britain, you Scots are less than sheep." Jack said, shaking his fist at George.

"I'm a Brit and I don't see it that way, you bloody vermin," said Jacob, his temper about to explode. Jannis grabbed Jacob and pulled him away as Jacob started for Jack.

"You know you can't get in a mess now, dear, especially with your condition the way it is," Jannis persisted, pulling him away. She could see by his reddening face that his blood pressure was out of control. George stepped between Jack and Jannis, seizing Jack's hand that was raised to strike Jacob and with the other hand now clenched in a fist hit Jack in the face knocking him to the ground. Jack lay on the ground and holding his hand over his nose and mouth, keeping the blood from running down to his shirt. Jack motion to the Constable, who had turned to return, to let it go. It was over, but not for Jack, though. He would bide his time, nurse his hatred, and have revenge...even if it took twenty years.

Chapter 4

The sheep station was small in size compared to others in Australia. It covered 30,000 acres and was bordered by small towns and a river. The main house was one-story and configured in an "L" shape. The small part of the "L" accommodated the kitchen and sleeping quarters for Jannis and Jacob. The large portion of the house was for entertaining... Jacob's great joy. He loved to have social occasions in this room. The area was large enough to hold twenty-five couples, dancing and whooping it up. Jannis was just as thrilled to have these parties, because it meant that she could have Jacob by her side for the duration of the party. Jannis knew these parties were taking their toll on Jacob's health, but she couldn't stop Jacob from enjoying himself. He would probably drink himself to death long before any accident would kill him, but Jacob worked hard and she felt that he deserved to play hard if he wished to. These parties would last as long as two to three days and, sometimes, a day longer solely to recover from the effects of alcohol consumption. Australians had developed a reputation as great beer drinkers, and it was at parties like Jacob's that the reputation was validated. The large party room was just off the kitchen, convenient to the food and beverage supply. The station office was located beyond the large room. This was where Jacob kept the records for wool production and cost of operation. Adjacent to the office was a lavatory. The lavatory was built to accommodate both men and women. A large verandah encircled the entire house; of course, it was enclosed by wire screen for outdoor activities on bug-infested nights. The house and out buildings were protected by a seven-foot high fence with heavy square iron netting, to keep the kangaroos (Roos) out, along with other wild animals. The heavy-duty fences were erected because the animals dug up gardens, over-turned barrels and troughs, kicked in walls, and knocked down the laundry lines. All the stations were constructed similarly for the same reason. Keeping the roos out of the pastures was a problem all its own, but the sheep dogs were a great help in controlling that issue. Horses were kept in a large corral next to one of the out buildings used as a barn for feed. Not far from the barn was another smaller building for the chickens and ducks. The ducks were content as long as the water ditch Jacob had dug didn't clog up during the hot season. The stream ran through a large pen just behind the chicken coop and out to a covered pond where a pipe was attached to a pump in the kitchen for the house water supply. The stream continued beyond the pond to the bullock paddock. This water supply system was one of many things Jacob had devised to make life easier on the station.

George worked hard and, as he worked, he never lost sight of his dream. He saved his pay and, for the next year and a half, every shilling he could save was socked away. Jacob supplied room and board for George and Winifred free, so saving money was not hard to do. All George needed to provide was their clothing and Winnie made most of those. George and Winifred soon had other ways to spend their money that would slow down their saving capability... their children. John arrived after George and Winifred had been wed for a year; and, every year thereafter, like clockwork, a new face would arrive. Six years and six children into life in the new land and four years after he paid off his obligation to Jacob, he was still looking for his dream to come true. He had not considered children in his grand scheme, but he loved Winnie and the children. He was a proud father, indeed, when his burgeoning family would take their places for Sunday services.

Jacob never regretted his decision to hire Mildred as a cook; she more than earned her keep through the tasty meals she prepared. Jacob liked George and Winifred and they developed a strong bond. Jacob and Jannis became involved with George's dream and were helping George to find the right land location and seeking financial assistance if he needed it. George soon found a bit of land in Stanhope and secured the land by making a down payment.

From the house, Jannis heard the shouting of the men and felt fear in the pit of her stomach. She had heard this sound before and knew what it could mean.

"Hold his head...don't let it move!" George shouted. Jacob was lying on his back in the wagon; the men held the horses down to a slow gait in an effort to immobilize him as the wagon swayed over the rough road. The road was deeply rutted from the effects of rain and searing heat that had dried the ground to concrete-like hardness. After a snake had startled Jacob's horse, he had been thrown to the ground, landing on his head. The fact that he was still alive was a testament to his tenacity. Jacob was barely conscious and he knew his time was limited. George knew it, also. George knew that Jacob's will to live until he saw his wife was all that was keeping him alive. George had observed this previously. Jacob was of a single-minded breed and once he saw his beloved wife, he said in a calm and controlled tone, "Jannis, I love you. Don't forget what we have discussed over these past few years." And with that, Jacob closed his eyes and passed into the great beyond.

Jacob's last words were a mystery to George, but he felt it was not for him to know. Jannis, however, just knew exactly what Jacob meant. As a couple, they had more or less adopted George and Winifred. They had not been blessed with children of their own and desperately needed someone to be their family. Unbeknownst to George, he had been selected to be their heir apparent long before he came to Australia. Neither Jacob nor Jannis had ever divulged to George the reason for their sponsorship of him to Australia. After George arrived with Winifred in tow, Jacob and Jannis were not uncertain about whether they should share their intentions with George. After all, there was an element of uncertainty at first; and, later, they just ran out of time. "You know, I really like Winnie...she is the best thing that could have happened to our George," Jannis would tell Jacob and Jacob would respond, "You always had a good eye, haven't you, lass. I think they will make a great family and show us proud when we're gone." Jannis interrupted Jacob, "Don't say those things! You know how I feel about death; that kind of talk scares me. You know how hopeless I would be if anything happened to you." Tragically, Jannis' worst fear had been realized. Jacob was gone and she was alone.

"Don't worry, Mrs. Mallory, we will always work the sheep as if Jacob was here," George said in a whisper, as he put his arm comfortingly around her shoulder. This gentle touch was the first time that George had ever shown affection to Jannis, and she leaned against him in such obvious relief that he was taken aback. He continued to hold her tightly and she took great comfort in his quiet strength.

Jacob was buried in the family plot on the station. The burial plot was on a small hill over-looking the valley and the river. Jacob had set this plot aside for himself and his family...the family that he and Jannis would never have. Many years before, a horse had kicked Jacob, rendering him physically incapable of having children. Jannis had never considered replacing Jacob with another man, even though she had wanted children so badly. He often told her she should leave and find a man who could give her the children she wanted, but Jannis would never leave Jacob...she loved him more than she wanted children. This is how they arrived at the idea of sponsoring George to leave their legacy to. They had some friends in Scotland search for a young man that they could sponsor and endow with their worldly goods. From all reports they knew George was the young man they wanted.

During the funeral service, George read from the Bible to comfort Jannis and the others, even though neither he nor Jacob was all that familiar with religion. As he read, Jacob's final words to Jannis replayed hauntingly through his mind, don't forget what we discussed over the years.

The next few days were spent in the house where Winifred devoted herself to Jannis' comfort by both deeds and words, saying, "You know he is still here in every part of the station and in every part of us", or "Jannis, dinnae worry! George and I will not let anything happen tae you or your station." During those days of dark grief, Jannis was at some other place in her mind. She was on a hill over looking the station, holding Jacob's hand and telling him of all the wonderful things they were going to build in this valley. Without any apparent warning, Jannis returned to the present and the immediate situation, "Winnie, I have been dealing with an agonizing problem over the last few days. I must speak with you and George."

Winifred felt the tightness of fear in her stomach; she wondered if this would be the end of their jobs. How would they survive if what she was thinking came to pass?

"Go get George and Millie and bring them to the office," Jannis said, sternly.

"I will just be a minute," replied Winifred in a quivering voice, quickly leaving the room to look for them.

George was the first to enter the office. He found Jannis seated behind the small desk...where Jacob had often sat when giving orders to George and the crew. Millie came in just behind George, with Winnie following close behind.

"Close the door, Winnie, and have a seat over there by the wall; George, you sit here," Jannis said as she pointed to the chair in front of the desk, "and, Millie, over by the other wall." Jannis had composed herself and looked to be as much in charge as Jacob had ever been behind the desk. She opened the top drawer of the desk and removed a stack of legal-looking papers.

She looked directly at George fixing her gaze into his eyes, and then she began. "Being of sound mind and in full charge of my faculties," she read. They all realized that they were hearing the Last Will and Testament of Jacob Mallory. Jannis read quickly through the legal terms and, when it seemed like eons had passed, she then concluded, "I, Jacob Mallory and I, Jannis Mallory," George couldn't believe what he heard next, "do hereby declare that upon the death of either of these parties, willfully and with forethought, enter into partnership with George McLean for the operation of this sheep station to the mutual benefit of both parties with equal ownership of said property."

George sprang from his chair in disbelief and said, "Mrs. Mallory! Jannis, you cannae give this station in ownership tae me and mine. I'm nae your family and you should give it tae your family."

"Jacob and I have no family here, and no family to speak of anywhere else," she faltered and then went on. "We have felt that you and Winnie are our family. Jacob and I discussed this with the legal authorities before writing this will and this is our wish and final decision. This is the way we want it, and this is the way it will be! You have been working and helping Jacob run this station for these past years and we agreed that you could run it by yourself if something happened."

George was compelled to say, "But, Mrs. Mallory, I huv a dream of starting a cheese factory, scrimping and saving to that end. If I huv tae run the station, what will happen tae my dream? It'll..."

"No, it won't, George; please call me Jannis. Jacob and I have been aware of your dream and we have anticipated your leaving." She paused and looked at Winifred, who, by now, had begun to be caught up in the conversation.

"George", Winnie said, in the stern tone that George knew, but had not heard since the difficult birth of John, their oldest. "Listen tae what Mrs. M... oh, I mean, Jannis has tae say before you put your foot in it."

Jannis continued, more forcefully this time, "As I was saying, Jacob and I had been looking forward to the time you completed your debt. We have been moving goats and cattle to our other property in Stanhope, not far from here. We thought that a joint venture in that business would be a good opportunity for us both. Now that Jacob is gone, it would seem that our joint venture timetable must be moved forward." Jannis looked into George's eyes and he felt as though she was searching his soul for an answer. "What say you, George?" Millie chimed in with Winnie as a close second.

"I'm not sure," George paused and looked out the window at the front gate to the station. "I'm at a loss for a plan; I wish I could look into Jacob's blessed, smiling, red face and ask him which way tae go. I could always depend on his advice." George folded his arms and bowed his head as if to somehow look into his soul for the answer of the honor beyond his words, but had no idea of this, and wished he could consult Jacob.

A long time passed with no one uttering a word. It was a tense moment in the lives of George and Winifred, who had held this dream for so long with faltering hopes of realizing it. Now, out of the blue, they were standing on the threshold of a new life, freely given to them by their friends and benefactors, Jacob and Jannis. Their generosity was too much for George to comprehend; he had learned to love and respect them as his own, with no thought of reward other than their friendship. On the other hand, he could carry on with his dream and make them part of it. George's thoughts raced...the work would have to be divided between business as usual at the station and the building of the factory. There would not be enough workers to do it all, so more men would need to be hired. George would recruit them from Kyabram. So George accepted the offer and set about the work with a willing spirit. When he did make the trip to Kyabram, the first person he encountered was "good old Jack". Jack had not heard of Jacob's death and was more than curious about why George, who seldom left the Station, was in town. George remembered Jacob's warning long ago about Jack's reputation for gaining power and riches through any means possible. He was reluctant at first to renew their acquaintance. In spite of his misgivings, George decided it would do no good to hold a grudge.

"How are you, George? We haven't seen you for a while. How is everything at the Station?" Jack asked.

At that point, George realized that Jack didn't know about Jacob or the joint venture, so he said, "How are you going, Jack? I guess you dinnae ken that Jacob was killed."

Jack appeared stunned, "No, I didn't. How and when did this happen?"

George explained what had happened and, when Jack appeared genuinely sorry about it, George began to feel more at ease with Jack. He was always so busy working that he had never had the time to dwell on yesterday's news. George had put the incident out of his conscious mind years ago. Jack, as smooth as ever, began to reel George in again. George trustingly told Jack about his ideas for the cheese factory and about the extra men he would need to run the station, as well as some construction people he would have to hire. Jack told George that he had a place in Stanhope and would be glad to help George with the men and the materials for the factory. What he didn't tell George was that there would be great personal profit to him. He began to plan how to exact his revenge, right then and there. George, in his innocence, thought that bygones were bygones and carried this news back to the station.

Jannis felt it was a bad idea to trust Jack, but Millie, with typical Scots' stubbornness, maintained that she knew Jack was a good man. "My brother and Jack's brother are good friends to be knowing each other for years," Millie said with an air of authority. "My brother said he would trust Jack with his life and knew he was basically a good man. He was verra disappointed with the marriage of Winnie tae George. By now, I'm sure all he thinks of is their happiness." Millie didn't know Jack; she was only judging him by her obstinate measuring stick of success. In actuality, her brother had discovered the truth about Jack... that he was a scoundrel...after he entered into some dealings with Jack that benefited Jack alone. They were no longer friendly. Millie hadn't spoken to her brother in many years and she was only repeating what she had remembered. George felt that there was truth in Millie's viewpoint; after all, hadn't Jack apologized to him? Their stories matched and that was an end to it as far as George was concerned. Their doubts would be discounted, as it seemed in everyone's best interest that they consider the past as over. In this still new and harsh country, people needed to rely on each other and Jack was offering to help.

Soon the work on the factory began in earnest and, within a month's time, a large rectangular building had been completed. This was the first of three buildings that George had planned. The buildings were twenty-five feet wide and eighty feet long, with six large vats down the center. At one end of the buildings, a mezzanine was placed over the end vat, where the finished cheese would cure. The vats were eight feet by sixteen feet and two feet deep. Each vat was specially designed for a particular type of cheese...one for cheddar, one for Swiss, one for cottage, and so on.

There were hoists and racks of every description in the building. Stacked on both sides of the vats were containers of ingredients to make the various types of cheese ready for transport. The orders were pouring in and the factory grew from one building to several buildings with large vats in two rows inside each building. The factory was now able to make various kinds and types of cheese in large blocks, rounds, and small parcels. George now had trucks transporting cheese to Sydney, Melbourne, and Brisbane, with the possibility of expansion all over Australia. George and Winifred had produced seven children over the years. George was 20 and Winifred was 18 when they married and they had a busy life for 20 years. Now, with the factory in full production, it seemed as though they had achieved a measure of success. Soon, the boys would be able to take over the operation. The sheep station was also in excellent shape, now including cattle, goats, and a small herd of sheep. Jannis was involved in the business and was able to handle the operation of the station. George's two oldest boys, John and Ron, seemed to like the work they were doing, especially the money they were earning. The other children were busy in school, with the exception of Graham, and didn't have much to do with the business. Winifred kept him close by because he was small for his age and didn't fit in well at school. He was sent to school and returned home, crying, "Mum, I don't want to go anymore! The others tease me because I can't talk right and I'm too small to fight." Winifred thought of his size and distress and was swayed. There was no further discussion about Graham's schooling. George privately felt that Graham would be better off if he went to school and learned to get along with others; but he did not verbalize those feelings. Graham went everywhere with Winifred. She liked his companionship because George often traveled back and forth between Stanhope and the Station on business. By now, the family lived in Kyabram, located about halfway between George's two operations, in a two-story house with four bedrooms upstairs and a shared bathroom at the end of the hall. Winifred's and George's room was the largest and nearest to the bath. Their room had a separate door to the bath, with another door to the hall extending through the center of the upstairs. The children's rooms were on both sides of that hall. Lelia and Mary had the room closest to their mother, because in those times girls were watched very closely. Across the hall, Arthur and Graham shared a room and opposite from them were Ron and Alan. John, as the eldest, had a small room on his own. The three-shared bedrooms were almost as large as Winifred and George's and John's room at the far end of the hall was a little over half the size of the others. John liked his single room and he had it decorated with all sorts of pictures of animals. He fancied himself as a great white hunter in Africa some day. Ron and Alan shared their room but neither one of them had any concrete future plans, so their room was messy and sparsely decorated. The children's bunk beds were a problem for Winifred; they were in a constant state of disrepair. Alan and Ron were the primary culprits; it seemed to Winifred that they were more interested in wrestling and jumping on the beds than anything else. Arthur was more concerned about girls, even at a very young age. He insisted on being called "Dasher", but no one really knew why. They assumed that it was to impress the girls at school. Graham didn't share Arthur's interest in the girls until much later. He was content to be with his "Mum". Lelia and Mary were the complete opposites of Ron and Alan. Their room was always neatly kept with the beds made, everything in its place, and their closet...well, their closet was a sight to behold. They were always dressed in proper attire, hair neatly combed and shoes cleaned and polished. The boys, on the other hand, were typical boys, and their rooms reflected that.

Chapter 5

Working long hours and traveling began to take its toll on
Winnie and George. He was unable to spend time with
Winifred; he was either in Stanhope, at the station, or points in between.
"George, would you please take time off tae be with the children and
me" Winnie begged. "I nae see you anymore; you seem tae be thinner
than ever before! I'm afraid that you are working yourself tae death!"

"Now, Winnie, you ken I cannae stop now. The factory is going well
and it is much too soon for the boys tae take over," George reasoned.

"I don't care." Winnie said heatedly. "Maybe one of the foremen can
give you a spell off, at least for a couple of days."

"All right," George said in an effort to placate her. "I'll see if that
can be done. Now go tae sleep because I have an early day tomorrow."
Then he rolled over and went to sleep. Winifred lay awake, worrying
about how she and the children would survive if something happened
to George. She could not help remembering how hard it would have
been for Jannis if George had not been there to take charge when Jacob
died.

Winifred made up her mind, in that instant, to take George to
Melbourne where they would implement their retirement, just as soon
as the factory and station were running smoothly with the boys in
charge. George awoke early to find that Winifred was already up and
downstairs cooking breakfast for him. "You'd best hurry and come

down before this food gets cold," Winifred shouted up at him. She had prepared George's favorite breakfast of bacon, eggs, toast and a large helping of potatoes; even the ever-present tea was ready. The effects of cholesterol on the heart were not unheard of and George loved what was later to be called "heart attack on a plate." His constant hard work and style of living, combined with smoking, were bound to take their toll on George's body.

"Remember your promise tae me, George, about taking some time off. I want tae go tae Melbourne day after tomorrow and I expect you tae go with me," Winnie reminded him.

George knew Winifred well enough that she either had or would have the train tickets in her little hand when he returned in two days, so he acquiesced. Two days later, George returned to the house and asked, "Are the valises and Graham ready?"

"Yes, the bags are ready; but Graham won't be going. This is for just us...you and me."

George couldn't believe his ears; Winnie usually did not go anywhere without Graham. "Are you sure?"

"Yes! Now pick up the bags. We don't want to miss the train," scolded Winnie gently. George hurriedly picked up the two bags on the floor and was about five steps behind her. He rushed out to the buggy, which was waiting just beyond the front gate. The driver flicked the reins and the horses moved forward down the street to the train station.

The station was a long building running parallel to the street on one side and a set of rails on the other. Narrow gage rail was all over Australia. These trains would remind readers of the Disneyland train station at the entrance of the park. They were about the size of the trains that went circling around the park to each one of the theme parks. The Australian trains were coal-fired steam engines with passenger cars attached. The passenger cars had several doors on both sides of the car with pew-like wooden seats extending from door to door. The baggage car was nothing more than an old converted livestock car; in fact, it still smelled of its former passengers. Winifred took one look at the baggage car and declared, "My bags will stay with me." George said nothing, for he knew once she had set her mind on something, it was futile to argue.

"You hold one on your lap and I'll take the other," Winnie said.

"Are you sure that's what you want to do, Winnie? Maybe there won't be anyone in this row for the trip and we can place the bags next to us," George observed as Winifred boarded the train.

"Maybe you'll be right and we'll be lucky, George," said Winnie.

The trip took six hours, so Winifred packed a lunch that she brought out about halfway through the trip.

"Here, George, have a sandwich, some fruit and cold tea! I ken you must be hungry."

George took the sandwich, but he refused the fruit.

"George, now eat this fruit or you'll be ill on this trip," bossed Winnie affectionately. To keep the peace, he took the fruit and the sandwich. The sandwich was good, made with Millie's homemade bread and sliced ham. George loved anything that Millie cooked; she was probably the best cook he encountered. He always stopped at the Main House on the station for a meal. Winifred hadn't inherited the talent for cooking from her mother; but the children enjoyed her cooking. She wasn't a bad cook, just not quite as good as Millie. Millie did seem to have a gift because everything she cooked turned out well. Clickity-clack, clickity-clack, the train clattered on; soon Melbourne was in sight. At this point in time, Melbourne was the second largest city in Australia. The center of the city was built around a square. This design was in the old European style and was structured to allow ease of shopping, transportation in and out the city, and access to government buildings. The Yarra River bordered one side and the train station adjacent to the market place bordered the opposite side. Streets leading out of the city center were later to become major arteries to the suburbs and were designed so that the city center was the hub and the streets leading outward were like the spokes on a wheel.

Winifred, in her methodical way, had planned each of the three days of their stay in Melbourne. The first step of her plan involved establishing a bank account. The second step was locating a house for them to retire to. The train arrived in the late afternoon and they went directly to the hotel... the very hotel, The Richmond Club Hotel that John was later to own and operate. As they checked in, Winnie announced, "We're George and Winifred McLean. We'll be staying for three days and we would like a room close to the loo."

Winifred was up early, filled with thoughts of her plan; but George seemed to be a little slow to awaken. Winifred thought he was just very tired and not accustomed to a relaxing day away from work.

"I dinnae feel verra well, Winnie," he said.

"Dinnae worry, dearie! After a day or so, you'll be back tae your precious work, then you'll feel a whole lot better. Now, get out of that bed and we'll be off," Winnie retorted.

"All right, I guess that's what it is; let's be off then," he said, rising very promptly and dressing.

George and Winifred took the last two seats in the back. The tram clamored along on the tracks toward the center of town. George didn't know where they were going; as usual, he just followed along. In Australia, it was a man's world; but George behaved differently; he was easy-going and laconic. He allowed Winifred to have her way, even though it was highly unusual. Normally, men were considered to be the dominant spouse and whatever they said was law. When families were out together with the children, the men acted as though they were walking by themselves. George respected Winifred so much that it was impossible for him to behave like the typical male of that era.

"Winnie, where are we off tae?" George ventured.

"The Bank," she quickly answered.

"The Bank! What on earth for?"

"I want tae set up an account for our retirement. Now that the factory is doing well, you need tae slow down and relax a bit!"

"But, I don't want to slow down." George protested.

"Now, George! How many times hae you told me that we can retire when the factory is up and running?"

He knew that he was in for it again; she had made up her mind. In his typical manner, he decided to go along with her and whatever her plans were.

The Bank of England was an impressive building, particularly so for that day and age. The large doors at the front were ten feet high and six feet wide... heavy wooden doors with plate glass panes from top to bottom. The front of the Bank had large granite columns rising to the second floor and supporting a granite balcony across the entire front of the building. The interior was no less ornate; the floors were marble panels that gleamed as though polished after the passage of every customer. The counter in front of the tellers was so high that only their heads and the top of their shoulders could be seen. Neither George nor Winnie had ever been inside a building like this; they just stood in the doorway, gaping at the majestic surroundings.

A voice from behind them said, "May I be of assistance?" Startled, they looked for the person behind the voice and saw a guard behind a granite podium at the side of the entrance.

Awed, Winifred answered, "Yes, yes, you can! We're here to open an account."

"Right this way, Madam." He directed them to the lady behind a desk.

"May I help you, Sir?" asked the lady. She was addressing her questions to George...again in the manner of the day.

"Yes, you can," answered Winifred, not George, who was still somewhat tongue-tied. "We are here to open an account."

"What kind of an account?" she asked, still directing her gaze at George.

"A retirement account," responded Winifred, determinedly.

George just stood there watching the conversation as Winifred attempted to divert the lady's attention away from him. "We are here to open an account that will earn enough interest to allow us to retire in a few years," continued Winifred. The woman finally realized that Winifred was the one who was going to do the talking for the two of them. They sat down and Winifred described her expectations of the account. The banking business was completed in record time and they were again on the tram.

"You know, Winnie, I believe that you could run the factory if you had tae," George said, impressed with Winnie's bank dealings.

"No worries over that, George! We'll be down here in Melbourne shortly, spoiling our grandchildren, and our boys will be running things. I expect good things from the girls, too; especially Mary. She is such a bright one."

The tram was on its way to Richmond, a suburb of Melbourne, where Winifred had read of a house for sale. The tram rails were right down the center of Bridge Road, with traffic on both sides traveling in opposite directions. A station was located every three or four blocks to allow passengers on and off the tram. It was a pleasant ride for them; this was their first tram ride and they went from one side of the tram to the other, taking in the sights. George was still looking out the back of the tram, when it stopped and Winifred arose from her seat to get off. She was halfway down the aisle before she realized that George was still sitting there.

"Come on, George." Winfred shouted.

"I'm coming, just hang on a minute" George said.

"You must hurry before the tram starts again," Winnie pleaded.

"No worries; I'll wait for you, mate," said the conductor. "No need to be in a rush; nothing is that important, except maybe a pint."

George laughed, "Right you are, mate! Just where are the pubs round here?"

"There's one round the corner."

"Maybe I'll see you there later, mate."

"G'day to you, then," responded the conductor as the tram started to roll down the tracks again.

"Winnie, where to now?" George wondered.

"Just a block down Waltham Street. There's a house I want to show you."

"A house?" George was surprised again.

"Yes, a house. What did you expect we were coming out here for?"

They located the house, which had three stories, including the basement. George liked the house immediately. The real estate agent was at the house as expected that day, Winnie had seen in a broacher at the bank they were showing it. He was rambling on about the price and the advantages of the large lot, but the talk went in one of George's ears and out the other. He was more interested in the actual house and property. The property featured two trees in front on both sides of the walkway. The house sat near the front of the lot with a big open area in the back. George thought this area suited for a garden and, perhaps, some sheep and hogs. Winifred was inside the kitchen, which was located on the basement floor in the back of the house. She was amazed by the modern conveniences not yet available in Kyabram. "Gas stove, electric refrigerator; just think of it!" Winnie exclaimed out-loud. Of course, Winifred's kitchen at home had indoor plumbing, a hand pump on the sink counter, but all these other things were not available. As she ascended to the first floor, she saw a grand open area with two smaller rooms at one end. One was a coatroom and the other was a loo. The third floor consisted of the bedrooms; three of them...two small ones and one large one with access to the upstairs loo. "This is perfect," thought Winifred as she said to George, "Don't you just fancy this?"

"Ye-yes, I actually do; I especially like the loo inside, where does the uh---, well, you know, go?"

"It is attached to the city sewer system," answered the agent.

"It's what? You mean there's no septic system?" asked George, with obvious shock.

"No. The line goes to a sewer plant outside the city. It will all be explained in the sale documents when you purchase the property."

George turned to Winifred and she responded to his look by saying, "How much?"

"500 pounds."

"We'll take it," said George and the deal was cut.

With the papers signed and the money exchanged, the couple was on their way back to Kyabram. Winifred was relieved that they had gone to Melbourne and secured their retirement. The purchase of the house was a bonus...now she could relax because their life was assured... or so she thought

Back in Kyabram, Jannis watched as the cattle, now mixed in with the sheep, grazed. She hoped George would return soon; she felt uneasy at the station without George there to keep things running smoothly. George had advised her that the cattle would do fine mixed in with the sheep; of course, everyone else had insisted that the sheep would have to go. She did remember, though, that her beloved Jacob had agreed with George when they decided to use the station's assets to develop a cattle herd...the very cattle that provided the milk needed for cheese. The station was becoming self-sufficient, as well as the factory; strange how these two concepts complimented each other in business.

Jack was also watching the progress of the business with an avaricious eye...waiting like a spider to pounce on his victims when the time was right.

He thought that George would be a formidable foe if a face-to-face confrontation occurred. Jack mused, "Too bad that I can't separate Winifred from George. I bet I could sway her to let me into the business. They still have no idea that I'm married. I need to gain their trust by asking Winifred and Millie look for a bride for me because I'm so lonely. A lonely man is an open invitation for most women to do some matchmaking. They seemed concerned about me after the disappointment I suffered over their marriage; at least, I'm sure Millie was." Jack's plan to get Millie involved in finding a wife for him was a "shoo-in", because everyone knew Millie fancied herself in the role of matchmaker.

Jannis was waiting when the train came to a stop and George stepped down. Winifred was right behind him and he held out his hand to help her down. Before Jannis could say "G'day", George was back in the railcar retrieving their valises.

"Winnie, how you going?" said Jannis, gently touching her arm.

"Oh, it's you, is it, Jannis. How you going?"

"I'm fine. Was it a good trip? You and George have a good time?"

"Yes, and I persuaded him tae do a few things for me, you ken?"

By this time, George had retrieved the bags and was standing next to Winifred. "G'day, Jannis, how you going?"

"Fine, and you?"

"I'm a bit tired, from the trip and all," said George, as he picked up the bags again and headed to the waiting buggy. "It is good to be back in

Kyabram. I dinnae remember when I have been so tired." He reasoned, in typical male fashion, that his illness was due to the long, hot trip.

"How you going?" came a shout from the other end of the platform; and, wonder of all wonders, there stood Jack. "George, Winnie, it's good to see you back! Jannis, it's good to see you, too."

"G'day tae you, Jack! What are you doing here?" asked George, as Jack reached them.

"I have to pick up a shipment from Sydney that should be on this train."

"Not this train. It's from Melbourne." "Really! Then both trains must be late, because the train from Sydney is due now," Jack said, glancing briefly at the conductor who had just left the last car.

"You're right, Jack, it seems that they are both late," replied the conductor as he walked past them without slowing down. "The Sydney train will be here two hours from now. G'day to you all!" He disappeared into the office before Jack could respond with one of his customary wisecracks.

This was fortunate for Jack because he had to mind his manners if he was to represent himself as a good man. "I'll bet you are tired and hungry; how about I shout you to dinner? Then you could go home and have a good night's sleep without having to cook or clean up." The offer seemed genuine and Winifred thought Jack was trying to heal the bad blood between them.

"That would be lovely, Jack. Thank you very much," answered Winifred before Jannis or George had a chance to think. Finally Jannis echoed, "That would be nice." Off they went to the hotel restaurant.

The hotel was an interesting building with only ten rooms to let on the second floor. Stairs ascended from the lobby in the center of the building to the second floor hallway. There were five rooms on each side across the back of the building, with the community bath across from the head of the staircase. The rooms were small with barely room for a standard-sized bed and dresser with a large ewer in a washbowl. Each room boasted its own window with lace curtains and a pull-down shade. The shade protected the room from the afternoon sun at the front of the hotel and from the morning sun in the rear. To the right of the staircase and left of the check-in desk, the restaurant area covered the front, rear and far right of the building. The kitchen and meal preparation area was located underneath the staircase and behind the desk...an unusual location, to be sure. The tables were set for four people. If groups came to dine, two or more tables would be lined up to accommodate the number of diners to be served.

George and Winifred sat next to each other, leaving Jannis and Jack to sit next to each other. Jannis was uncomfortable with this, but didn't say anything. She was aware that George and Jack had put aside their differences and she didn't want to cause any problems.

"This is rather nice, don't you think?" announced Jack, after helping Jannis to her seat. Jannis was taken aback by Jack's chivalry because that behavior was not customary in Australia.

"Yes, it is," responded George. He gave Winifred a stern look as if to direct her to mask her apparent distrust of Jack's motives. She still felt ambiguous about Jack and it would be some time many more years before she would realize that her lack of trust was firmly grounded.

'I need to obtain their trust and allegiance if I am to achieve my goal,' thought Jack as he passed the menus around the table. The menus didn't offer much in the way of variety. It was mutton, swine, and beef... the diet of the colonists from Scotland and Ireland.

I didn't personally care for cottage cheese after an incident where Norman force-fed it to me when we lived in Park City, Utah. Norman believed, at least in my case, that adversity built character. However much character I gained from that experience, I still have a strong dislike for cottage cheese; as a matter of fact, it was years before I could eat any type of cheese.

They were not familiar with a diet that included vegetables, other than potatoes and turnips. This lack of proper nutrition created serious health issues. It was normal for Australians to lose their teeth before the end of their teenage years. George and Winifred had better dental health than the others, but they were beginning to have problems. Other health problems involved the vast consumption of alcohol; the Aussies were well on their way to becoming the most notorious beer-drinking nation on earth.

"Well, George, what'll it be?" Jack asked.

"Don' know, maybe a grand steak with potatoes," George answered.

"George, are you sure?" Winifred looked at the menu. "Perhaps a nice piece of mutton would be better for you."

"Woman...don' tell me what I want! I want a steak." George shot back in a peevish tone not typical of him. George seemed tired and irritable from the trip, so Winifred didn't snap back at him. Strangely enough, it was Jack who came to Winifred's defense.

"George, Winifred is only thinking of you."

"I ken and I'm verra sorry. I think these long days are getting tae me."

"That's all right, George. You go and have wha' you want! I'm verra sorry, too."

Everyone placed their order; and as usual, George and Jack had a beer. The beer mugs contained well over a pint each; so it was not long before George and Jack were feeling calm and relaxed. Suddenly George's face went pale and he couldn't seem to breathe right. Jannis noticed George gasping for breath and looked sharply at Winifred.

"Oh my God! Help us!" shouted Winifred as she jumped up and grabbed George's hand, as he toppled his chair backwards in his desperate struggle to breathe. He landed on his back, Winifred still holding his hand for dear life. Meanwhile, Jack came around the table to see what he could do to help. George continued to gasp for air and his face began to turn blue. They thought he was choking on a bit of food, but the Heimlich maneuver wouldn't be discovered for another thirty years. The only thing they could do was force George into an upright position and pound on his back to dislodge the blockage. Jack tried to reach in George's mouth to see if he could extract the blockage from George's throat; but, lacking the proper equipment, it was a futile effort. People gathered around them as they struggled to save George. Winifred held George close to her as he looked into her tear soaked eyes with the love he always held for her; life passed from his body. Winifred was a strong woman, but this was too much for her to cope with. She wept uncontrollably as she held George in her lap, rocking back and forth, with Jannis grasping her shoulders from behind. Both women had lost someone they loved...Jannis, an "adopted-in-kind" son...Winifred, a husband and partner. Jack reached down to extricate George from Winifred and to help her to rise. Winifred looked into Jack's eyes and, in her great grief, thought she saw a friendly and comforting face she could count on. Jack looked back at Winifred, pretending to be what she needed.

Jack's wife didn't appear at the funeral or the memorial. He specifically told her not to come to Kyabram because the death was one of the workers at the station and no one of importance. She did not even consider questioning him.

So, it was Jack who helped Winifred through the next few days with the funeral and the consoling of her children, particularly Mary. Mary was very close to her father. Jack even took over temporary operation of the station and factory until Winifred and Jannis could get back to it, or so they believed.

The funeral was a very sad occasion; the procession and graveside memorial was lengthy. Winifred tried to be strong for the children's sake, but she was unable to control her weeping during the memorial given by the local priest, Father O'Flanhary, of the church where Winifred had dragged an unwilling George.

"Will we see Dad again, Mum?" asked Graham as he looked into her tear-drenched eyes.

"Of course we will, Pom," she replied, using her favorite nickname for him. Father O'Flanhary had just finished the service and everyone was moving toward the graveyard gate. They placed George's body in the family plot by the north wall of the church...the same place he had frequently retreated after church service. He would lean against the stones on the wall of the church and smoke his pipe. When standing there, he could see the plot where he and his family would rest for eternity. He often thought about that while he was puffing on his pipe. George waited there for Winifred and the children to finish congratulating the Father on his sermon. He would wonder if there was enough daylight left to finish some project he had started earlier that morning. Winifred had quite a time just getting him to attend services, so she was tolerant of his quiet time there, smoking and pondering. The good Father always found time to come over and talk to George. They had a common interest in farming and cheese production, so they often conversed for an hour or more. As a result, George frequently "lost his daylight" on Sunday.

George didn't mind because he looked forward to their friendly chats. The mourners all felt his presence there with them, wearing his rumpled wool suit that was, at least, one size too small; the aroma of his pipe still swirling around. His tobacco had a pleasant smell, reminiscent of fresh apple with a hint of heather. George mixed his own tobacco and did not share the ingredients with anyone.

Winifred felt the warmth of everyone's good wishes and took solace in the knowledge that George was there, somewhere, watching over them.

Millie could feel that same solace, but was already matching up Winifred with Jack. She hoped that Winnie would consider Jack to fill the void left by George's passing...after a proper mourning period, of course. Millie had always secretly wished that Winifred had chosen Jack instead of George, even though George had never given her any reason to be unhappy with him. 'Jack is a man of position in both communities of Kyabram and Stanhope, while George hadn't finished realizing his dream before his death,' thought Millie as she stood beside Winifred and Jack. 'My greatest desire is tae see Winnie achieve the lifestyle I have always wanted her tae huv.' Again, she felt a surge of joy that this might now be possible. She had always lived her life vicariously through her daughter and she focused on how this current sad situation could be used for furthering her goals. The people were passing by to console Winifred, while Jack stood there and gave every appearance of sympathy and concern. This was one of Jack's best performances in a lifetime of great performances; his apparent remorse for George's passing and his concern for Winifred were acted out as if she was his dearest family member.

'I will make sure that this is the end of George's legacy here in Kyabram,' thought Jack as he automatically shook the hand of one of the mourners. 'I have done what was necessary to obtain Winnie's complete confidence. Now I can exact my revenge,' mused Jack, struggling to keep a smile from his lips.

Winifred thanked everyone as they passed by her for their kind thoughts and deeds. It was obvious that George was very well liked and respected in both Kyabram and Stanhope. Jack continued to stand beside Winifred as the people offered their condolences. Millie could finally see an end to the line of mourners, so she turned to Winifred, "Should we go tae the house or go with Jack and have a bite tae eat?" Her motive was to guide Winifred gradually toward Jack.

"Mother, I need to see to the children," replied Winifred. She still considered them as such, even though John was nearly twenty and the youngest, Graham, was almost ten.

"Maybe after you settle them at home we could go relax at the Hotel," insisted Millie.

"I couldn't go there, Mother, it would remind me of George."

"Might I suggest we drive to Shepparton for a bite then," said Jack in a soothing tone. "You know that I have just purchased a new automobile and it would be a pleasant ride. It would also give you a chance to relax and compose yourself."

"Maybe that would be good after all. Thank you, Jack," responded Winifred, much to Millie's secret delight.

She turned away from them to attend to the children, but Jack felt as though he was inching closer to his goal. Millie was also pleased; she had her goals, however self-serving they might be. She had no idea that their goals, while both involving Winifred, were in diametric opposition.

"Come along, children! John, would you get Mary and Arthur into the car so we can go home?"

"Of course, Mum," responded John. He knew, as the oldest, that he would bear the responsibility of taking his father's place. John would never shirk his duty, but his real objective was to enter the hotel/restaurant business. He was a handsome bloke and he knew it. In school, he seemed to slide by with little effort by trading on his looks and charm. As he grew older, he would become more adept at using these assets to his advantage. Late in his secondary school years, his teacher, Miss O'Donnell, would find him irresistible and an affair would ensue. She was his first taste of womanhood and he would always remember her fondly.

Winifred was not entirely certain that the affair had occurred, but she would always maintain her suspicion. The affair did not reach the light of day and that was good for the reputation of the family, especially now in their time of distress. John brought the car around and Winfred said her good-byes to Jack.

"Winnie, I'll be by to fetch you and Millie in about an hour. I have something to take care of first," said Jack, placing his hand somewhat possessively on the window of the car. John quickly moved the car away from Jack. John didn't care for Jack, but there was no identifiable reason.

Jack got in his car and drove to Stanhope to inform his wife that he would be gone on business for a fortnight. His absence would make it an ideal time for her to visit her sister in Sydney; after all, hadn't she been hinting about visiting her sister for some time now? Jack packed her up and took her to the train station; and "click" went the first domino into place. Jack had set his political aspirations on the Governor's House in Canberra, but it would take more money and power than he possessed at present. With the factory and the station added to his other holdings, he would have that power. No one knew of his great ambition, except his Asian partners in Tokyo. Jack had entered into an agreement with wealthy Japanese bankers to remove the "white only" immigration restriction placed on the Australian Colonies by both the Crown and the Australia authorities. The Japanese felt there was an immense potential for previously untouched wealth in opals and other precious metals in Australia. They were determined to tap this source. Through their unscrupulous partners like Jack, they financed houses of prostitution in all the large coastal cities to raise money to bribe politicians for immigration policy changes. Sydney, Melbourne, and Brisbane were the primary targets, because they were the largest cities and because of their shipping ports. Jack was the local connection to the politicians in these cities. His selection of Kyabram as a center of operation was logical because it was conveniently located, but nearly isolated in the Bush. His function was to filter the money back to Japan after taking a hefty cut for himself. Jack's status as a liaison between the politicians and the Japanese moneymen would increase his level of power and eventually land him in Government House. With his wife on her way to visit her sister, he could concentrate solely on Winifred and the factory. Jack knew if the factory fell into his hands, the station would follow. He could use his influence to have Jannis taxed out of the property or he could create a boycott of the milk produced at the station to accomplish the same result. He had thought about this chess game for years; now was the time to make his move.

"G'day Winnie, and to you, Millie! Are you ready?" he greeted them after Graham answered the door.

"We'll just be a moment, Jack. I need to leave John with some tasks to keep his mind from wandering to the "Sheila's". We'll be back tonight, won't we?" Winifred asked as she parceled out instructions. "Yes, of course," replied Jack as he helped Millie into the back seat of his car.

Jack planned to keep Winifred away from home as late as possible, without damaging the respect that he had earned in the days following George's death

The drive to Shepparton lasted a little longer than Jack had anticipated, but that was good for his plan. The road wasn't paved and the recent rain had caused ruts and potholes that made the drive slow going.

"Jack," Winifred said as they drove into the town "where are we going tae huv a bite?"

Shepparton had two places to eat...A hotel/restaurant similar to, but much nicer than the one in Kyabram and another small diner. The small diner at the south end of the main street offered a limited menu; the hotel, on the other hand, offered a better selection than at Kyabram. Jack, still determined to impress Winifred, preferred the latter. "Winnie, why don't you select one...but the hotel has a more appetizing fare and it would please me to have a nice, relaxing meal with you."

"Go on, Winnie, that sounds verra nice," piped up Millie, adding her two-cents worth.

"Well, it sounds verra nice, perhaps that would be best," responded Winifred.

'Ah, sweet victory will be mine, at last,' thought Jack. Winnie seemed to be more trustful of him than before. Jack parked the car in front of the hotel. The trip had taken its toll on the shiny new condition of his car. The roads in rural Australia were graded, not yet paved, and were still dusty and dangerous. A fine, red dust had settled all over Jack's car from the bottom edge of the side windows all the way down to the tires.

Jack went around to open Winifred's door, but he was not in time. She smiled, giving Jack even more confidence of his ultimate success.

"Come along, you two," shouted Millie from the top of the stairs, "We hae nae a lot of time before the sun goes down, making the return drive verra perilous."

Jack had deliberately scheduled the timing of their arrival to offer him more opportunity to spend time with Winifred. "It'll be fine. We still have plenty of time; it's only two o'clock. See here...on my pocket watch. Oh, Oh! I am wrong! It's actually a quarter to three, but we still have plenty of time to spare. Don't worry! If it gets late, we can stay here at the hotel. The owner is a friend of mine who will gladly put us up."

The truth of the matter was that Jack owned the hotel in partnership with his friends in Japan; of course, the manager was sworn to secrecy. Jack anticipated all along that they would be staying the night before they left Kyabram, but he offered Millie and Winifred false confidence that they would be home that night. His dilemma surfaced only when he needed to convince them that the delay was not planned. He was a master strategist, so this problem would be easy to resolve. The manager greeted them at the doorway to the restaurant.

"G'Day, ladies, how you going?"

"G'Day, to you," they responded in unison.

"Three for dinner," said Jack as he entered behind them.

"Very well," responded the manager as he led them to a large table arranged in the front of the room. The table was located near the window so they could look out and observe the street activity. The surroundings were a little nicer and the room was a little larger than the one in Kyabram, but the hotel design was nearly a carbon copy. It was true that the fare was better. The menu offered fish, pasta, and other delicacies things that Winifred had only heard about. Jack had developed a taste for these items when traveling abroad and was able to arrange for shipments to be sent to his hotel.

"Would you like to try some of these unusual items?" asked Jack, when he noticed Winifred looking at all of them. She simply couldn't make up her mind, so Jack suggested to the waiter that he bring a sample of all of the dishes that they were unsure about.

"I will check with the manager for you," said the waiter as he walked away toward the manager.

"Give him anything he wants and don't act as if you recognize him. Understand?" instructed the manager and the waiter returned to the table.

"We can do that, sir. Do you all want the same?"

"No, just for the ladies! I will have this."

"You know, this is very nice of you, Jack! I think George would approve of our friendship," Winnie said, complimenting Jack.

"Thank you, Winnie. I always respected George, ever since the first day we met. We did seem to get along, except for that unfortunate incident when you arrived. I regretted that day for years."

"I know, Jack, it was a terrible misunderstanding and I, too, regretted it; perhaps we should have been friends all these years."

"After all, we are of the same background, being British subjects and all," chimed in Millie, pushing them together in a not too subtle way.

"Right you are!" answered Jack, just as the waiter brought the teapot and cups. "I'm glad we've had this day to speak to each other, but I am sorry about the reason that brought us here." He was hard-pressed to bring sincerity into his voice; he was not the type of bloke to forget his humiliation of that fateful day.

The waiter poured the tea and Winifred held the cup in both hands, gathering the warmth from the tea and offering Jack a look of warmth, also.

Millie saw this look and thought, 'Maybe, just maybe, this could work! That is, if I can push a little, but not too hard.'

"You ken, Jack, maybe you could help Jannis and I with the factory and station," Winifred said, abruptly. She surprised herself, because she had been lost in thought before the outburst.

"Yes, I could, Winnie," responded Jack.

"You ken, I think that would be just famous," added Millie, happily.

"Yes, it would, Mum. You know Jannis and I are nae always sure of what tae do and we could use some help. I think that Jack, with his business sense, could set us on the right course."

"I would be happy to help you out, Winnie. You know I have always had your best interests at heart."

After that statement, they fell silent and began to eat their meal, which had just arrived.

Jack finished first and looked at the clock on the wall above the doorway. "Good Lord! Look at the time! We need to get back before dark." His watch indicated five o'clock.

"Don't worry, Jack! I told John we would be late."

"Late, yes, but if we don't go soon, we will have to stay the night. The road is no place to be after dark."

"You mean we must stay here tonight?" asked Millie.

"Yes, I'm afraid that we will," answered Jack.

"Oh, that would be all right, I told John we could be staying overnight."

"Well, then I must organize rooms for us," said Jack as he got up and went to the front desk.

His plans were coming to fruition much more rapidly than his wildest dreams. When he returned, he said, "I've organized two rooms for us, so I will see you both in the morning."

"Jack, let's nae go now. We need tae talk more about the factory and the station," Millie begged.

"That would be nice, I should go over the bookwork to figure out where George was at," answered Jack, trying to curb his enthusiasm. He waited for Winnie to comment, but she just sat and looked at him with the same trust she had exhibited earlier.

"You know, Jack..." Millie started to say, just as Winifred said, "I don't really know where we stand. We rarely spoke of it."

"That's all right, when we look at the books we should be able to pick up where he left off," replied Jack in a most officious manner. "You can feel confident that we will be able to continue his dream."

The hour was growing late, but Winifred didn't seem to mind. It was nice to talk to someone about her doubts. She gazed around the room and thought how nice the setting was and how George would have enjoyed the dinner with them.

Millie was still concentrating on how this whole outing could benefit her. "It seems as though Winnie is getting on well with Jack. Should I continue tae push or just let nature take its course? Nae, let it go," she said to herself.

The sun had long set and the night sky surrounded them as they talked over past experiences. The wind had risen to a cooling breeze and Winifred was very comfortable. Millie began to yawn and excused herself. "I'm off tae bed; come up when you're finished. Good night tae you, Jack. I will see you in the morning." She headed to the front desk for the key to her room...all courtesy of Jack.

With Millie gone, Jack felt he could step up the pace to charm Winnie. "Winnie, may I call you Winnie?" asked Jack in very humble voice.

"I think that would be nice."

"Thank you, Winnie! I know that was what George called you and I wouldn't want to intrude."

"That would be fine; I think George would approve."

He was building their relationship, brick by brick, hoping to distract her from any misgivings. This would not be easy, for as soon as Winifred was through grieving, she would become more aware of the business.

Winifred looked closely at the room and noticed for the first time that it had an oriental decor strangely out of place out here in the Bush. Jack decorated it to familiarize the Aussies with the oriental culture. His ulterior motive was to effect a subtle change to the government immigration policy. At the far end of the large room was a statue of something that Winifred had not seen before, except in storybooks. This beast… a dragon…stretched across the center entrance. She hadn't noticed it before, even though it was colored with bright reds and oranges. The tongue was painted green and appeared to flicker in and out as the ceiling fan blades sliced through the incandescent light. The changing light seemed to give life to the feathery protrusions from its long, snake-like body. Oriental paintings lined the walls on both sides of the dining room. Jack had these paintings sent to him from Japan, along with the Japanese cook he had in the kitchen…all part of his plan to make Australians aware of the Asians in illusive, insinuative ways. Some of the officials at Government house were in the pockets of Jack and his Japanese partners and they, too, were in favor of multi-national immigration. Jack and his partners were pushing hard for laws to further their fortunes needed the new immigration laws so they could further their fortunes by the exploitation of the Aussies.

Winnie continued her perusal of the room; it was rich in Far Eastern art and tradition. The tables were covered with red and royal blue tablecloths, with large decorative centerpieces. This adornment was so different from the hotel in Kyabram with its wooden plank tables covered with white linen and plain wooden chairs. There the walls were covered with dust from the streets, occasionally interrupted by a piece of local art hung in a haphazard manner about the room. Winifred liked what she saw.

"Winnie?"

"Y-yes."

"Where are you? You seem to be somewhere else," asked Jack, startling her.

"Oh, Jack! I was just looking at all these beautiful things and wishing that I could hae such nice things of my own."

"You will, Winnie, once we look at the books and make sure everything's right."

"Oh, you sound so much like George when you say that," reminisced Winifred, "I can hear him now."

"Don't fret; we will be all right," said Jack. It was getting much later than either of them realized. The waiter and front desk clerk were turning off lights as they stacked chairs on the empty tables.

"You finished?" asked the waiter as he passed by with a chair in each hand.

"Yes, we are," replied Jack as he motioned for the desk clerk to bring the bill.

"Shall I put it on your bill along with the rooms?"

"Yes, that would be good."

"Then, it's good night to you!" he said as he walked toward the front desk, leaving Jack and Winifred at the table as the last light was extinguished. They each went to their respective rooms. Jack's focus was now on revenge. He thought that Winnie was ripe for a relationship in which he no longer had an interest. At this juncture, it would only complicate matters.

Jack was up early and made sure with the day clerk that he would not be recognized as the owner of the hotel. Winifred and Millie descended the stairs just as he finished. Jack felt uncomfortable about how narrowly they missed hearing his orders.

"How you going, Jack? Is everything all right?" asked Millie as she set her small bag down on the running board of Jack's car.

"Yes, everything is fine. I was just inquiring as to how the road is. They said it rained between here and Kyabram last night." His luck was holding… it had rained! Once again, he was able to dissemble to cover his discussion about his real role in the hotel business. "Let me help you into the car," continued Jack as he held out his hand to Winifred. They were on their way home.

The roads and their maintenance were a vast improvement from when Winifred had arrived in Australia, but they were still dirty and dusty. The red silt was billowing up behind the car as they sped along at twenty-five to forty-five miles an hour. The road was just barely wide enough that an oncoming vehicle could pass without exchanging paint, depending on where the vehicles met. Fortunately, there were not many cars on the road at this time. Jack drove along, keeping the conversation light, holding on to the good will he had so carefully cultivated the night before.

Millie was sitting in the middle of the back seat like a queen, her head turning from side to side in an effort not to miss any of the scenery. Suddenly, Jack stopped the car.

"What is it?" questioned Millie.

"Just a roo," responded Winifred before Jack could answer.

"Look, there he goes! Oh, look, there's more approaching. Do you see them, Jack?"

"Yes, there they are. Something must have stirred them!" answered Jack, just as the roos passed with three or four dingoes hot on their heels. The dingoes really had no chance to catch the roos, so they had developed a chase and wait strategy. The larger dogs would chase them to a pack of smaller dogs and the slower roos would fall prey. The dingoes are the renowned wild dogs of Australia and are considered its largest predator.

Jack eased the car forward again. The road had a long sweeping turn just before the river. The river crossing occurred at the shallowest part; no bridge had yet been constructed. The river bottom was hard and had been firmed by dumping gravel and small rocks, packed down by workers with large trucks. Jack eased toward the edge and then into the water, which was at a depth of about half a meter. The river crossing itself spanned one hundred yards, so he moved the car slowly not to flood out the engine. Jack had crossed the river many times and had been stranded in the middle more than once. His thoughts, as he slowly forded the river, turned to his success. He thought that Millie was on his side and had made the transition from George to him. As the water rose over the front bumper and began to rise to the radiator, Jack slowed down to five miles an hour and the water receded.

"I hope we will nae flood the engine," Millie worried, as she tried to focus her attention from the water surrounding the car.

"Don't worry, Millie! It will be all right now that I have slowed to a mere crawl."

"Mum, you worry too much. Jack wouldn't let anything happen tae us, now would you, Jack?"

"No, I would lose my life before I would allow anything to happen," responded Jack while thinking; 'Now I've got her!'

It was late afternoon by the time they pulled into Kyabram. The car had completely dried and was again covered with the red road dust. John was waiting impatiently in front of the house for them to return. He didn't like Jack and had a difficult time hiding that.

"Well, it's nice of you to come home, Mother." John said in an irritable tone.

"And G'day to you," countered Winifred in an authoritative tone.

"I'm sorry, Mother! I have been concerned and worried."

"I know, John, but it was all right. We were with Jack and he wouldn't let anything happen to us."

John looked at Jack, aware of the change in attitude. John felt uneasy around Jack, but had no real basis for that uneasiness. John helped his mother out of the car and opened the door for Millie.

Winifred leaned on the window opening. "Jack, we had a wonderful time and we should get together later, maybe tomorrow, tae look through the books so we can see how we are doing." She then turned up the walkway to the house with John following closely behind, a puzzled look on his face. He glanced back at Jack, just in time to see Jack's slight smile. Jack drove off to Stanhope to begin the next phase of his vengeance.

Chapter 6

J. W. Chelmsford, practicing Solicitor of Law, and Jack's confidential friend, stood at the door of his office as Jack drove up. The old house he used for his office had once been the home of Jack's father. JW, as everyone knew him, had completed his study of law in England and had been sent to Australia as a representative of the Crown. His primary function was to insure that the Crown didn't lose any of its control over the economy in this part of Outback Australia. There were several solicitors, as they are called in English Law, strategically placed around the country. Jack and his father soon convinced JW that it would be more profitable to direct some of the economic benefits to them. The house hadn't been painted since Jack's father died. The window screens were dangling half-off the windows and the porch was in a sad state of disrepair. JW didn't waste any time on upkeep of the property; he was too busy removing riches from the colonists to the Crown; and now, of course, to Jack. He was far more interested in the local barmaids and the "drink" to be wasting time on repairs. Soon he would be back in England, entitled to a rich lifestyle in the upper class. His great hope was for an appointment to the Bar in London.

The center of the porch sagged under JW's weight as he walked across to greet Jack, who was stepping down from the car's running board.

"Jack, how you going?"

"Fine, how you going?"

"I would be better if I could stop eating everything in sight."

"Yeah, you should give it up," returned Jack as he reached to shake JW's hand. And give up the ale. That wouldn't hurt, thought Jack, eying JW's huge girth. JW stood about five foot nine inches and was almost the same in width; his beard matched his hair, uncombed, but clean. His eyes sparkled under his huge eyebrows. They shook hands and turned to go into the house. JW lumbered ahead, with Jack following closely behind.

"What is it I can do for us, Jack?" asked JW as he walked around his desk to sit down. JW knew if Jack needed legal work, it spelled profit for him as well.

"As you know," started Jack, "George McLean has passed away. A lot of money is waiting to be made if I can obtain control of the factory and the station that supplies the milk for the cheese."

"But," interjected JW, "without my help you won't get it! So there must be something in it for me as well."

"Yes, I recognize that fact. There will be some compensation for a solicitor who sees his way clear to help and, later, conveniently forgets everything about this venture," answered Jack with a hint of sarcasm in his voice.

"What you need is to convince the widow to give you that control."

"Yes, I know, and I could achieve that given enough time, but..."

"But you don't have the time," interrupted JW. "I think I could organize the paperwork, but her signature is necessary."

"That's right, so what do we do?" questioned Jack, as he leaned forward, unable to control his anticipation of the up-coming wealth.

"I could prepare a Quit Claim Deed giving you control and ownership of all the factory property. All that would be needed is her signature and that would give you not only control, but also ownership. Of course, the trick is to obtain her signature."

"I think I can do that. She is beginning to trust me and her mother has become an ally that I hadn't counted on," said Jack, excitement building in his mind. The two men sat looking at each other across the oak desk that JW had transported from England when he received his Australian appointment. JW pushed back his chair and looked up at the ceiling fan as it spun slowly around, struggling to move the hot air fast enough to cool the room. He was thinking of the steps necessary to get back to England with the small fortune he had been gathering over the years, of his future appointment as the Magistrate in Canberra, and then on to London.

"JW," interrupted Jack from JW's daydream. "You need to organize that paperwork soon and quit thinking about the Magistrate appointment. I think we can assure that after I get control. You are well aware that I have the contacts to appoint you; so, don't worry, it will happen."

"Yes, I know that alone could be worth some legal advice in the direction you are heading," said JW in response to Jack's promise.

"I don't need advice, I need a solution, JW!" answered Jack. As he was speaking, the smile left his lips and his face became stone cold. JW felt a measure of fear at Jack's very intensity.

"What you must do is gain her confidence that your only concern is for her and her family's welfare. You must convince her that you will run the business as she would want it."

"I don't have time to court her."

"I don't think it will take that much time, but you should be prepared to spend as much time as it takes right now, because she will never sign it over to you without that confidence."

"There must be a faster way, JW! Well, perhaps I have her partial confidence since she wants me to look over the books tomorrow," mused Jack, thinking out-loud.

"That's good, Jack. Maintain that confidence and buy me some time to organize the paperwork," said JW, as he reached for a law book on the shelf behind his desk.

"Just how much time will you need?"

"I must review various legal points of reference to insure that our agreements will stand the scrutiny of the court, if it should ever go that far. Give me a month and, in the meantime, you can further your relationship with her."

"Okay, but I will only give you a fortnight to have the paperwork ready. Am I clear?" Jack responded, with viciousness that JW had never heard from him! JW knew enough about Jack's behavior that it would be go very badly for him if he didn't deliver what Jack wanted.

"Of course, I do," he said. He quickly opened the book he had retrieved from the shelf earlier to search for the reference material he intended to use.

Jack got up and headed toward the door, turning back to JW when he reached the doorway. "Don't forget! I want results within a fortnight."

"Uh huh," mumbled JW, as he continued to scan the law reference while Jack stalked out to his car.

Jack was consumed with his revenge. He would not rest until he had achieved his goal...no one was allowed to make a fool of Jack.

'Maybe we could take over by the end of the year. That way, the New Year tax wouldn't be too much,' thought Jack as he headed up the walkway to the front door of his house, a seemingly modest dwelling of the day on the outside, but entirely different inside. Jack had imported furnishings and expensive paintings that were not visible to anyone but his family. His wife was not aware of his Japanese connections; after all, he was involved with an import business in Sydney and Brisbane. Her impression, if she ever thought about it, was that he was holding these expensive items, pending their sale and transfer to points within Australia. Sometimes, the furnishings changed because Jack was rotating them through his various businesses to hide them from the tax collectors.

JW reviewed his law books until late into the night, and was still unable to find a legal way to affect a takeover without Winifred's signature.

'The only way I see to do this is very risky, at best,' he thought, 'and we need a way to conceal this from her notice until it's finalized.'

He looked at the clock on the wall just as it began to chime two o'clock in the morning. JW yawned as he got up to prepare for bed. 'I'll start to put something together tomorrow,' he thought as he began to undress and get into his nightshirt. The temperature could cool off around this time, so it was necessary to wear nightclothes and to retrieve the blanket that had been discarded earlier in the night.

JW got up early and began to formulate a plan that, if Jack was as smooth with women as he claimed, would enable him to acquire the business... not on the "up and up", but still legally. The main impediment was to obtain Winifred's signature on a document, without her realizing that she had signed over control and ownership of the factory. He planned on creating a document giving Jack complete control to manage, expand, and transfer money within the company without her express authorization, in addition to a majority ownership of the factory. He would, in essence, be able to sell or transfer complete ownership to himself. The document would declare that Jack could assume complete ownership within a year after the initial signature. As a reward for the management of the factory, there would be no compensation to Winifred, other than a small monthly annuity for her maintenance. The maintenance annuity would have a clause stating that it would increase at two percent per annum and that, upon her death, this right would pass to Graham. JW thought that, with this compensation, she would not be inclined to fight the takeover. He would have to tell Jack this, even though he knew Jack wouldn't like it.

The document would have to bear the official stamp of an officer of the court. JW would have no problem with the stamp; he could easily have that taken care of by the Magistrate in Shepparton. The document would have to be stamped before Winifred signed it, in the event that Jack was able to obtain her signature without her noticing the seal. JW sat down and began to draft the paper, which he came to think of as his crowning achievement. 'If I succeed in this, Jack will owe me more than even he could pay. I will have my way paved to Canberra and, eventually, to England,' JW thought to himself as he began to type the first part of the document.

Jack drove to Kyabram to see Winifred and uphold his role in the plan. Millie was standing at the gate as he drove up.

"How you going?" she asked, as he opened the door and stepped out.

"I had a nice drive over here. How you going, Mrs. Gunn?" he responded, with a huge smile for Millie's obvious delight in seeing him. She still was holding on to her design for Winnie to be Mrs. Carrigan.

"Dinnae stand so formal with me, Jack," Millie said as she opened the gate to let him in.

"I must show respect, Mrs. Gunn, or my mum would have my hide." he said, with as much honesty as he was capable of.

"Is Winnie ready to go to Stanhope?" Jack asked.

"Not quite! Could we be speaking for a moment, Jack?" Millie asked as she gently edged him out the gate and away from the view of the house. Jack didn't know what to expect from her, but she seemed very insistent.

"As you know, I had no part in the marriage of George and Winifred. They had the Captain marry them in route," she began, "Then I told her afterward that she had been promised to you and should not have married George."

"I know that and I don't hold you responsible," interrupted Jack, with dulcet tones. "They were in love and I can understand that of course, I felt badly at first, but, as I came to know George, I was glad they were together. They made a very nice couple," he said. "I feel very sad about George passing. I can only hope I can help both of you get what you deserve." Jack's words were as fraudulent as his demeanor. "You must realize I still think of Winifred with George and probably always will, they were meant to be with each other," he continued, "and, even though I still do love Winnie, I couldn't do anything that would not be right for her," he finished abruptly. Winnie had appeared at the gate.

"G'Day, Winifred and how are you going?" asked Jack.

"Oh, I'm fine and you?" she answered back as she passed through the open gate to the passenger side of the car. "What were you two gabbing on about?

Anything I should know?"

"Nothing really, just weather and such," Millie said as she rounded the rear of the car to go back to the house. Winnie got in and Jack closed the door and they left for Stanhope.

As they drove down the road, Winifred said, "Jack, what you said to Mum was very nice and I do feel affection for you as a good friend!"

This was a complete surprise to Jack. "How long had you been standing there?" he asked, wondering if he had gone too far in his declarations to Millie.

"Oh, just long enough tae hear what you said about George and me. That was verra nice! Thank you, Jack."

"That's all right. I do feel that way, you know" he commented, trying very hard to conceal his real motive.

They soon arrived at the factory office and Jack parked the car in George's old parking space. It was only a small victory, but Jack felt he would be the only one to park there. He was beginning to feel confident that this subterfuge would soon be over. They went up the steps to the office and Jack helped Winifred off with her coat. He hung up their coats and sat down behind the large desk, while Winifred sat down in the small chair next to him. They began to go though the mail and the other papers that had accumulated on George's desk.

In the meantime, JW had drafted the legal paper in his head and began to formalize the documents that would give Jack control and avoid a costly legal entanglement. The objectives, now firmly cemented in JW's mind, were for Jack to obtain administrative control and, as time passed, complete control. All of this would be hidden in the legal jargon for ownership with no recourse for Winifred or the McLean family. Of course, the remaining difficult issue was obtaining the Magistrate's seal on the document after Winifred had signed it.

That was the only part that JW was skeptical about, for if she realized what she had done, she could stop the sealing of the document by the Magistrate. The whole shady deal would come out and he and Jack would be jailed.

Jack spent most of the day at the office going through the business paperwork with Winifred. In the afternoon, JW sent a messenger to summon Jack to his office that afternoon.

"It seems I'm needed at my solicitor's; could we continue this later?" asked Jack.

"That would be fine. I think John is on his way over to fetch me anyway," she said, without looking up from the papers.

Jack quickly got into his car and drove to JW's.

"What is the problem now?" He exploded as he entered the house without knocking.

"We don't knock anymore?" asked JW as he looked up at Jack.

"No, we don't when you send someone to get me while I'm working on getting next to our target" Jack said, half-shouting now.

"Calm yourself! You need to know that this paperwork may not work as we have planned."

"What do you mean?"

"The Magistrate could be blocked from sealing it, if Winifred realizes what she has signed before you can hide it," responded JW in a panic-stricken voice.

"You scare too easily! Nothing will happen. Besides, the Magistrate will seal the document on my word alone."

"That may be true, but if Winifred intervenes prior to the seal, it could be beyond his control. That would cause us all kinds of trouble, not only on this deal, but it could arouse interest in all your other activities!" JW said, commandingly.

"You could be right! Maybe I should check with the Magistrate on how to proceed. I'll be back later tonight; just continue on with your work." Jack had not forgotten about Winifred at the factory and decided to go by and tell her he had to go on another errand; but, when he arrived at the office, she had left. He decided to see her the next day and left for Shepparton. The road was not long but still had its dangers, so Jack drove slowly and kept his eyes focused on the road ahead as far as he could. But, with the night approaching, it was becoming harder and harder to see. He thought to himself as he drove, 'How can I overcome this and get her to sign without any trouble?'

It was dark when he arrived in Shepparton, but it wasn't all that late because during mid- to late winter, the sun set very early. The winters in this part of Australia were not very cold, but the temperature shift was enough that a jacket was needed. The temperatures would occasionally dip into the freezing mark, but not much beyond. This temperature shift was not as common as in Melbourne, but seemed cold since everyone was still accustomed to hot summer temperatures. The rain would pour for days on end and, if the mild wind were factored in, it would seem very cold indeed.

Jack drove to the Magistrates' house and charged up the path and banged on the door. It opened almost immediately and the butler asked, "May I be of some assistance, sir?"

"Yes, you may," said Jack, pushing his way in. "I need to see the Magistrate."

"Shall I tell him who is calling?" asked the butler, who was concerned about this angry man who had come to call.

"Yes, tell him it's Jack Carrigan to see him on an important matter."

"Very good, sir, please wait in the study."

The butler disappeared down the hall and left Jack standing near the entrance of the study. Jack was nervous and did not want to wait one minute. The Magistrate was at the other end of the house and not in a mood to be disturbed. He was entertaining a young lady from the hotel/pub downtown, while his wife was off on holiday in England visiting her mother. He had been to England several times in the two years since Jack had arranged his appointment to the Magistrate position. He was bent on living as well as the Magistrates in England, so he arranged to have his very proper English butler brought over on his last trip. The butler was indentured for five years and had been promised a substantial position at Government House if he met expectations.

"You have a visitor, M'lord," announced the butler, stopping just short of the door in an effort not to enter at an inopportune time.

"Not now, Rupert," snapped the Magistrate.

"But, Sir, it's Jack Car..."

"I'll be right out. Tell him to have a drink and I'll be there in two minutes."

"Is that all it will take?" interrupted Jack as he entered the room, much to the butler's dismay. "Get your clothes on, Lucy, and come back in an hour; Jim and I have business."

Lucy started to say something and Jack raised his hand to his lips to signal her to be quiet and do what he said. She picked up her clothes and put them under her arm, pushed her way past the startled butler and went down the hall to the study where Jack had been told to wait. The butler was astonished by the even more surprised by what Lucy was or, more accurately, was not wearing. He had never seen a fully naked woman leave a room with her clothes under her arm before. His experiences with naked women were limited to peeking at his sister when she bathed in the large tub in their kitchen.

Jack pushed him into the hall and closed the door behind him. "Look, Jim, I know there should be some sort of protocol here; but I am in desperate need of some advice."

"I don't care what you need, Jack! Don't think that you can barge in here again."

"Jim, need I remind about how you came by your position? I am aware that we need to act as if I am the lowly merchant, but this matter is of utmost importance," said Jack, trying to retain control over the situation.

"All right, Jack! I well know who is responsible for my position, but this had better be important, because Lucy was about to give me a night to remember."

"Don't worry, she'll come back and you can continue where you left off; besides, I can arrange it so you two can go to Melbourne and spend a week doing whatever you want to do."

"Well, what in the hell is so dammed important?" asked Jim, still not mollified.

Jack decided to back off for now, especially with factory takeover such an important issue. So, he held his tongue and marshaled his thoughts about what he was going to tell Jim. First looking at the floor then at the ceiling, trying to pull his thoughts together, Jack seemed indecisive; Jim began to think that he had an opportunity to control Jack. Jack continued to think without speaking, which, to Jim, seemed to last an eternity. Finally, Jack looked straight at Jim and spoke very slowly in an effort to make himself understood. "Jim, here is my dilemma...if Winifred McLean discovers that she has signed an important document prior to affixing the seal on it, she could stop my planned business takeover. I need you to guarantee that she will not realize what's happening. I need your assurance that the documents cannot be challenged in court by anyone. This is of great importance to me."

Jim looked at Jack and, for the first time in their rather shady relationship, he sensed the presence of genuine malevolence. Jim had known Jack for nearly ten years, but he had never seen this level of intensity. Jim was relieved that he was not the recipient of all Jack's hatred and determination. The ruination of the McLean family would not cause Jack to lose a moment's sleep.

"Okay," Jim begrudgingly responded. "The first order of business is to draw up the documents."

"I have someone taking care of that now," Jack interrupted, impatiently.

"Good! When they are complete, I will review them to insure they provide for every eventuality."

"I'm sure the documents will meet those criteria and then some!" said Jack with a slight grimace that could have passed for a smile. "But, remember...the most important part is the seal."

"You let me worry about that," said Jim with a sly smile of his own. He saw Jack's request as the final assurance of his own goal to be Prime Minister. He would enlist Jack's financial help by proving, once and for all, that he was worthy of Jack's support and the corresponding support of Jack's Asian friends. "Get me those papers as soon as you can, Jack, and I will take it from there."

"Do you need them before or after she signs them?"

"Before! I must see them before and we must make sure that I have the exact date that she will sign them. Otherwise, it's all for naught! We must be very clear on this."

"That finishes our business then, Jim. I will bring you the papers within a fortnight."

"Goodnight to you, Jack. Oh, by the way, could you have Lucy come back since you were the one who dismissed her?"

"I'll see what can be done, Jim, but don't forget... a fortnight or sooner," Jack reminded him, as he saw the partially open door. When he realized that the door had not been closed he wondered, "Could the butler have been listening?" Jack looked down the hall and was relieved to find that the butler was nowhere to be seen.

"Don't forget; I need to see the papers before signature," shouted Jim as Jack left.

Jack mused on the whole episode as he got into his car. "That chap is an idiot if he thinks that I will help him to be Prime Minister." Jack had always been aware of Jim's goal and had been using it to manipulate him. As Jack drove back to Stanhope in the darkness, he was very pleased with himself for his ability to use people for his own gain. Of course, he hadn't forgotten to tell Lucy to go back to Jim's; after all, he still needed Jim to complete the takeover.

The two men had been so engrossed in their scheming that they were unaware there was a listener by the slightly open hallway door. The butler had heard enough to put those two conspirators in prison for a long time. He reflected for a moment and decided to record the date and the substance of the conversation that he had overheard. He recorded his observances to use to his future advantage. He could use a favor to shorten his indenture period and have some "ready cash" stashed away. He had developed a relationship with a woman in town, but could not bring his plans to fruition until he was able to rid himself of the indenture. Surely he could gather more information on what he had overheard and put it to good use. Even Jack, who prided himself on his skill as a master manipulator, couldn't have imagined that his revenge would include so many variables. JW would receive payment for his part, so would Jim; and, now there was the price for the butler's silence. Even without knowledge of the butler's involvement, Jack began to add up all the people who would need to be bought off, and, for a millisecond, began to doubt the worth of the factory in hard currency, not withstanding his desire for vengeance. True, the factory was currently a small operation; but, with his connections throughout Australia, it had potential. In 1939, he could not have anticipated that the world would be at war in less than two years and that the factory would become a major food supplier to support the war effort.

Jack arrived home shortly after midnight and was surprised to find JW at his door. "What are you doing here?" he demanded.

"I finished your paperwork. Knowing just how badly you want this to be over and done with... I wanted you to have it before I change my mind."

"What do you mean, 'change your mind'?" Jack interjected.

"I have been working on this all day; but I liked George. Somehow, this just doesn't seem right!" said JW, with as much courage as his alcohol haze would allow.

"What are you saying? My good will alone could propel you to Government House as Representative of the entire district. With my connections, so much is possible for you; but, without them, nothing will happen. You do realize that, don't you?" Jack was very conscious of the need to intimidate JW.

"I, I, I guess, you're right. Here are the papers; did you see the Magistrate?"

"Give me the papers! You go home and sleep it off! You'll feel better in the morning," said Jack, ignoring JW's question. JW was not aware of the extent of Jack's influence with the Magistrate, because Jack was careful not to reveal the extent of his connections to anyone. He did not trust; therefore, he kept his resources close to the vest. He operated with cunning, using weaknesses against all who revealed them. He was not above blackmail, but stopped short of allowing his victims off the hook. JW staggered off in the general direction of his own house. Unconcerned, Jack had the important papers in his hands and there was time to rectify any errors. Even though it was nearly time for the monthly statements of account, the ledgers were not due for several days. Jack scanned the paperwork as he walked into the house. Truth be known, Jack had not finished even rudimentary education, so he had difficulty with reading comprehension. He relied on intimidation and aggressiveness to compel others to interpret for him. These tactics had worked for many years, so no one was aware of his weakness.

While closing the door behind him, he noticed a light on in the back of the house and had a chilling thought that maybe his wife had come home early and be the ruination of his plans. His fear was not unfounded for he, himself, had left the light on in his mad rush to go see the Magistrate.

'This is becoming a nightmare of apprehension even for me,' he thought, 'this must be over and done with very soon... I'll take these papers to Jim tomorrow.' And with that, he fell asleep on top of the bed, fully clothed. His next thought did not occur until he rolled over on the bed and felt the warmth of the sun on his face.

"What time is it?"

"Eleven o'clock! Oh my God, I should have met Jim by now." He jumped up and changed from the previous day's clothing. "I'll have to rush over and have Jim check these papers." He put on his shoes; he ran to the loo, combed through his hair and splashed water in his face to present semblance of cleanliness. Then he was in the car, heading back to Shepparton. As he pulled up to the Magistrate's house, just in time to see Julie leaving, so he was sure Jim, was in no condition to review the paperwork. Jack knocked loudly at the door, cursing Jim under his breath. Much to his surprise Jim opened to door.

"Jack, I was actually expecting to see you back much earlier." Jack's surprised look vanished and he pushed his way through the doorway. "Well, it's good to see you too, thanks for the cheery greeting!" Jim retorted as he moved aside to let Jack in. "Your timing couldn't be better, even though you're later than I expected. Lucy just left."

"Well, I slept in. These drives back and forth are killing me, but I have the paper work here. Look it over and see if it will hold up legally." He handed the papers to Jim, who took them and walked down the hall to the study.

Jack sat an interminable time while Jim read and reread the papers. The door opened to the study and the butler peered in to see Jack sitting across the desk from Jim. "Would there be anything you need, M'lord?" he asked as Jack turned to see who had entered the room.

"Nothing for me. How are you, Jack?" asked Jim still studying the papers. Jim was not concerned over the butler's presence because they had an agreement on his indenture for five years. Jack, on the other hand, had no agreement with the butler and was suspicious of everyone. In spite of his suspicious nature, he was not aware of the butler moving closer to the table, where he was able to read most of the top page of the paper that Jim had finished reviewing. The nature of the scheme clarified in his mind, but he innocently asked, "Sir, would you care for tea?"

"Yes, that would be fine" Jack slowly responded, giving the butler more than enough time to finish the page.

"Very good, sir! Milk and sugar?"

"No, just milk." Like many other Australians, Jack had milk with tea as a common practice.

As the butler left to prepare the tea, Jack asked "Can you trust him?"

Jim disregarded Jack's query and went on to say, "I will stamp this paper with the seal, but you need to hide it from her when she signs it.

As I have stressed to you before, I must know the exact date she will sign it."

"I plan to have it signed two days from now, which will be on the 30th," Jack answered, still staring at the door where the butler had exited.

Jack turned just as he answered Jim with the date as the butler arrived with the tea and asked,

"How much milk, sir?" as he poured the tea from a pot to Jack's cup. The butler was concentrating on the date he heard as he entered the room. 'Two days from now, the 30th, November 30, 1939,' he thought to himself. 'I'll write that down along with the other information! This may serve me well when I need a favor.' He excused himself.

"My previous question to you comes to mind. Can you trust the butler?" asked Jack.

"Yes, besides he can hardly read or write." This was not true, but Jim didn't know that. His wife had hired the butler specifically to spy on Jim; and she was receiving regular reports in England from the butler. The servant went to his room and wrote down the date and the legal phrases he had seen for future reference.

"I'll get the stamp from the office and place the stamp on the paper where it will not be easy to notice if you cover the second page with the first. It will resemble a bill."

"Are you sure?"

"Look at this! What does it look like to you?"

"You're right, it does."

"Jack, let me get my coat and hat and we will go to the office. Then you can return and put your plan in action." said Jim as he moved to the closet to get his hat and coat. Jim always wore a suit coat and hat; he felt that his attire demonstrated his status in the community.

They arrived at the office just as the Constable was leaving to go to Stanhope, relating to a disturbance at the factory. "Mr. Carrigan, it appears someone was hurt at the factory, will you be going to Stanhope soon?" he asked as he met him on the steps.

"What happened?" asked Jack.

"Just a minor accident; someone ran over a loader's foot with a truck. Luckily, nothing was broken, but the bloke whose foot got run over punched the driver. Now I have to separate them for a while."

"I don't need to be there for that. Please tell Mrs. McLean that I'll be over tomorrow."

"I'll tell her. What time do you think?"

"Don't know, possibly early afternoon. And thanks Constable." said Jack, concealing his connection with the Constable by being properly respectful.

"Jack, c'mon. We need to seal this so you can complete your task on the correct date." said Jim.

They went into the building and up to Jim's office, where he had one of the secretaries bring in the seal.

"Will there be anything else, your Honor?" she asked as she left the seal on his desk.

"No, that will be all. Please close the door for me, thank you." She closed the door as she left and both men set the papers on the desk next to the seal.

"Now, what we need is for the seal to be concealed when she signs this," said Jim as he placed the top page exactly the way he wanted it, over the second page. "This is the way you need to present it to her, Jack."

"Then I need her to sign on this line, right here?"

"Yes, that will make it legal. When she signs it, move immediately to the next set of bills so she will not suspect."

"Where are you going to place the seal?"

"Right here, just above the signature. Now remember, hold the papers like this or she will see the seal."

"Just like this?"

"Yes, exactly like this and move quickly or she will notice." he said as he applied the seal. "This will give you the factory, as sole owner." Since JW had inserted a section to cover any potential problems, he added, "You are required to pay her a small allowance for life."

"I don't want that."

"No, this is a good move. Now, it will seem as though she did this willingly and will save you a prolonged court battle. Again, this is a good move, not only that it has a provision for her son Graham."

"How much is the so called allowance?"

"It's 2,000 pound a year and can only go to 10,000. Also the one for her son is incremented from 500 to 2,000 in any circumstances. That's nothing compared to what you will make, and it promotes the idea that you actually bought her out."

"You think this is good?"

"It's a stroke of genius, I can't believe I thought of it," responded Jim with a touch of awe in his voice.

"Alright! If you think It's good, then I guess it will work." Jack was still apprehensive.

"Trust me, Jack! Now let's go over to the hotel for some tucker."

As they left the building and headed to the hotel, Jack could feel victory within his grasp. His tension seemed to flow right out of his body and the creases on his forehead disappeared.

Jack arrived early to pick up Winifred at her house, but Arthur met him at the door. "G'Day, Mr. Carrigan! Mum and everyone went to the factory."

"What do you mean by 'everyone'?"

"Mum, Gran-mum, John, and Graham." replied Arthur.

Jack knew Graham would be with her, but he was unclear why the others went also.

"Why did all of them go?"

"Mum wanted to go to Shepparton to shop after she finished this morning."

Jack knew he better get to the factory quickly before she had finished or it would be another month before he could get her in a position to sign the paper again.

"Thank you." As he drove away Jack was panicking at the thought he might be too late, but, as usual, his face showed very little emotion.

He arrived at the office just in time to see Winifred and the others entering the building. He gave a sigh of relief; he was just in time. Jack pulled his car into the parking space that was once George's and turned off the engine and went inside.

Winifred greeted him as she hung her coat on the rack and bent down to help Graham. "G'Day, how you going?"

"Just fine and you? Are you ready to get this work done so you can go shopping?"

"How did you know that?"

"Oh, I stopped to pick you up and Arthur told me."

Jack paid particular attention to the location of everyone in the room. Winifred moved over to the desk in the center of the little office and Graham followed close behind. Millie stood over near the right side of the desk with John just over her left shoulder. Then, Jack walked around the desk to be along side Winifred so he could see what bills and other correspondence she was working on. There was already a stack of papers on the desk, so Jack thought he could mix the important paper in with the rest and she would never know until he decided to show her, on Monday.

"Let me see what we have here?" Jack said, as he moved closer to Winifred and slipped his paper into the stack. Jack felt no one saw, and he was right, with the exception of Graham. Graham was at eye level with the stack of papers, and even though he was curious, he wasn't concerned about what happened.

"Well, let's get started," enthused Jack as he handed Winifred the paper. His hope was that she would sign it first and then it would be buried under the others he could recover it later.

Winfred took hold of the pen and Jack laid the paper under her hand and she began to sign. It seemed like an eternity had passed when Graham asked his mother for some water. She looked up to

Millie to get it then returned to the signing. Jack couldn't believe it was finally signed. He quickly moved another paper on top and she looked at it and him and he motioned it was another bill that had to be paid.

Everything was proceeding on schedule, when Graham returned back to his mother's side. Curiosity finally got the better of him and he reached up and pulled out the second page of Jack's paper and asked, "Mum, why does this one have bumps on it?"

"I don't know, let me see."

"It's just an invoice, Winnie," said Jack as he reached for the paper, barely missing as Winifred pulled it out to read. Jack simply stood there, hoping she would not understand what it said.

"You...bloody bastard, you...no good rotten bastard!" shouted Winfred as she slapped his face as hard as she could. Jack took the papers as he backed away from her and began to laugh. Everything happened so fast and yet it seemed to everyone as though the events were in slow motion. Then his eyes shifted to anger and he raised his hand as if to strike Winnie. Seeing this, John lunged at Jack, trying to get past Millie. As John pushed against Millie, Jack sensed the attack, backing up and reaching into his coat for the small revolver he always carried with him after the incident with George, those many years before. Millie, after seeing the gun and knowing what John was intending, stepped in between them just as the gun went off. The bullet struck Millie in the breastbone, and ricocheted into her neck and penetrated her larynx passing into the lower portion at the back of her head destroying that part of her brain. The bullet continued up through the back of her skull and out to hit John in the right cheekbone, then glancing off to lodge in the ceiling. Millie died instantly and John fell to the floor, unconscious. Winifred could not believe what had just happened.

Everything was over in less than ten seconds, but it seemed like it took years for Millie and John to fall to the floor. They both lay there; Millie on her back in a pool of blood, John lay on his face with his feet close to Millie's head, at a forty-degree angle from her body. Jack and Winfred stood behind the desk, gaping at each other in a moment that was frozen in time.

"What have you done, you bastard?" screamed Winifred, as she moved to check John. Still disbelieving this turn of events, Jack instinctively knew that he needed to cover his actions and hide the papers. Without the papers, no one could prove anything, but an accident had occurred. The only stumbling block to the cover-up was whether or not Graham could remember seeing the paper… poor Graham seemed to be in total shock.

Someone had run to get the Constable after hearing the shot and the shouting in the office. Jack began forming his story in his mind, so that he would be a victim more than a combatant. The constable arrived and Jack quickly took charge. "Constable, I need to talk to you outside."

"Very well, Mr. Carrigan, what is it?"

"We have a situation here that requires your help." Winifred was more concerned with how John was doing than with what Jack was doing. She had no fears that the law would be anything but fair. She had no realization that the Scots people might not be given fair shake. In the meantime, Jack was busily fabricating a story about showing Graham the revolver, when poor Graham accidentally pulled the trigger. The tragic incident was only an accident, and nothing more. He had the all-important papers hidden within his jacket and he could afford to wait a while before seizing Winifred's factory.

This whole episode could turn out to be a blessing in disguise for his plans. Winifred would probably be so distracted by what happened that she would hardly notice the business takeover and simply take her whole family to Melbourne.

As the month passed, Millie was buried in the family plot, and John was recovering with no real memory of what had transpired. Graham, on the other hand, felt responsible for the "accident" as Jack had represented it and never really regained any ability to refute Jack's statement. Winifred's grief over her mother's loss was strong, for even though they had their differences over the years, she still loved her. Winifred spent the next month with her family gathered to her at home, while Jack ran the factory, and Ron helped him. Ron had no idea what had happened…he believed it was a simple accident. Winifred, with the concurrence of Graham and John, never discussed it again. Jack

waited not just one, but two months. On January 31, 1940 he presented
Winifred with the paper she had signed in November. This confirmed
her vague recollection of the events of that fateful day, but the document
had already been filed with the court and the case was a closed issue.
Jack had won.

"This paper gives me sole ownership of the factory and you are no
longer involved," he said with a smirk.

"That's fine, Jack," Winifred said sarcastically. "I see JW was kind
enough to give me and Graham something and that will be enough to
get by, because I have been squirreling some cash for a long time. Just
keep the factory and welcome to it. One day you will get yours and I
hope I'm alive to see it!"

"I told you before that you would pay for what you did to me, and
now you have," he said as she pushed him out the door and closed it.

Winifred turned her back to the door, aching for all her losses…
George was gone, Millie was gone, Graham's speech would never be the
same, John had a great scar on his face and an embittered heart, and
she was alone, bereft and deserted. She sat down on her bed, with her
solitary memories and wept.

Morning came both too soon and not soon enough, for her eyes
were puffed and reddened from crying all night and her heart was
broken. Her sadness originated from deep within and her weariness
possessed her whole body. 'You know,' she thought, 'I need to start over,
maybe in Melbourne. That's it…we will sell the house here and begin
over again in Melbourne.'

The house, placed up for sale that very day, sold quickly and before
she knew what was happening she was standing on the the platform,
waiting for the Melbourne train. Ron decided to stay at the factory, but
all the rest were going with her to Melbourne.

"Don't forget me, Winnie," cautioned Jannis, as she hugged each
one of the children.

"I won't forget you…or Jacob…or any of the people who have
touched my heart. Please come and visit us when you are able."

That scoundrel Jack had missed one vital part of his nefarious scheme and that was the station. It was locked up in trust for Jannis, with multiple signatures required to obtain control. Jacob and Jannis had been in business too long to allow any room for error or subterfuge. They had known what could happen, what with the world filled with scoundrels like Jack and unsuspecting women like Winifred.

Winifred and her children boarded the train, the whistle blew, the drive wheels spun on the tracks, and the train began to move slowly forward…a new life for Winifred and her family.

Chapter 7

On December 7, 1941, President Roosevelt said, "This is a day that will live in infamy." Pearl Harbor had been attacked and the United States was now at war with Japan. In retrospect, it would appear to many historians that the American President and the British Prime Minister were aware of the attack prior to the actual occurrence. History reveals that at the beginning of World War 1, when Roosevelt was Assistant Secretary of the Navy and Churchill was First Lord of the Admiralty, a British steamship of the Cunard Line was torpedoed by a German submarine in 1915, ten miles off Kinsale Head, Ireland. This vessel was unarmed and carried American citizens on board. The Germans asserted she was carrying war contraband and that Americans had been warned against taking passage on British vessels. Feeling against the Germans rose to a fevered pitch, and engendered popular sentiment for America's entry into the war. Roosevelt and Churchill had a plan to bring into the fray a nation to supply the material needed to defeat Germany. The British and French were in a state of near-bankruptcy and needed material support to continue "the war to end all wars." In 1941 history was to repeat itself. Europe was on the verge of another world war; Japan had been island hopping and with the invasion of Manchuria; had been at war for the past two years. England gave the impression of negotiating with Hitler as a stalling tactic to remain out of a war, but the negotiations were just that, a stalling tactic. It was clear that Hitler wanted to dominate the world and would not stop unless he was defeated in an all-out war. It was also clear that France and Britain could not defeat him alone.

The people of America were enjoying a life that was far from the ravages of war, with no real urgency to engage in a war so far from their shores. Both leaders Roosevelt and Churchill were aware of the popular sentiment. Just as certainly, they knew that in order to get the material rich and industrial power of the United States into the war, something must happen to enrage the American people.

Australia was in the path of the Japanese as they continued to island-hop and Britain knew that they would soon be drawn into a war with the Japanese. In their role as protector of the Common Wealth, they would have no choice. Jack, on the other hand, would heartily welcome his old friends, the Japanese, in the name of power and money. He could only hope that the Allies would not be able to move quickly enough to turn back the Japanese before they could gain a foothold in Australia. His need for constant contact with his partners, dictated that they supply him with a short wave radio that he kept at the hotel in Shepparton. The radio needed a large area for the antenna, which was camouflaged on the hotel roof as supporting wire to hold the sign. Jack had the radio itself hidden in the storeroom of the hotel. Jack had everything well planned that he sent one of his minions to operate the radio in Tokyo, while he would operate the one in Shepparton. This would eliminate any language barrier, while presenting an image of two amateur radio operators were talking to each other. They would develop a code to hide the transfer of any real information. As far as Jack was concerned, he was in the "catbirds seat". All he had to do was sit back and reap those riches. The only glitch to his plan would be the Allies entrance into the war.

Jack's partners were businessmen and were not privy to military information about the planning of a strike at Pearl Harbor. The Japanese military were planning a knockout blow to the United States and prevent their interference of their plans for domination of the South

Pacific Region. Japan's military saw this planned domination as to replenish their limited renewable resources. Jack, of course, was unaware of the military plan, which would later sever his Japanese connection as a simple matter of survival...his survival. At this point in time, Jack felt that the Japanese would control the South Pacific Region and eventually, placing him in a high-ranking position with control over the economic structure of Australia. The strike on Pearl Harbor, that Jack was unaware of, changed the complexion of the war and the world forever. America became a world power and a primary destination for immigrants from all over the world. The American economy received a much-needed shot in the arm and the depression was left forever behind. The brave men and women of the Free World would not only win the war, not only, but also America would prove its industrial might by flooding the war effort with more material than could be used. The evidence of the U.S.'s material successes would remain all over the world at the end of the war; military jeeps would become the main transportation vehicles everywhere and anywhere that the Americans had been stationed.

Australia became a staging point for the Allies in the South Pacific Theater. Americans began to send troops to Australia in late 1942 to early 1943. This would impact Winifred's family forever. The older boys enlisted in the Army, but Mary did so also. She was stationed at Townsville, Queensland, where there was a huge support station for the American Army. The Americans had established this base to receive the wounded and dead from various islands, and to supply the front to push the Japanese back to Japan. The war was starting to turn with the Battle of the Coral Sea; the American war machine began to crank up and with the industrial might of America it would not be long until the Allies would be victorious. Soon after the Battle of Coral Sea, May 1942 came the Battle of Midway, June 1942. These victories gave the Americans the balance of sea power in the Pacific, and won the Americans the right to establish supply bases in Australia.

It is during this time that Mary meets John Reese, and is easily swept off her feet by this fast-talking, smooth American. She becomes fascinated by his stories of America and soon believes everything he tells her.

"Oh! John, please tell me about the States; its sounds so grand."

John says "America is a land of great opportunities and Australia is a fine place, but that Australia is at least twenty years behind America. Many new and exciting things in America would probably not ever be found in Australia. The cars, trains, and even the airplanes are larger, faster, and more elegant than anything you could imagine. The houses are large and filled with modern conveniences such as indoor plumbing, electric lights, electric stoves, and garages with two cars in them." All the things he described had a profound effect on Mary's mindset and she imagined how nice it must be to have a home of her own with all the conveniences at her fingertips. Mary would dream of America and of John in America when she was alone in her barracks. She would picture a large two-story house, with acreage surrounding it, a stream running through the backyard, large patio where the family would gather. These dreams were as real to Mary as Winifred's dreams about George so many years ago, lying in her bunk aboard ship. Mary was convinced that John loved her and fantasized about how wonderful it would be to be married to the man she loved. Mary had romanticized America and her future with John to the point that romance became a reality.

Mary and John were at their normal meeting place, a local hotel in town. They would meet as much as they could to discuss their life in America even though John really had no plans for her in his life after the war. He was already married and only wanted to add to his conquests.

"John, when we go back to the States, will we live in Washington where you are from or will we live in another state?" Mary asked innocently, catching John off guard.

"Gee, Mary I don't know, it will…," he sputtered.

"It will what?" asked Mary, more forcefully.

"Well, Mary as I have mentioned before, the Army won't allow us marry, so I don't know if I can take you with me… but I will send for you." he said with a little hesitance in his voice.

Mary correctly read the hesitancy and quietly headed toward the door as she put on her jacket and turned to leave. She knew or thought she sensed his insincerity and knew she would not travel to the States unless they were married.

"Wait!" shouted John as he got off the bed attempting to prevent her leaving.

"Wait for what?" Mary retorted, as her hand turned the knob. John took her hand from the knob and held it close to his heart and took her other hand, holding them close together.

"I love you, Mary, but it is very difficult to get permission to marry from the Army. I will try again, but if I can't marry you, I will still send for you after the war. You must believe me."

Mary gazed into his eyes and thought she saw sincerity...she gazed deep into his eyes and thought she saw that special sign of love that only women can see in a man. They stood there for what seemed an eternity looking at one another, he, waiting for the consent that would achieve his goal of sexual relations...and, her, for that commitment of everlasting love and devotion. She placed her head on his bare chest; he had taken off his shirt earlier as she had her jacket because of the heat and humidity. She felt safe and liked the hair on his chest that tickled her nose; she began to laugh as she leaned back away from his embrace. She needed to leave and run over in her mind the sense she had from his hesitance.

"John, I know you will send for me because of the love we share, I also know that we will be very happy no matter where we live."

"Yes, you're right! Tomorrow I will go see the Commanding Officer and try again to get that permission." he said with as much false enthusiasm as he could muster.

Mary was reassured, but there was still that hesitance about John's commitment and her passage to America at the end of the war, as Mrs. Reese.

"Oh, my god!" exclaimed Mary looking at her watch, "It's almost past time for my shift. I need to get over to Headquarters before I'm missed."

"Wait, Mary my love, we have a few minutes."

"No, I will see you later. I only have time to fix myself up and get across town to the base." She moved from his arms and headed through the door and down the hall. She disappeared down the stairs at the end of the hall and left him standing in the doorway of the hotel room he had rented for what he thought would be another conquest. John's motives were nowhere close to what Mary thought they were. He was only out for a fling. The war had done only one thing for him, give him more territory for his extra-marital activities. He was only interested in Mary for sexual gratification. She was so naïve that his promise of marriage and passage to the great country of America were all she could see.

Mary was across the quad, up the stairs through the front door, in the office, and at her desk before the other secretaries realized she was five minutes late. "Mary, where were you, with that Yank again?" asked one of her co-workers.

"No, I was in the loo," responded Mary as she began to type some correspondence on her desk from the day before. She knew she would have to keep her activity as much a secret as possible, not from her friends and co-workers, but from the officers. The Australian forces were of the same mindset as the Americans; when the war was over everyone would go back to their own lives in their own countries.

Marriages between the different forces of the Allies were frowned upon, to say the least.

John, as a matter of fact, had no intention of asking his commanding officer for permission to wed. He only wanted a singular sexual relationship and to go home without any excess baggage. 'I need to gain her confidence soon or I won't be able to get her into bed,' John thought as he closed the door behind him. He needed to get back to the base also, because his shift was due. John and several other GI's were on burial duty at the base and with the war raging in the islands, allied casualties were high.

"It's about time you got back, Corporal." shouted Sergeant Rankle from across the room.

"Yes sir, I'm sorry I was late sir, but I had an important personal matter to attend to." John declared in his best military manner.

"I don't need to hear any excuses for your tardiness. I realize this isn't the best duty; day after day, burying and transporting these unfortunate souls, but it must be done," snapped back Sergeant Rankle. "We need to have these poor Americans ready to transport back home as soon as possible. The British don't seem as anxious as the Americans, and the Aussies are home anyway, so let's get at it."

The work crew spoke in unison, "Yes, Sir," and they headed to the transport trucks that brought the bodies from the docks on the seaport on the other side of Townsville.

This was perhaps the worst detail of the war and it sickened all of the men who worked on it. John was so tired of the detail that he would do anything to get out of it. He had even tried to fake stomach flu to get a week in sick bay, he drank some nasty concoction that created for him, the symptoms of the flu, with fever, cough, vomiting and cold shakes, but it only lasted until he went to sick bay, because the medics were wise to all the tricks of the trade. He was cured and back on duty in two days. John wasn't sure it was worth the trouble but the whole group continued to try various methods of ridding themselves of the detail. John had a new reason now to get out of duty... his thoughts were occupied by Mary, and how to convince her to give in and give him what he wanted, namely sex. He had tried everything he knew he gave her numerous gifts, the false promise of a life in America.

'What would it take?' he thought, as he helped unload one of the body bags. "What will it take, what *will* it take?" he repeated out loud as he went to the next body bag.

"What will it take to do what, mate?" asked his Aussie counterpart at the other end of the bag.

"Nothing, nothing really." answered John. He had not confided in him about Mary, as the Aussies were not pleased about the American's relationships with their own girls.

"You mean how you are going to get that bird to go to bed with you, right?" responded the Aussie, with a glint in his eye. "Don't look so shocked, mate, we know what you're doing, of course we don't approve, but it would seem that bird is for you and is lost to us, anyway you look at it." John just stood there, shocked at the openness of his mate.

"What you need to do is marry her and everything will fall into place."

"You know the Army won't let me."

"Maybe the Army won't, but Australia will, and after that marriage the Army will give in. Trust me, mate I've seen it before." He exuded such confidence, that John began to think along those lines.

'I could marry here, have my fling and not apply to the Army, so when I leave forget all about it and I can go home without any excess baggage.' John thought to himself as a smile came over his face.

"What do you think, Yank? You could get a pass, go to Ayr for the week and do it there."

"That's a great idea and just before I go home, I could approach the Major for permission to have the Army authorize the marriage, which they will deny. Great idea! How can I thank you?" asked John.

"Well, you can start by pasting a smile on your face and after, shouting a few rounds at the Pub tonight."

"Then it's settled, that's what I'll do!"

"You bet it is, Yank! Tonight, at the Pub, now get back to work," said the Aussie as he hefted another bag with great strength and confidence, as though he had won a great victory. This was a victory of sorts for him, because Australians were great beer drinkers and whenever they could get free beer, it was a small victory.

John felt confident. As the day wore on, the stench and gore no longer bothered him as much as it had in the past. He felt sure this would bring Mary where he wanted her, in his bed. That night he didn't see Mary, for he had a debt to pay at the Pub. He would also use the next couple of days to get everything in place for the trip to Ayr. His Aussie friend and told him that he could obtain a civil marriage in Ayr and that it was a pleasant place for a honeymoon located by the sea.

"You know, Yank, these Aussie girls are very stubborn and will be hard to handle after they see what it's like in the States. I've been there during this war and the conveniences you have are at least twenty years ahead of us."

"I think I will be able to handle her," John said, as he played along with the conversation, knowing full well he had no intention of taking Mary back to America.

Soon his plans were in place and they were in Ayr. The breeze flowed in from the ocean and seemed to cool that March evening in 1943. Mary and John had married that very afternoon and John's goal was in sight. Mary was beautiful; the white sheer nightgown outlined her slender body as the moonlight exposed the splendor that John had waited for. She stood with her back to the window, confident that the moonlight was showcasing her. Then, she moved toward John.

"I feel so wonderful; we'll be the happiest couple in the States when this dreadful war is over" said Mary as she moved closer to John.

"Yes, it will be a life of unbelievable happiness." He took her in his arms. She eagerly stepped into his embrace, anticipating her first experience in lovemaking with her own true love. Her embrace was so enthusiastic and earnest that John felt a slight moment of inferiority in the face of love. That thought passed as her nightgown fell to the floor to expose all her loveliness for the first time for any man. John slipped out of his robe to confirm all the stories that Mary had heard of men and time stood still for the next brief moment as they looked deeply into each other's eyes.

Mary could only think about the marriage earlier in the day when she and John shared the vow, until death do us part. She held his hand tightly during the ceremony and thought only of the ceremony and not the consummation.

Fortunately, John proceeded slowly with her. He had to call on his considerable acting skills to pretend it was his first time and that love, not lust, was his motivating factor. She sensed his every move and responded in kind to his gentle touch; then, he moved his hand to the small of her back and gently lowered her to the bed.

She felt so many emotions and her body seemed to belong to someone else…someone who was feeling ecstatic and lethargic at the same time…'what would happen next,' she thought. She felt a slight stab of pain and instinctively pushed toward him. John moved slightly and slowly and she began to move in unison with his movement. *Mary's last coherent thought before she began to drift away in her mind to a place where there was only a great sense of giving and sharing and awe.* Time stood still as they made love; nothing else existed…it was only them and this moment. Mary wanted to exist in that moment for the rest of her life. That wondrous moment ended with waves of ecstasy flowing through her body, masking all other senses. It was heaven to her; it was unbelievable. She had lived her whole existence on earth just to be here and now with the man she loved so much. It was flight through all the senses that the human body could offer. As John slept, she wondered anew at the strength of her emotional bond to him…how glad she was that she and John shared this special moment… one she was sure would go on for the rest of their lives, together. She knew he would always be there for her, as she would be for him. She was never to change that belief, even as events transpired that put that great love she felt to the supreme test. The next few days together passed in a haze for Mary; she thought she was the center of his universe. In retrospect, those days would be all she had to hang on to, for John was to receive his orders to return to the States.

Their marriage still had to be kept a secret, and this secretiveness caused Mary many anxious moments. The morning sickness she had didn't help matters. True to Mary's luck, the sickness started about one month after their honeymoon at Ayr. This is the part which changes the picture and reveals the huge flaw in John's plan. The Army really frowned on their soldiers impregnating foreign women. He would have a great deal to explain, if in fact the Army was to discover what had happened. John decided to talk Mary into leaving the service and moving to Kerang, to hide her condition. He explained that this would be the best way to ensure that he could bring her to the States with the least amount of problem. He Convinced her it would be better if she should deliver in secret; thereby, keeping the Army unaware of the entire circumstance.

"This," he said, "is the best way to achieve passage to the States, because my Commanding Officer will never allow us to marry." John had no intention of taking Mary or, for that matter, a baby home with him. He already had a family in the States and he was not prepared to deal with that issue.

"How on earth will this be easier to achieve passage?" asked Mary in a brief moment of reality, the reality that maybe John was not honest in his explanations.

"It's easy," he replied. "The fact that you are pregnant and having the baby will only benefit us."

Mary searched his eyes for hidden meaning, but John was well practiced in the art of deception. He gazed at Mary with an attitude of assurance.

"John, how will this help us?" Mary still seemed uncertain.

"The Army will send for you when I get back to the States and tell them what I have left behind. They would never leave one of their own, and I will be able send for both of you." John said, attempting to cover his real intentions of leaving her there and never sending for her. He didn't even plan on telling her when he got his orders; he would simple not come around any more. Mary seemed to believe John's latest fabrication and didn't ask any questions for the rest of the evening. She just acted as the housewife she knew she would be soon and left his arms to continue her cooking. She had prepared his favorite meal, corned beef cabbage with cornbread. The cornbread mix and all the ingredients were from the PX, because the Aussie's were not accustomed to these Irish-American meals. They ate mostly mutton and very few vegetables, perhaps their diet explain their lack of good dental health; false teeth were common for people over thirty. Cornbread was an exclusively American dish and it was hard for Mary to get it right. It would leave the oven ether very hard, spongy or crumbly. Hard as she tried, it was never quite right. John would let her know it was not as up to his mothers' standards. On one occasion, he slipped and mentioned his wife's name, Betty.

"Betty!" Mary shouted. "Who is Betty?"

"She is my mother, and that's what her name is!" he shouted back.

"You never called her that before and I don't think it is polite for you to call your mother by her Christian name. I would never call my mother Winifred," Mary shouted back.

"That is her name and we do things different in the States. Maybe you will learn that before you're called for."

She was unable to understand any of these implications until later. He always complained about the cornbread…Mary would never cook this meal again after he left her.

John had to return to the base and said "Mary, I should be back next week and I will bring more supplies. I have a friend at the base that has been helping me get more supplies than I could normally get as a Corporal."

"How nice. Would you ask him if he wants a home cooked meal, for his help, the next time you come?"

"That would be great," John quickly answered. His devious mind began to calculate a possible connection between his friend, Norman, and Mary.

If he could create enough interest between them, he could return to the States unnoticed. After all the trouble Mary had caused him over the issue of marriage and sex, it is a testament to his character that he would think it possible to sway Mary's affections to his friend.

Norman was a large man with barrel chest, standing over six feet tall. His black curly hair was his most attractive feature; it looked more sculpted than alive. His eyes were so piercing that his unnerving gaze seemed to stare straight into your soul, but his soft smile would give you a clue to his demeanor. His voice could be commanding when he needed it to be; but generally he was gentle and could make you so comfortable that you felt as though you had known him all your life.

His chest gave the correct impression of great strength, and if his legs had matched his torso, he would have been an awesome man. His legs looked as if they belonged to a boy; his thighs were small but his calves were somewhat muscular and added to his strength.

Norman was older than most of the servicemen by about five years and was drafted into service late in life. His skills were needed in the war effort because he had been a superintendent and knew how to handle men. In his youth, he had attended military school after his mother had divorced his father.

His father still had the old country ways from Cornwall, England so he agreed that the proper place for Norman, especially considering the divorce was at military school.

The service needed these types of people to train the new troops because when he was drafted, the war was not going good for the Allies. He spent the first part of the war as a Drill Instructor, but his temper got him into trouble and he was demoted. Before he knew it, he was in Australia, shipping bodies back to the States. He was accustomed to hard work, and soon he regained his rank of Staff Sergeant. He fancied himself to be an amateur boxer and would spend a lot of time at the gym working a speed bag. His great upper body strength was demonstrated when he once snapped the swivel that held the bag to the return mounting and sent the bag flying. John just knew if he could get Norman and Mary together that they would click and he would be off the hook.

Mary had moved to be close to John after she resigned the service. They had acquired a small house in Townsville off the base, 4 Hirst St. Townsville, Queensland, Australia.

"How you going, love?" asked Mary as John and Norman entered house through the door. She embraced John and gave him a hug and lasting kiss.

Mary looked over John's shoulder and asked. "Who might this be?"

"Oh, this is the man I told you about, Norman Cooper, Sergeant Norman Cooper."

Norman smiled as he asked. "Oh, how are you? I've heard a lot about you from John."

"And I've heard about you. Have you been in Aussie long?"

"About six months, between here and New Guinea. I was shot in the foot and after recovery it was decided I would be better used here at the Base in Townsville."

"What do you do there?" asked Mary, as John had never confided in her about the nature of his duties. John felt it was below his ability to only be placed far from the glamorous front lines.

Loading prepared bodies for shipment back home was the final indignity. Norman was not concerned with the nature of his duties and regaled Mary with all the grizzly details.

"We load the bodies of the dead soldiers into wooden coffins and send them to the States. Most of them are blown to pieces, so we try to load enough to give the approximate weight. Often, we throw in different body parts--."

"Stop right there!" Mary interrupted. "I simply can't listen to anymore of this; it's starting to make me ill. Now I know why you didn't tell me what you do, John."

"Yes, I knew it would be painful for you to think about."

Mary continued, "Norman--."

"Curly," he interrupted Mary.

"Very well. Curly, I need to ask one final question then I will leave it alone. Do you get any dead soldiers other than Americans?"

"Yes we…" Curly started to say when Mary interrupted again, "Aussies? Could I ask…?"

Norm laughed, "Remember. Only one question!"

"I know, I said only one," Mary smiled then frowned, "but I need to check on my brothers to see if any of them were brought in."

"I'm sure if you gave us a list we could check, couldn't we, Sarge?" John finally chimed in when he could see the conversation wasn't revolving around him. He was a bit jealous, but told himself that all was going as planned. Mary and Curly were hitting it off just great.

"Yes, get the list together with name, rank, and where they were stationed or what command and I will have the research done."

"How can I thank you, Norm...Curly?"

"How about some of that home cooked food John has been bragging about?"

"Just set yourselves down and it will be right up."

Norman sat down at the end of the table and Mary turned to go to the kitchen with John right behind her. "You just sit down and keep each other company. I have a few things to do to get the meal ready."

"I just thought you might need some help." John held her close to him; he was still a bit jealous of the way Mary and Norman were getting along. This was odd but he blamed it on his great acting ability...the act that had Mary believing that she would to be sent for after the war.

Her family was happy for Mary and thought she would be a new American and they would have ties in the States, something everyone wanted for Mary, a grand life in a new land. Her mother, Winifred was especially proud of her and knew her daughter would be as happy as she was with her George.

"No, no...that's alright, luv, get a couple of beers out of the fridge and keep him company while I finish up."

"Hey, Sarge, do you want to try the best in the world, Victory Bitter; Aussies not only know how to drink it but we also know how to make it," shouted Mary from the kitchen.

"That sounds great, thank you." Norman shouted back from the front room.

The next two months passed with Norman and John visiting Mary more frequently. They were more of a threesome than a couple. John felt his plan was working; soon he would be gone, and with his typical insensitivity John thought that Mary would forget about him and become Norman's problem. In the fifth month of Mary's pregnancy, John got his orders. There was a big push to island hop toward Japan and it would require more soldiers...soldiers like John. He told Mary that after his tour at the front, he would be sent home; then he would send for her. Mary thought she would hear from John in about two or three months, while John felt certain that he would never hear from her again. He didn't count on her ingenuity and determination to be with the man she loved. John had been gone for two months and Mary still had not had a word from him. She went to the post everyday and the same result was there, nothing, not a word! She had been in constant contact with Norman during this whole period, but of course he was reluctant to tell her what he already knew. He knew that John had left her with his child…he would not return and he would not send for her. He visited her house frequently, always answering her questions with 'It's classified.'

Finally, Norman couldn't stand it…he had to tell her the truth about John. It was preying on his mind and the weight of the lie was making him feel guilty. He had fallen in love with her and this guilt was beginning to be too much. He thought,

'How am I to tell her without losing her in the process, I really don't want to lose her, even though I know she will soon have John's child. All that matters is that I love her and will take the responsibility for the child.' So he said,

"Mary, please sit down, I have something to tell you." His tone made her assume the worst possible news… John had been killed and Norman didn't know how to tell her.

"Mary, I need to talk to you. Please wait until I'm through before you answer me."

Now Mary was totally confused. Was this about John's death or was it something else? Her mind raced a hundred miles an hour.

"Mary, I don't know how to say this any other way. John…"

Mary's head bent down as if already burdened by the news of John's death.

"John was never going to send for you," Norman continued. "His whole purpose was to have sex with you and that's all. He considered the child a mistake and you will never hear from him again.

I'm sorry, I wish I could be more kind, but I've never been very good at mincing words. I'm so sorry." Mary fell to her knees and began to weep uncontrollable. How can this be? She wasn't sure whether she was mourning John's loss or rage for allowing this indignity against her person.

Norman pulled her up from the floor and held her close to him. He had always wanted to hold her, but this was a different feeling than he had experienced before. He realized that he loved her and needed to tell her. Mary felt his strong arms surround her and felt some measure of comfort even though she was completely devastated. How could John lie to her and pursue her solely for his own gratification? This inequity just couldn't register in her brain; she gave him all her love and devotion and all she received in return was rejection and a child to care for.

"I will not let this stop me from getting to the States and, when I do, I will find John and make him pay for what he has done. I swear this on the head of our child." Mary fumed as she laid her head on Norman's shoulder. Her grief had solidified in that short period of time into anger.

"Are you okay?" asked Norman as he held her even closer. "Can I help in any way? Please don't cry anymore. I can't stand to see you this way."

"I don't know what to do. The child will be here in November and I have left the service. John was helping with support and that was all the support I had. You know we are married?" Mary stuttered as she continued to cry; again, her sorrow was not one of self-pity, but of great anger...anger at herself for being so foolish as to believe John's lies.

"Yes, I know, but it can be annulled. The States won't recognize the marriage because he didn't get permission."

"What does that mean?"

"It means you are only married in the eyes of the Australian court and that claim is not valid or recognized in America."

"So...my baby is a bastard, without a name."

"That is the truth as I know it right now."

"Do you know where he is?"

"No, I don't. He shipped out to the Front and after that none of us here will know where he is. He will be unreachable until he returns to the States, if he does."

"What do you mean, if he does?"

"If he isn't killed," Norman answered as he looked down at Mary's tear-filled eyes. He hoped she would look to him for further comfort, but she cleared her eyes and gave him the look of determination that would become familiar to others in her future. That look of determination allowed her to control her emotions and she began to formulate a plan in her mind to get to America and confront John, if he survived.

Norman looked back at her and wondered, could she possible love me as I love her and more importantly, will I be able to convince her I'm not like John. Norman realized the importance of not appearing to be like John in any way. Mary and Norman were wondering what the other one was thinking.

'I bet he sees me as an easy mark. I wonder if he knew all along that John was going to leave me here for the next guy?' Mary thought as she regained some coherence. 'John didn't think there would be a baby. Now that I think back on it, he tried to make sure that I wouldn't get with child; but the first night was his downfall. He later claimed to be overcome by passion. After the first night, I remember how he made sure that we were careful to avoid an accident. I should have realized something was wrong. When I told him I was pregnant, he didn't want to believe it.' Mary replayed this scene over and over in her mind while holding on to Norman as if for dear life.

'I wonder what she is thinking. She seems very comfortable in my arms. Could she possibly care about me and is afraid to say it because of this mess with John? I had no real proof of anything, just a feeling that he was going to leave her here and not send for her.' Norman kept rehashing the events in his mind. Finally, Mary pulled away from him and searched his eyes trying to gage his thoughts.

"Will you be ok?" he asked.

"I will be fine now that I know 'the rules'," she snapped.

"What do you mean 'the rules'?"

"You know…how you Yanks are going to treat the Birds here in Aussie."

"That's not fair, Mary, not everyone is like John."

"Maybe not, but from now on I'll be on my guard." Her hurt was rapidly being replaced by anger. "You Yanks are all alike."

"Not true," he interrupted, placing his hand gently over her mouth to stop her from continuing. "I, for one, am not here to treat 'the Birds', as you say, badly. I must confess that I am in love with you. It would be a great honor if you would marry me and come to America as my wife."

Mary stood there with her mouth agape staring at Norman. She had no idea he fancied her to that degree…and there she was with another man's baby in her womb. She stood, stock-still and silent, for what seemed an eternity for him. The look of love in his eyes was unmistakable.

"Would you go to your Commanding Officer and get permission to marry me properly, and not only have the Aussie marriage?"

"Yes. If you will just say yes, I will take you to him now and ask him while you are present."

"You would do that?"

"Yes I would."

"Then the answer is yes, but only if mum approves," she said, doubtfully. She sounded doubtful because this approval process might scare him away from her. It would be a test of his sincerity. Norman didn't move a muscle; in addition, the statement didn't catch him off guard. Norman believed in the importance of her mother's opinion because he had a great amount of love and respect for his own mother.

Lillie Park was a strong, independent woman, who married a Cornishman, who expressly offered work in the mines in the Western United States. She spent a hard life with Norman's father… for mining is a tough business, working fifteen hour shifts daily, except on Sunday where a short shift of twelve hours was the schedule. It was common practice for the miners to work all day and drink late into the night.

Norman's father was different. He did his drinking at home, but Lillie was left to raise the children. He considered it his job to provide and hers to raise Norman and his three brothers. Lillie also ran a boarding house in her spare time. She ruled the roost and was the driving factor in her children's lives. She ruled with an iron hand and if a child got crossways with her, she was not above making a trip to the wood shed. She taught Norman to be honest, above all other things, in his dealings with life. She once said to him "If you are honest and do not cheat anyone in life, you will always win out." So he carried this concept with him his whole life, and he found it to be true. Of course, he had some minor setbacks, as does everyone; but, with honesty as a first consideration, he would do fine.

Now his problem was to convince Mary of this basic honesty, which appeared impossible at this point.

"Mary, I know it's hard to believe me, but please give me a chance to prove myself to you. I love you and will love your child as my own," he said with sincerity. It was this sincerity that gave Mary a hint of the characteristics that she had looked for in John.

"I think if we see what my mum thinks about this and obtain her agreement that we might have something that we could build on," she answered, as she wiped the tears from her face. As she did so, she realized that she must look terrible. If he was interested in her at this time maybe he was telling the truth and could see beyond a pretty face and a reputation in tatters.

"When will you be ready to go?"

"We have to take a fortnight. You know how far Melbourne is and Mum would be disappointed if we only stayed one day."

"I will put in for some leave I have on the books and we should be able to go in a couple of weeks, if that would be all right?"

"Yes I think so," she said hesitantly. She knew the need for a speedy resolution, but was still tentative…it was so much to absorb at one time. "In the mean time, ----Yes."

"I would like to call on you and spend time with you in these two weeks. We could go to dinner and, if the base has a new movie we'll go, as well as anything else you'd like to do."

"That would be fine, but only as friends, right now."

"I wouldn't have it any other way, until you feel comfortable to move on."

"That would be wonderful," she said, feeling much better about the evening.

"I know you haven't eaten so would you care to go to the local restaurant?" Norman asked, hoping she would say yes. He did not want to leave her alone to dwell on her doubts.

"I would love to! Just let me clean myself up a bit and we will go." Bravely, she managed a smile and disappeared into the loo.

This is how her relationship began with Norman (Curly, as she would learn to call him.) They seemed a good fit together and Curly would come to love her, as he had no other. They went everywhere together and were soon as inseparable as any couple could be. Mary was as happy as she could, or thought she could, be. Curly talked about his second love, mining. He said all he ever wanted to be was an underground miner, and to that end he was probably the best of anyone you knew. He could look at ore and tell you where it was mined and, if given time, probably who mined it. Everyone was amazed by his ability to tell so much about what most people considered just plain rocks. It was fascinating to listen to him tell about where and how he and others mined the ore that was used to make so many things taken for granted in everyday lives. Just to think of the appliances, automobiles, airplanes, tools, and too many other things to mention was mind-boggling.

Chapter 8

It was time for the big event… the long-awaited, much-discussed child was coming. Fortunately, Curly was available to transport Mary to the hospital in the early evening, where they waited and waited and waited.

As is usual with the birth of a child and very true to their contrary nature, I did not make an appearance until I was damn good and ready. My poor suffering mother's labor began when her water broke and did not subside until I was born, about six hours later than expected. It was much before that when I bonded with my mother and I have always loved her for that labor of love and for all the other issues to follow.

"Breath, Mary, breath out, if you don't help, the baby won't come." Nurse Mattie said, as she held Mary's hand in support and comfort.

Mary shouted, as she tried to rise up, "I can't breathe out and push at the same time. Can't you help? It won't come out!"

"Hey! Hello! What if I don't want to come out?" Does anybody care?" I screamed back from within my comfort zone. No one remembers what it's like to be born, but we were all there when it happened, upside-down, floating in fluid, warm, all nourishment provided, protected from the weather, every need taken care of, and the only problem was the dratted umbilical cord. With every movement, this giver of life could potentially end life as I had briefly known it…it must be dodged with every movement I made, whether pushing, pulling, or stretching…I was doing all those things. The memory of birth is not retained and that is very probably a good thing. Imagine, if you will, the trauma involved; ask your mother…the very person to whom you have been tied, literally and figuratively, for the past nine months. First, the comfortable sac, surrounding my body and the fluid I'm floating in, breaks. The fluid spews out, leaving the sac closing in around me AND my mother's body begins to expel me…EXPEL ME…through an opening that seems impossibly small. Suddenly, this safe haven that I have enjoyed since my conception doesn't want me anymore. I begin to move down the birth canal, still fighting with the umbilical cord and a force not my own pushes at my feet, my arms crushed at my sides, and an unbelievable pressure squeezes and elongates my head. A viscous substance provides a measure of relief, as it eases my passage. As you begin to pass down the birth cannel the umbilical cord makes its last attempt to wrap around your neck, arm or anything that is sticking out. Your head starts toward the opening and your mother's body pushes at your feet to keep you moving and the birth canal begins to crush your head; your arms are pressed to your sides. Your shoulders are pushed down toward your waist until you begin to look like a narrow stretched out alien. While you are pushed, pressed, crushed, and dodging the cord; you hear from outside "I see the head! Push, Mary, push." A man's voice exhorted, with as much excitement in his voice as if he were at a Rugby game. It was completely understandable…this was his first delivery. Doctor William A. Duhearst III had just finished his residency; and Mary was his very first birth and he was this excited because all during his residency he had not been afforded the opportunity to deliver a child.

"Don't worry about the breathing, just push and let Mother Nature do the rest. Push, Mary, push! Look I see the shoulders…it's a BOY!" Nurse Mattie shouted, as pleased as if she had accomplished this birth all by herself. And I made my entrance into the world, kicking and screaming…not at all sure that this was a place where I wanted to be. I heard the doctor and nurse reassure Mary that I was just trying out my lungs for the first time. I just wanted my body to assume its original shape, so the pain from that effort was making me unhappy. My mother looked upon me for the first time and her pain disappeared. I have heard that, when the maternal instinct takes over, all other physical concerns recede…comparable to a combination of an adrenaline rush and a mental block. She was not able to hold me in her arms until they cleaned me up, but, at first glimpse, I heard her say that I was so perfect, so beautiful. She clearly must have been blinded by motherly love, because I was covered with blood, mucous, and that bluish-white substance that eased my passage…furthermore, I was exercising my lungs to make this new, strange, and uncomfortable place aware that I was not accepting this indignity of being displayed like a prize bull for all to see.

Norman stayed until the next afternoon, offering Mary support and comforted. When the doctor made his visit, he questioned Norman about his status…was he the father? Norman stated that, although he and Mary were friends, the father had abandoned her in this unfortunate state. This was not strictly true, for over the past few months, they had begun a relationship that would beget an adventure of a lifetime, with all its joys and perils. The doctor explained that he needed information to complete the birth documents about the father. Norman suggested that they enter 'Unknown American Sergeant' in that section.

He told the doctor that he wouldn't mind using his name, just to make Mary happy, but that wouldn't be acceptable to the American Command. Of course, all this was said out of Mary's hearing.

"I would be happy to claim fatherhood, but I can't at this point in our relationship. I plan to marry her; but, quite frankly, I haven't had the courage to risk rejection yet." Norman explained. The doctor told Norman that he understood and hoped that the parentage issue was something that could be worked out later. After thanking the doctor, he left.

I was soon cleaned up and brought to Mary, she held me close and I felt safe again. I had just been removed from my safe haven and didn't have any idea where I was or what would happen to me, but I was back within familiar surroundings again safe in my mother's arms. You hear that saying, "safe in your mother's arms. But I don't think anyone realizes what it really means. Mom would always love and protect me. I remember some of the times she was there for me. Later in America she would marry a man, Lonnie, and my brother and I would set the desert on fire. Being the oldest, Lonnie wanted to punish me, but mom stepped in to say that both of us should be punished and not just me. Another time she told a truant officer in Liverpool I had gone to Scotland and would return later that day. I had really gone with a friend of Mom's and she covered for me. There had been several instances like these and I am sure I will think of them later.

Over the next few years, Curly and Mary became even closer and they began an ardent love relationship that Curly was never to recover from; in fact, he was fated to love her until the day he died and, who knows, perhaps beyond. Mary, on the other hand, would love many times, not always too wisely or too well. The couple would spend endless hours together and Curly kept his promise: they were married in August of 1945. They took up residence in the same house she and John had shared, 4 Hirst Street, Townsville. She didn't care for the arrangement but it was the only place available. They traveled to Melbourne to visit Winifred as often as they could. Winifred loved her grandchild and spoiled him in every way. It seemed that this was the happy ending to a misguided start. The war was nearing the end and it was expected the Yanks would go home and probably leave some of the wartime wives in Australia.

Mary was determined go to America and she was not to be left behind. Curly had promised not to leave her, but she was unable to forget that she had been promised much before and had been left holding the proverbial bag. The day finally arrived when Norman said, "Mary, I will be leaving next week on a troop ship. That means I will have to send for you and Alan."

"Norm, I cannot bear to be left behind because I know what that will mean; you will not send for me and I will be left here to raise Alan by myself."

"No, you won't, I promise. See, I have your travel chits for the trip to San Francisco on the Mariposa."

The S.S. Mariposa was the identical sister ship of S.S. Monterey. These liners were the luxury vessels of the day, built by the Matson line. The Monterey, Lurline and Mariposa were considered to be the queens of the liners. These prewar ships were built like floating palaces. They reached a length of 631 feet, a width of 79 feet, with twin screws propelling them though the water at 23 knots. They carried 472 passengers in first Class and 229 in cabin Class, with a crew of 360 to provide for the passengers' every whim. The Mariposa was built soon after the Monterey, and joined her sister ship on the seas, operating between San Francisco, Los Angeles, Honolulu, Pago Pago, Suva, Sydney, and Melbourne. At the end of the war, these liners were conscripted by the Military as "Bride Ships" to transport most of the wounded, nurses, and new brides to the States.

"The ship will arrive before June, then, you will be in San Francisco in late July."

"Oh, this is so exciting! You'll be right there waiting for us on the dock?" Mary needed constant reassurance about that part.

"Unfortunately, you will have to call me just before you arrive. Then I will come and get you."

"You won't be there? Why won't you be there?"

"I can't be sure of the arrival date because the schedule only estimates sometime between the 15th and the 25th. There is no way of knowing exactly when you'll arrive. Then, I will need time to travel from the mine to San Francisco and take you back to New Pass Mine where I will be working."

New Pass Mine is located approximately in the center of Nevada, about four hundred miles from San Francisco. The trip would be long because of the two lane roads and the large trucks that slowed the traffic to a snail's pace over the mountains.

Mary was still afraid.

"I will call you from the ship, if I can, several days out of port which will give you a day or two of notice. That should give you time to get there."

Norm agreed that it was settled. Mary went on to say how happy she was. "This has been my dream for a long while, to use all those many modern conveniences that John spoke about."

Curly didn't disabuse her of the notion that the mine had modern conveniences; in actuality, life at the mine would be more primitive than what they had in Australia. The cabins were small, very like a motel room, without a shower or toilet. The only shower available was in the main change room and it was used in shifts. The women were allowed to shower according to a schedule based around the mine shift changes. Even then, they had to solicit the foreman to have someone watch so none of the men were around. The toilet was an outhouse, plain and simple…a small square building with one door and a hole in a plank where you sat to do your duty. In other words, the lavatory arrangements were more basic than when Mary's mother first came to Kyabram.

So… Norm left Australia and Mary missed him, but could not curb her nervousness over his promises about the ship and the journey to America. She worried about whether the travel chits were real or not. She replayed his promises and her fears over and over in her mind everyday. It did not help her state of mind that she had not heard from him since he left and had no real idea where he was. Was she really going to America? Curly, along with others from his company, was placed on an Aircraft Carrier to dump equipment overboard as they zigzagged across the ocean on the way home.

The U.S. Government (in its infinite wisdom) decided to dump jeeps, trucks, cars, and tons of other equipment over the side. The equipment could have been sold for civilian use. But the government did this to preserve competition in the private sector. Curly told me about this much later and about the Jeep he could have had for $200. I often thought that it would have been great to have a World War II Jeep. I have always liked four-wheel drive vehicles; they were able to go anywhere and climb any obstacle. These Jeeps were a great benefit to the Americans in their war with the Axis Powers. They were easy to maintain, easy to move (because of their size they could be transported in great numbers, and could go great distances on very little fuel.

Finally, in late June and not a moment too soon for Mary, the S.S. Mariposa arrived in Sydney Harbor and began its preparation for the trip to America. The repairs and general maintenance on the ship would take about a week and then she would load her cargo of 'hopes and dreams' for the long voyage to San Francisco. Mary would also begin her journey to both, a fast-lived and short adventure. Winifred traveled to Sydney to see her daughter and grandson off to America. Winifred again felt all the feelings that she herself experienced before her own trip…the mystery, the adventure, the excitement and the fear. She felt compelled to advise her daughter. "Mary, you must watch what you eat on board! Greasy food will make you ill, so be sure you watch."

"Oh, Mum, please. You think I don't know about those things, but I do. After all, you, yourself have told me so many times."

"Yes, Mary, it might have left your mind with all the excitement; but, many years ago, I was as you are now," Winfred replied. As she thought back to her adventure and to her love, George, she fell silent, slipping back in time to see George standing before her with his soft smile and gazing into her eyes with the same warmth and love that he had always shown her.

"Mother? Mother…are you all right?" Mary was concerned about her mother's dazed look. Winifred assured her that she was just perfect and that Mary would be fine also when she was reunited with Curly. Instead, Mary contemplated about how she was going to find John when she actually got to America. She had strong feelings for Curly, but she couldn't control that sense of betrayal and anger after the way John treated her. She would have satisfaction or know the reason why.

"Mary, now be sure that you huv the telephone number and address of Curly's work, so you will be able tae call him from the ship. Then he will meet you in San Francisco…Mary! Are you listening tae me?"

"Yesss! I am listening. I was thinking of all the things I have to do to get ready; it's long trip."

"I ken that, but you should huv everything you need on board. Your grandmother and I could only take what we could carry."

"Yes, Mum, we have a limit also," Mary answered absently, still thinking about how difficult the trip would be with an active three-year-old in tow.

The day finally arrived…it was time to board the ship with the rest of the passengers. There were many trophy wives of soldiers and sailors; and at that time Mary was reminded, as if she needed reminding, of John's betrayal of her. She wasn't even a real trophy, but a hidden one. Mary's anger grew in enormous proportion and the desire for revenge became her ruling emotion. "I need to find John and hurt him in some way. He cannot be allowed this victory without pain."

She loved her son, but the false marriage and the lies he had told her were all-consuming. Worst of all, she hated the way he had maneuvered her relationship with Norm. She cared for Norm, but not with the same intensity of feeling that he offered to her. After all, she did marry him and planned to be a faithful wife, in spite of her unsettled feelings for John. John was her first love and she wondered how he could hurt her so much, and still not dampen that love…maybe it was the child who connected them forever. It was beyond her understanding; she just knew it was so.

The dock area was a scene of intense excitement. Winifred harkened back to that last day in Scotland prior to boarding, the bustle of busy people toward the ship's gangplank all the way to the section where customs processed the passengers. Winifred remembered about the first time she saw George leaning over the rail in agony and of how much she had loved him from that first sighting. How strange it was to love someone from the first sighting…how very unusual! She was transported in time back to those days when she held him in her arms and comforted him. Her memories skipped through their years together until she recalled their last moment together on earth…his eyes, looking at her with undying love and devotion. "I love you, Winnie." and he closed his eyes.

"Mum, Mum!" Mary peered into her eyes. Winifred could barely hear Mary asking if she was all right.

"Oh, yes, my dear, I'm fine," Winifred stoutly declared as she removed her glasses and wiped a tear of joy from her eyes.

"Are you sure, Mum"? Mary inquired, just as Alan jumped from her arms and sped away toward the gangplank.

"Catch him before he gets tae the gangplank or you may never see him again." Winfred shouted as Mary ran after him.

"Now I have you! Just where is your mother?" A large man in a uniform gathered him up into his arms just as Mary arrived.

"Is this little rapscallion yours?" he asked sternly.

"Yes, he is. You can bet the spanking he will get will warm his little bottom."

"He is just excited about the adventure ahead of him. I have been the same way for most of my life, so please just keep him under control and nothing will be said. So, you see he won't need a warm bottom after all."

"Well, I guess I can hold off on the bottom warming this time; but, Alan, if you run off again, no 'excitement of the day' excuse will save you."

"Ma'am, if you hurry to the gangplank and check in, I think they are taking pictures of the children with Sister Kenny on deck."

"That would be smashing! Mum, did you hear? Sister Kenny is on board and she is taking pictures with the children." Mary shouted to Winfred just as she came around the corner before the gangplank.

"What did you say?" Winifred asked as she stopped to catch her breath.

"You know, Mum, Sister Kenny."

All of Australia and the entire world, for that matter, knew of Sister Kenny, who was famous for her work with children suffering from infantile paralysis. She had shocked the medical community with her unorthodox method of treating this disease. She first encountered the disease, more commonly known as polio when she was a nurse and visited a young farm girl with a strange crippling disease. She had not seen this condition before and wrote to a Doctor McDonnell to ask his opinion. He wrote back to her, saying that it sounded like infantile paralysis, for which there was no known treatment. He encouraged her to do the best she could and wished her luck with the outcome, and with that small amount of encouragement, she did her best. Using her knowledge of muscles and muscle reactions, she applied hot, damp rags to the girl's legs, so that the muscles wouldn't waste away. The little girl recovered. During this polio outbreak, twenty children in the district contracted the crippling disease. The six treated by Nurse Kenny completely recovered, even though her methods were the exact opposite of what doctors were using. She tried to share her methods with them, but they wouldn't listen. When World War I erupted, Nurse Kenny joined the service and eventually earned the designation of "Sister Kenny". After the war, she returned home; but by 1932, a polio epidemic was sweeping Australia. The word spread about Sister Kenny's treatment methods and, within four years, four Kenny Clinics had successfully treated six hundred patients. She could no longer be ignored. But even a Royal Commission for her treatment would not support her effort fully. In 1940, at age of 59, Sister Kenny left Australia for the United States where she felt her efforts would be better supported.

The United States was in the grip of a severe polio epidemic. She demonstrated her techniques and, gradually, her methods were accepted. In 1942, the Sister Kenny Institute was opened to train therapists in the use of splints; American doctors had adopted her techniques. She became an American heroine and, in 1952, was voted the most admired woman in the United States. Sister Kenny died during one of her trips back home to Australia at the age of seventy-two. Two years later, in 1954, a vaccine for polio was discovered. Sister Kenny's treatment restored dignity and physical independence to thousands of people. Today, the Kenny principles are part of rehabilitative medicine around the world.

(Courtesy of 1998 Australian Broadcasting Corporation)

True to the sailor's word, there was Sister Kenny, sitting on a deck chair with children all around her, as the flash bulbs on cameras were popping. She sat back in the chair, dressed in black except for the white and gray striped lapel and the gold pin that held her inner garment close around her neck. Her hair was white and cut close, she exuded dignity and grace as she held out her arms to the crowd of children around her. She smiled at all of the children and even with the commotion from the reporters and everyone around she held fast her concentration on the children, she cared more for them than for the fame she had achieved.

"Mum, do you think Alan will hold still long enough to get a picture?"

"I would think he would. You ken Sister has handled a lot of orangutans like him in her time."

"Let's try. It would be the photo of a lifetime."

"Yes, give it a go."

"Next!" The man standing next to her shouted as the photographers readied their cameras.

"How about you, little man?" the man assisting the photographers asked, taking hold of Alan's arm.

He squirmed and wiggled all the way to Sister Kenny.

"This will only take a minute." the man said to Mary as he grabbed another child standing next to Alan and headed to the deck chair where Sister Kenny was seated. I have kept that photograph to this day. The little blonde girl is standing next to her and I'm on the other side held in a death grip by Sister Kenny. She somehow knew I was about to bolt and she said to me "Be a good lad and get this picture for your mum."

I knew from the tone of her voice that I was going to be included in the picture regardless of any other mischief I had in mind. Her voice was very gentle and soothing; but there was also an element of steel there; I knew she was in charge.

She held me just high enough that I couldn't get any leverage to bolt before the picture snapped.

Flash and pop, the posing was over and I was released to my Mom. She grabbed my arm and we headed for our cabin.

The ship was long and the passageways were somewhat narrow as they descended to the lower decks where the 'brides' were to be settled.

"This is so much nicer than your father and I had on our trip," Winifred said to Mary in a moderate voice because she really did not want Mary to hear. She was just thinking out loud.

"What, what did you say, Mum?" asked Mary as she steered Alan toward the stairs leading to even lower decks.

"Oh, nothing, I was just remembering my first time aboard a ship."

"Yes, Mum I have heard those stories and it is just as exciting to me, but, of course, you didn't have this little mischief-maker to contend with. Oh, here we are, Room 125, Deck C."

The door opened to a small room with two single beds and a full bathroom. There was some extra room to sit and look out the porthole, if one had cared to. There was a lamp over the bed and one on the ceiling in the center of the room, next to the closet door.

"Look at this, Mary, your own closet and loo." Winifred was excited. "You can have your meals in here and nae huv tae leave." Winifred looked around and remembered the circumstances when she and her mother traveled. They were in the aft section of the ship, sharing an area not much larger than this with many other women.

There were no private loos then and they were on a schedule for most of the necessities during the six-week voyage. Winifred could only remember how unbearable the voyage was until she and George were able to spend time together. "This will be a lovely voyage, Mary. You and Alan will get tae ken each other, form a bond and…"

"And, what Mother? I will be a complete wreck by the time this voyage is over and you know it."

"You will be fine, Mary," Winifred said, unsuccessfully trying to hide a chuckle. She knew that Mary would be fine and her attachment to Alan even stronger by journey's end.

The call to shore came; this meant that all non-passengers had to leave ship. Winifred grabbed Mary and held her to her breast so tightly that Mary couldn't breathe. They both knew it would be a long time before Mary would return, if ever.

"I love you, my beautiful child! I will miss you more than you can imagine. Please dinnae forget tae write and tell me of your adventures," Winifred said as she held back the tears she would shed later away from all eyes.

"I will, Mum, and I will come back when we have the time."

With that, Winifred faced Alan, who looked like he wanted to do a little adventuring on his own.

"Come here, give Grandmum a kiss. We must nae forget each other." She had Alan with his face buried so deeply in a neck crease that he also did not think he could breathe. She kissed the top of his dear little head; then releasing her grip to get a better hold, kissed his face several times before he could wiggle free. "I will miss you, you little mischief-maker. Be good for your Mum and help her. You're the man of the house now until you get tae the States."

Alan hated it when people said, "You're the man of the house and we are depending on you." How can a three-year-old be the man of anything? We are still being told what to do and when to do it. He guessed that statement was designed to make them feel good and at the same time, impart to him some sense of responsibility. The last call came and we walked Grandmum back to the gangplank.

She briskly headed down to the dock and turned to wave to Mary and Alan as the crewmen hoisted the gangplank to the side of the ship and released the lines. The huge ship began to back away from the dock as the whistle blew, the band assembled on the dock played the Australian Anthem, Sister Kenny waved to the many "brides" standing on the boat deck, and they waved back to everyone.

Tugs pushed the ship to the entrance of the harbor and soon light smoke belched from her stacks and they were on their way to the United States. Moving under her own power, the S.S. Mariposa once again headed to the open ocean on a 'grand voyage'. The passengers may not have been as grand as she had held in the past, but they were a precious cargo of new lives and hopes. Some would go home to reunite with families and some would go to start new families. Others were bound for hospitals to heal. Some of them would not be destined to heal, but would be carried home for burial, granting final closure for those who loved them.

The trip was an uneventful one for Mom, but we did form a bond that would last forever. The only real incident occurred as a result of a slight misunderstanding...one in which I locked myself in one of the watertight lavatories on the boat deck and turned on the water. Locks and lads and lavatories were a daunting mixture. A bit frightened by all the hullabaloo, I refused to budge and Mom had to convince a sailor to open the door by removing the hinges. The time seemed to drag on forever, perhaps aided (or hindered) by the fact that the sailor had been sampling from the liquor locker. He had as much trouble with the door as he did remaining upright. Mom said that if she hadn't been so upset with me, it would have been very comical watching him trying to get the hinges off and swaying back and forth simultaneously. I was finally rescued and given a hug; then came the reprimand, as expected.

Aboard ship, Mary tried to call the number Norm had given to her; but each time the call would not go through. The excuses were myriad: the lines were down, the circuits were busy, or no one answered. The ship was only a few days out of San Francisco when Mary finally was able to get through to Norm. The connection was very poor to begin with and they spent a lot of time screaming, "hello, can you hear me, hello?" into the phones. Miraculously, the lines cleared and they could hear each other. Mary quickly tried to get Norm to be in San Francisco in four day's time, but the radio went dead. "Must be a sunspot or something; I hope he got that," the radio operator said, as he turned the switch on the radio to off.

"I hope he got it also, because I won't know what to do if he's not there," Mary said as she headed for the cabin. She was extremely concerned that Norm wouldn't be there to help her with the Immigration by verifying her identity. The next two days were difficult for her; she replayed the phone call over and over in her mind, hoping Norm hadn't been cut off before he heard her tell him when they would be in San Francisco. The night before the ship docked was the longest night Mary had spent in her entire life. She learned a lesson from this episode and many other delays and problems in her life: that whatever was to happen would…nothing could prevent it; not all the worry in the world would change a thing. She tossed and turned, thinking of all that could go wrong, her greatest fear was being sent back to Australia. These thoughts and many others would rob her of much needed sleep that night. The next day, July 25, 1946, dawned with bright sunlight peeking through the porthole just between the curtains. The light across Mary's eyes gave a sudden splash of color as the ship slowed in the passage through the breakwater. She awoke with a start.

"Where are we? Alan, get up and get dressed quickly. I think we'll will be docking soon and we must be on deck ready to look for Norm."

They hurriedly gathered their things together; in which case, Alan was probably more hindrance than help.

"Hurry! Let's get on deck, so we can see everything," she said, as she ushered Alan out the door, leaving the suitcases for the porters. They pushed and shoved through the corridors, along with all the other passengers who were trying to reach the upper deck. They emerged out into the sunlight just as the ship passed under the Golden Gate Bridge; it was the most impressive thing they had seen on the whole trip. Everyone just stared up at it in awe; not a sound was uttered. This complete silence lasted until the ship had passed well under the bridge and steamed toward the San Francisco docks.

"Look, that must be Alcatraz. I have heard so many things about the dangerous criminals there!" one of the women in the crowd said as the ship passed by.

'Alcatraz…that's where I would like to put John.' Mary thought.

'No, I really wouldn't, I just wish he could love me the same way I love him.' She remembered the wonderful times she had shared with him… she still loved him and she always would.

"Look, there's the dock to the right, Mary." Lisa said, touching Mary's shoulder and interrupting her reverie. Lisa was one of the nurses who had helped Mary during Alan's little lavatory incident. It was not easy for Mary to make friends on the trip; she had spent most of her time in the cabin with Alan. She regretted the loss of female companionship; but, in a very short while, she would be with Norm in New Pass. She hoped to make new friends and forget her need for Australia. She missed her Mum and the rest of her family; but most of all, she missed her departed dad. Mary and George were very close, so she missed him in simple ways, such as the smell of pipe smoke in his coat, when he picked her up and hugged her. He hugged her every night, without fail, on his return from the factory. She missed his soft-spoken voice when he read to her from the books that he so treasured.

She stood with her hands on the upper rail, while Alan stood on the lower rail, fitting right into her arms. She thought of her dad and wondered if he was looking down on her as she began this new stage of her life. The ship turned sharply in order to dock and everyone craned their necks to see if they could find loved ones on the dock. Mary searched every face for Norm's familiar features; she was not sure that he had been able to hear their arrival plans over the poor connection.

Norm did understand the time that the ship was to be there, but he was unavoidably delayed on the trip from New Pass. New Pass is located about four hundred miles from San Francisco. The distance alone was one hurdle to overcome, but another hurdle presented itself in the form of a truck accident that blocked one of the mountain passes he had to go through. He would not be able to get there until the next day. Mary looked into the sea of faces until her eyes were blurry, but she couldn't find Norm's face. It was déjà vu…she could not erase from her mind the thought that she had mistakenly believed in someone again. Did he leave her in the lurch, the same way John did?

"C'mon, let's find the gangway." She grabbed Alan's arm and joined the swarm of passengers exiting the ship. "We need to get off this ship and clear Immigration, before they change their minds and send us back."

The Immigration Line was long and each piece of luggage was being searched. This process would take the better part of the day; it seemed as though they were standing still in the middle of the line. With Alan hanging off one arm and her purse hanging on the other, with the porter bringing up the rear, she stood in line with all her possessions, but with her head held high. There were so many immigrants that they were packed in like sardines, and every movement forward had a ripple effect on the line. Immigration Officials opened bags and asked questions without making eye contact. 'Organized chaos,' might have accurately described the immigration process and it worsened when the man across the table realized Mary had a "wee one'" with her. Apparently the manifest didn't include Alan.

"And who might this be, Ma'am?" he quipped.

"This is my son; he should be on the manifest."

"He's not on it. Here, look for yourself!"

"He has to be, we filed all the papers in Sydney."

"Well, he's not on these papers. What are we going to do about this?"

"I----don't know; what ----do we need to do?" Mary was visibly shaken by this news. "Oh, dear Lord! What shall I do?"

"Please step around to this side and come with me," he said, making an entranceway for them by separating two tables. Mary began to cry; it was too much for her. She knew without Norm there it would be a mess and she was consumed by fear. She had nearly achieved her goal... the end was in sight, and now it appeared they were headed back to Australia. She followed him into an office over in the corner of the dock building and he closed the door behind them.

"Let me see the papers you have and we will see if we can resolve the problem," he said kindly, taking the papers and scanning them page-by-page.

"I can see that this misconception can be taken care with a redefinition of this little guy's status." His huge grin made Mary feel much better. "This is unusual, but if you will get the papers from Australia back to us within a reasonable time frame, we can allow you to take him with you."

"I can do that...I will do that! Mary breathed a sigh of relief that echoed through the tiny office.

"I'm going to stamp him as 'Excess Baggage', which will allow you entry onto the American continent without further delay. Is someone here to meet you? It says on the papers a Norm Cooper is to pick you up."

"Yes, ------ he is here, just outside." Mary resolutely answered, even though she had not actually seen him.

Meanwhile, Norm had made it to Sacramento and was calling the dock to let her know that he was on his way and would be there by tomorrow.

"Mary Cooper, paging Mary Cooper." The loud speaker crackled over the noise of the masses being questioned by the officials.

"Mary Cooper, paging Mary Cooper, telephone call." The loud speaker repeated again.

"You can take it here," the official said, handing her the telephone.

"Hello, yes! Oh, my God, Norm, is that you?"

"Yes, Mary, it's really me! I've been calling since yesterday, but the lines are bad because of the weather. I'm in Sacramento and I will be there tomorrow to get you. Don't worry...it will be okay."

"Okay, what do you want me to do until then?"

"Get a room and meet me at the dock about one o'clock."

"Okay, until tomorrow! That's what we will do." Mary, dazed and disoriented, started to walk out the door, but turned back and asked "Would you know of anyplace close by to stay, so I can be at the dock by noon?"

"Yes, there is a place! In the interim, you can wait in here, while I find someone to take you over to the hotel." Mary had no sooner sat down, giving a big sigh of relief, when a lady in a uniform appeared in the doorway.

"Ma'am, did you need some place to stay?"

"Yes, I do, but only until tomorrow."

"You'd be surprised, but this happens all time. The men never seem to arrive on time to pick up their ladies. Oh, well! Come along with me and we'll see what we can find."

She hoisted up one of Mary's bags and handed it to the porter, who was standing just behind her in the doorway. He bent over and grabbed the other two bags. Mom tucked me under her arm...we were off again.

The hotel was across the street and down the block. We were there in less than ten minutes and were registered and in our room in less than thirty minutes. The room wasn't any larger than the one aboard the S.S. Mariposa and, in some ways, less than elegant. The bed was wider and we had to share. I didn't have my own bed as I did on board ship. I didn't mind, because Mom slept so soundly that she didn't even hear the telephone ring for the wake-up call. The desk clerk had to come and bang on the door to get her up.

"Wake-up call!" he shouted.

"What...what is it?" Mom was groggy from her deep sleep.

"Wake-up call, Ma'am,"

"Okay, okay, we're up." Mom sat up and pushed at me to get us moving. We cleaned up and Mom showered while I listened to the radio and played on the floor. She had everything packed; we checked out and were in front of the dock by noon. We sat on the bags and, like many other 'brides,' we waited for the men to arrive. Some of the 'brides' were muttering over and over, "I hope he recognizes me and I hope he looks the same as I remember."

The day was warm and it was pleasant to wait, but as time passed, the 'brides' became more and more irritable with each passing minute. One o'clock came and went; two o'clock came and went; two thirty; some had been met, but some were still waiting.

"I knew it would be like this," one of them said in despair.

"Don't worry, they will be here. I heard the traffic on the bridge was backed up today," the official announced as he came out of the building.

"Oh, it's you, Mary, is it? I just heard from the tollbooth it would be another hour before they can get the traffic moving. Someone blew a tire and blocked two lanes." He was the same man who gave me the label "Excess Baggage."

"Thank you; thank you for your concern, I'm sure he will be here soon!" Mom responded without looking up.

The sun had moved lower into the western horizon…it was getting late. Mom had to decide if she should get a room for the night, since the Immigration Service had only paid for the first night. She knew that their payment was simply a courtesy and she could not expect the same for the next night. She had some Australian money, but she didn't know if she had time to exchange it for American money. Just as she was about to get up and cross the street to look for a room at the same place they had spent the first night, a large pickup truck pulled up in front of us. It was a 1946 Dodge Power Wagon, with bright paint and even though there were many scratches up and down the sides, it still shone brightly in the sun. Norm was sitting behind the wheel, wearing his wide smile that displayed the new gold crowns on the left side of his mouth. He didn't have those when he left Australia. Later he told us about his accident with Quicksilver; he had inhaled the gas as he was refining Cinnabar to recover mercury. He said he was 'salivated', for which no explanation was offered. When he jumped out of the truck and ran around the front to greet Mary, he stopped short of her. They just looked at each other for a long time, then, he engulfed her in his huge arms and hugged her ever so tightly. He was crying with joy, even though it was well hidden from those around us. He loved her; it was both a curse and a blessing that he would have for the rest of his life.

"I missed you and have so many things to tell you, but all that can wait until we get settled for the night," he said to her as he looked down to me.

"How have you been, little guy?" he said as he picked me up and pressed me to his stubble-bearded face and kissed me. I loved him and would always consider him my father. It was only later that I would learn the truth and be damaged by the lies of these years. He loaded the bags and we were in the truck and on our way across the bridge before we knew what was happening. Norm was never one to wait around, so we drove to Sacramento and spent the night there.

The next morning, he was up early. "It's six o'clock and we have a long way to go." I was so impressed, as a toddler, that he had such great strength that he could carry all our bags in one trip.

"We must eat before leaving; then, we should call Mum and tell her that we are finally together. I know she'll be worried!" Mom said, all the while dressing us both. It has always been a source of wonderment to me that moms seem to able to do two things at once, like get dressed and take care of children at the same time. Amazingly, we would both be presentable in short order. Norm agreed, and, by the time that he returned, we were ready.

"Don't you think it would be better if we called from New Pass once we get there; that way she won't worry about the trip through the mountains and the desert."

"You're right! Your idea is much better, but we do need to eat."

"Okay, I saw a place across the street. Let's go over there." He lifted me up into the truck.

While we ate breakfast, Mom and Norm talked about how much they had missed each other and shared experiences about their various journeys to be together. Then we were off through the Sierra Nevada Mountains on our way to happiness and a better life...or so we thought.

It was a long drive to Reno. The I-80 freeway wasn't there in 1946. It was only a two-lane highway with lots of trucks ON it and lots of potholes IN it. If you were unfortunate enough to get behind one of the semi-trucks in between passing turnouts, it was possible to spend a good portion of the journey at a speed of less than 15 miles per hour. This happened frequently and, when the turnouts were reached, there was a struggle to pass with all the other cars lined up behind you. You thought you were in a good position if you were right behind the truck, but that was not so. The worst position was right behind the semi; everyone else would pass you before you could pull out to pass the truck. We finally arrived in Reno, but it had taken all day and we had to spend the night once more.

The glittering lights of the city were centered on the downtown area on Virginia Street, where the casinos straddled both sides of the Truckee River. It was a sight to behold; Mom was awed of the lights that moved around the signs inviting everyone to join the fun and spend your money. We checked into one of the brightly lit motels close to the casinos and Norm decided to take us to one of them for dinner. I was fascinated by the rows and rows of slot machines and gaming tables crowded by people, all excited by the prospect of winning. They were shouting and laughing, rolling dice, watching the roulette ball spinning around, and playing cards. The very air was filled with feverish excitement; after all, the war was over, our soldiers were returning, the economy was on the upswing, and times were good. We went in the restaurant and had a good meal; I still believe that the restaurants are one of the best features of casinos.

"How many coins can you put into one of those machines before it's full?" Mom asked as we passed by one of the nickel slot machines.

"I don't think you could ever fill one of them up."

"You must be joking; look at the size of those machines. Most of it must be the mechanism that causes those wheels to spin around."

"Mary, here's twenty dollars! Go get this changed for some nickels and see how many it will take."

"All right, I will." This was the first and only lesson Mom would need to avoid slot machines in the future. She changed the twenty into nickels and began to feed them into the machines. I say 'feed' because the machine gobbled up all of the nickels and did not even burp back one coin.

"I think it is about to hit," called a voice from behind us. The voice belonged to a little elderly lady with a tattered shawl draped over her old and worn dress.

"What do you mean?" Mom asked. She turned to see who had spoken to her with some slang term she didn't understand.

"I mean the machine is about 'hit', 'pay out'; you know, win a jackpot."

"A jackpot?" Mom said, with a puzzled look on her face.

"Yes, Mary, a jackpot! You didn't think you were just playing the machine for the fun it, did you?" Norm asked, laughing.

"Do you mean that I could win something?" she asked.

"Yes, I won five hundred dollars three months ago," the lady said, but it was obvious she hadn't won since. She looked as down on her luck and hooked as anyone could be.

I later remembered this first lesson that gambling was an addiction and that whole families would suffer if the 'gambling bug' bit either parent. People gambled away fortunes, ending their lives in poverty on the streets of America from New York to San Francisco. Even though gambling was legal only in Nevada, it was still a problem for many across America.

"May I have another twenty, Norm?"

"Sure, why not, it will gobble up that, as well."

"Come on, honey, let me show you how to pull the handle to make sure you win," the lady said. You could see the gleam in her eye as she dropped the first coin in the slot. She had the 'fever', as Norm would later tell Mom. The machines around us were clanging and their lights were glowing as the excitement grew. Mom and her new friend were about halfway through the twenty dollars when the machines capriciously gave some coins back. The wheels lined up and a few coins fell into the tray below with a clang and the lady jumped with glee as she exclaimed, "You see, it does pay to play."

"What do you mean? We spent $15 to get $5." In that instant, Mom got the point; a point that the poor lady would never get. "Come on,

Norm, let's go," she said as she took me from his arms and bid farewell to the lady and to the slot machines forever.

The next day, we were on our way to New Pass Mine, located almost in the center of Nevada, about 40 miles northwest of Austin. In order to get to New Pass, we had to travel to Austin first, and backtrack on a dirt road to New Pass. Norm owned a house in Austin, which was a small stone building typical of the surrounding houses. It was constructed of a wood frame with stone facia on the outer walls. It consisted of one large room in the center, with a bedroom on either side of the house and the kitchen in the back, next to the bathroom. It was a nice cozy house, clearly in need of a woman's touch, but that would come with Mom and with time. The house was to be used on a part-time basis, because we would be at the mine most of the summer. The weather in the winters was very bad. The mine would be shut down for part of the winter because of the heavy snow pack. The snow was so heavy that the trucks hauling ore to the smelter in Salt Lake City were unable to run.

We spent that night in Austin, as well as the following two days, just getting the house in what Mom called "good shape". Norm went out to the mine, saying that he would be back in two days to gather the supplies for our stay at the mine. Those two days went by fast. Before we realized it, Norm appeared at the door and said, "Well, are you ready to go?"

"Yes, I am. It will be nice to get to the mine and see the nice house and conveniences I have heard so much about."

Norm looked downcast as Mom finished; he knew that he was in for a hard time once she saw the cabin at the mine. The cabin was only about half the size of the house in town and had no indoor plumbing or a kitchen, as such. The mine had a mess hall and soon Mom would be part of the work force operating the mess hall. The women would do most of the cooking, serving, cleaning, and general work around the mess hall. They were compensated for their work; but, in a way, the work was a blessing. It was better than waiting in the small cabins for the men to get off work. We arrived at the mine about noon...just in time for lunch, where Norm proudly introduced us to everyone. The mine employed about twenty men and eight women; only a few of the miners were married. Most of the men were what Norm called 'tramp miners', who went from mine to mine, working for a limited time to get a stake and then move on. They would 'tramp' around the country, eventually to be killed in an accident or die alone of complications associated with their hard living. Sometimes they were able to live to a ripe 'old age', which was about forty, at least in miner's years. They would often be buried in unmarked graves, with no one to notice or mourn their passing. All that they owned was either on their backs or in their bedroll. They might have a car or a pickup truck if they were lucky. Once in a while, one of them would have a bank account, but finding relatives of these silent men with no past was nearly impossible. Any money they might have left would go to charity, primarily established for miners. After lunch, we went to Norm's cabin and, to Mom's utter surprise, it was smaller and more primitive than she could have ever imagined. The cabin consisted of a one-room structure with one bed in a corner. In the center of the room was a pot-bellied stove to provide heat, with a flat top for a kettle. Wall shelves covered by a curtain; three windows, one on each wall perpendicular to the door, and a small window to one side of the narrow back door. There was one dresser to hold all of their underclothing and one small closet in the opposite corner from the bed.

Mary looked around remembering what her mum had commented when saying their farewells, 'It seems you will have it much better than your father and I had when we first started.'

'I thought we would have a much better start than this.' Mary thought, as she looked at the single bed. She could not imagine how they would ever be comfortable here. On a hook next to the door were the dirtiest clothes she had ever seen but before she could ask about them, Norm said "I'll get these down and move them to the change house. They are my work clothes for the mine."

"That would be nice, but where is Alan to sleep?"

"I'll have a double bed brought in for us and he can have the single. We'll be fine here after we fix it up a little," Norm said, struggling to infuse some hope in his voice.

"Okay, just give me some time to adjust." Mary responded, with a slight sigh in her voice.

"I know it's not what you expected, but it will get better," Norm consoled her, as he moved closer. As he hugged her, she felt an internal jolt; this relationship would not last. Women possess certain instincts; they can discern an outcome long before it happens...maybe it's the fabled 'women's intuition' that most men belittle because they don't understand it. She knew at that very moment that she did not love him the way that she thought she had. She knew they would not be together forever like they had promised in their wedding vows. In his defense, Norm loved her and would do anything to keep her, but he had no idea it was over.

They cleaned up the cabin and began to live as normally as was possible in such a desolate place. All I can remember is that it was a great time for me. I ran wild through the mining camp and it was fun sliding down the slag dumps and watching the parades when we went to Austin. Austin, as in all of America, had long, colorful, patriotic parades after the war. This was a time of great pride in America, they had just won the most devastating conflict of all time and the economy was in good shape. I can remember standing on the balcony of the International Hotel in Austin and watching the floats, horses, clowns, and Masons' parade by. For me, it was a wonderful time. The only dark cloud on the horizon was the monthly arrival of the INS agent to inquire when I was to achieve status. I was four, nearly five, years old; and I must have posed a great threat to national security. Mom and I came into Austin frequently where she began to drink and smoke very heavily. Her problem with alcohol earned her the nickname "Whiskey Mary"... a source of many difficulties in the future.

We had been at New Pass and Austin for nearly a year when the mine closed and we moved to Park City...Park City, Utah in the Wasatch mountain range east of Salt Lake City. The mine and most of the town was either owned or controlled by Norm's mother's second husband, John Allen. He had made a lot of money from the mine and other property deals. In fact, he built the Allen Hotel in the center of town. It was natural that he would arrange for Norm to work at the mine. We had a house on the mine property from which Norm could easily walk to work. I think this was one of the happiest times for Mom with Norm, even though she was fighting the alcohol and cigarettes. Mom and I would sled down the mountain in the winter and, in the summer we would run over the meadows to see Grandma Allen. These were carefree days for me. Later that year, Mom began to spend a lot of time at the local bars while Norm was at work. I, on the other hand, spent time with Grandma Allen. Mom and Norm fought incessantly, over every little thing. It seemed as though the marriage was unraveling; when, suddenly, Mom became pregnant with my brother. I have never been certain that child was Norm's, and it was always a source of concern for me, as well as my concern over the identity of my father. It is hard to relate to these issues of identity unless one has experienced them personally. Even then, it is hard to explore your origins in a sensitive manner without causing potential damage to your birth parents. In those days, things that were best left unsaid were left unsaid, sometimes to the great detriment of the identity-seeker. Time, the great equalizer, is not on the side of truth, justice, and self-worth.

My brother, William George, was born August 10, 1947, in Park City, Utah. My first memory of him was when my Mom held him up to the window, while Norm and I stood on the lawn below. Otherwise, I would have missed seeing him for a number of days. I was not that impressed with his looks; he was wrinkled and wasn't old enough to play with me. The hospital didn't allow visitors under the age of ten, and since I was only four, the chances of my visiting were nil, and the allowed visitation schedule in 1947 was very strict. As I remember it, the hospital was a red brick, three-story, square building with an ornate entrance. It was most impressive, but I would not be impressed with it later on.

Once, I went on a small excursion before bedtime and wound up in there for a tonsillectomy. But, again, I digress...........................

About three days later when Mom and Bill came home, there was an obvious change in Norman's attitude. He seemed to be more interested in Bill's welfare than in Mom's or mine. Maybe it was just Mom's imagination working overtime... maybe he was just really interested in his son. Mom didn't say anything and I was too young to understand what was happening, but I could feel the change. Mom was just happy that Bill was born without complication and would likely develop into a healthy man. Mom and Norm continued to argue and the situation became worse with each passing day. Their fighting would linger on into the night; I would listen to this and wonder what would happen to our family. These times were frightening to me, but I would retreat into my own little world where everything was safe and nothing could harm me. To this day, I avoid confrontation; unless I consider it to be a matter of honor...everything else can just go by the wayside. People, places, and things meant nothing...Norm and Mom were both drinking and this didn't help with the relationship. Mom drank all day long and would be passed out by the time Norm got home. Then he left for the bar to try and catch up. When he got home, she was usually awake and upset because he had gone out. This went on for several months, while Bill and I spent most of our time at Grandma's. Grandma was a no-nonsense woman and she didn't sugarcoat her feelings about their lifestyle, but neither one would listen.

One day when I awakened very early and very cold, Mom was packing our stuff out to the pickup. Norman was passed out on the bed.

"Quiet, don't say anything," she whispered to me as she picked Bill up and moved to the door. "Come on, move faster!"

"Mom, I'm sleepy."

"Quiet!" she said, grabbing me by the arm and pulling me along to the truck. "Get in; don't say anything," she said, sternly.

Just as she started the engine, Norman appeared in the doorway of the house. He stood there in his shorts and T-shirt for a moment as though trying to absorb what was happening, and then started toward the truck.

"Where in the hell do you think you're going?" he shouted as she put the truck in gear and started to pull away.

"I'm leaving you and all your goddamn drunkenness," she shouted as the truck finally began to move. Norm grabbed at the door handle and caught it with his left hand. Mom jerked, the clutch popped, and the truck lunged forward, throwing Norman to the ground, causing him to lose his hold on the door handle. I remember him lying on the ground in the mud, as we pulled away...destination unknown. We headed down the hill to the main road and on to Salt Lake City, where Mom fueled up and pointed the nose of the truck to the west and Washington State. I don't know how long we traveled before Mom pulled off the road to feed Bill. As she pulled the truck onto the shoulder, we began to sink into the mud. After we sat there for what seemed like hours, two men stopped and helped us get free of the mud. Mom fed Bill while we were waiting for the men to get the truck out of the mud. She was breast-feeding him and I thought that the men seemed embarrassed by her actions.

"Are you okay, lady?" asked one of them.

"Yes, I just need to get back on the road," she said, covering herself.

"We should have you out in a minute. You're not from around here, are you, lady?"

"No, I'm Australian."

"I thought so; I spent time in Sydney during the war and the accent sounded familiar. Well, you're ready to go," he said as the truck moved to the blacktop. Once again, we were off with the destination unknown to me. Once we passed over Dead Horse Summit, it was smooth sailing to a small town just outside of Seattle. I don't remember the name of the town, but I do remember the house and the two other children. We arrived early in the evening and were met at the door by a man. The look on this man's face was one of shock and dismay; he began to back away from Mom. A woman I later learned was his wife came to see who was at the door.

"Hello, John, how are you?"

"Hello, Mary, I'm...um...fine. And you?" he stammered, as he attempted to regain his composure.

"Who are you?" John's wife asked assertively, moving out of the doorway and out onto the step.

"I'm..."

"She's an old army friend," John interrupted, attempting to rescue the moment.

"An army *friend*?" Mom asked loudly. John decided that quick action was necessary, so he pulled Mom, with Bill still in her arms, and his wife into the house, while the rest of us were left outside to play. Mom didn't disclose what the discussion was about, but it seemed to me that they were in the house for a very long time. We played outside together in a friendly manner as I remember it.

"Alan, let's go," Mom called from the step and I ran quickly to her... this was another mystery to me in a lifetime of mysterious happenings. "We are going to stay at a motel that John has arranged for. Get your things together and let's go," she said, staring at John with a look of hurt and anger so intense that I was frightened. I would never see the look of being hurt, but I would see that look of anger and I would know that look from the inside. John gave me an odd, yearning look; in one single day, I had seen the full gamut of emotions and I didn't understand a bit of it. I didn't know that John had tried to obtain approval from Mom and his wife to keep me. They both turned him down; his wife, because she already had her children and didn't want to disrupt her life; and Mom, because she loved me and would not give me up for any reason, other than my best interests. We left that night and I was never to see John or any of those other people again. When I look back on that day, I think that, given the social mores of the time, nothing else could have happened. We stayed at the designated motel; the next morning, we were on our way back to Reno. Mom was to file for divorce in a place known as the 'divorce capital of the world'. During the long trip to Reno, she began to plan out-loud about how she was going take care of us. Who will ever know the emotional cost to Mom of what transpired with John?

Reno was a wide-open town with legalized gaming and a 'money can buy everything' atmosphere. Almost immediately, she found a job as a cocktail waitress at one of the casinos. We found a place to stay not far from her work and someone to watch us while she was working. That someone was a lady of color, as they were called in those days. She was short in stature and very compact; if she had worn a hoop skirt and a checkered bandana on her shoulders, it would have been difficult to tell the difference between her and the Aunt Jemima figure on the old syrup bottle and the pancake mix bag. I can still see her standing in the doorway, calling out to me and the rest of the kids as we ran out to play. "You children stay out of the street now; don't make me run after you."

We knew she couldn't catch us even if she wanted to; but we respected her, so we would come back. She was as much a mother to Bill and me as she was to her own two boys. I will never forget her or her warm house with those wonderful cooking smells that would greet me at the door and invite me in. Rita, or Aunt Rita, as we came to know her, would always remain a fond memory for me.

The girls who worked at the casinos were well acquainted. They all had similar problems, such as children without fathers and the need of childcare. They tried to help each other by pooling resources and sharing places to live. It was a good arrangement. The place where we lived was on 665 West Street, between Sixth and Seventh. That whole area is now a part of St. Mary's Hospital. It was an easy walk home from Harold's Club for Mom; even crossing the railroad tracks wasn't bad, and she could be home within five minutes. She liked her job and had the chance to meet many different types of people; some were good, some were bad. The casino provided a skimpy uniform that revealed as much of the female anatomy as was allowed at that time. The casinos were in business to make money and if this attire enticed a patron to spend money, then the desired effect was achieved. The casino paid for the cleaning, but it was the waitresses' responsibility to take the uniforms to the cleaners. Mary found a dry cleaner nearby and dropped off that day's uniform and picked up the next day's set on the way home. The casino gave them three uniforms, so they would always have a clean uniform for work.

The man who worked at the dry cleaner always exchanged pleasantries with her and chatted about her day. He knew her schedule and made it a point to be there to greet her. This man, Lonnie, had learned dry-cleaning in prison and was out on parole for good behavior. He was what is commonly referred to as a 'second story man,' a burglar. He had been serving time in Carson for some thefts in the Reno area. His parole time was nearly over when he met Mary. As usual, he greeted her as she came through the door. She replied, without paying much attention, that she had had a tough day. His question caused her to reflect on her future…a future that looked pretty bleak…with two kids and no husband to help her survive. She was in a situation for which there seemed no solution.

The Casino offered fair benefits, but wages were linked to tips. Sometimes those tips were not forthcoming and she struggled to make ends meet from paycheck to paycheck. Mary pondered what to do about their future. Going home to Australia was one option; but could she face everyone, especially her mother, after her divorce. But, her options were either Australia or survival here in the United States.

"Here you are," Lonnie said as he handed the package to her. In those days they folded and wrapped the clothes. He had hesitated in an attempt to get her to offer her name, but she was far away, thinking of other things. She absently smiled at him. "Thank you," she said and left.

'I must find out who she is,' he thought as he headed back to the clothes press.

Lonnie's boss chastised him for waiting on customers instead of remaining in the back, but Lonnie didn't even notice; he was thinking about the woman who had just given him that dazzling smile. That smile that made you feel that she thought you were the only person in the world. That smile, accented by her petite well-portioned body, her pleasant demeanor.

Lonnie's boss had a side deal with some of the cocktail waitresses to charge for cleaning that wasn't needed. He split the money with them; some went along with him, even knowing that it would cost them their jobs if they were caught. Lonnie was aware of how the scam worked; but, because he was on parole, he did not want to be involved. His goal was to go straight...if he could leave Reno and find a job out of the bright lights and the temptation of quick riches, he would be able to give up his life of crime. Now there was an additional problem... he had seen Mary, the special woman. He had no idea of her identity and the cleaning ticket gave no clue. The ticket showed a number where the name should be; it was an easy way for the casino to track the cleaning bills.

"I need to find out who she is; I would like to see more of her." Just then, he saw another cocktail waitress he knew, Jackie, leaving the back of the cleaners. She had just been talking to his boss, Jim. Jim was referred to as 'Fat Jim'; but not within his hearing, of course. Jim was a man of about 5'8 in height and about the same size in girth. He could hardly waddle through the aisles, even though they had been widened to accommodate his size. He constantly sweated, no matter what the temperature outside was. It was always hot inside the cleaners, but during the winter when it was cold outside, he would still sweat. His body was like a furnace, with his red face as the gage, the ever-present sweat pouring off his face in some futile attempt to cool him. He was repulsive to the girls; the advances he made would surely cause them to agree with his scheme to bilk the casinos, just to get rid of him.

"Jackie! Wait up," Lonnie shouted as he ran after her.

"What do you want?" she snapped as she turned to see who it was. She was relieved to see Lonnie and changed her demeanor.

"Hey," he asked, "Who is that girl who was just in here?"

"I don't know, I didn't see her. Can you describe her?"

"Yes, she's blond."

"That description fits almost all of us," she laughed.

"That's not all; she is small, has a great smile, and she speaks with an accent! British, I think."

"Oh, yeah, that's Mary. Yeah, Mary. She's from Australia."

"What do you know about her?"

"She has two kids and is either single or in the process of getting a divorce, I don't know which. She's been in the country since '46 and I think she is considering going home."

"How can I meet her?" Lonnie asked, just as 'Fat Jim' came through the open door.

"What's going on here?" he asked, thinking that Lonnie and Jackie were plotting some scheme of their own.

"Nothing!" Lonnie answered back sharply. "I just asked Jackie if she knew that girl who was in here before."

"What do you want to know for?"

"None of your business."

"Don't get smart with me! Lonnie, I know your parole officer and..."

"And what? I'm sure that the casinos would love to know about your schemes, so you best forget this," Lonnie fired back, as he went to the clothes press. Jim just stood there, relieved that Lonnie wouldn't push the issue. He knew the casinos would frown on his scheme in a 'big way'; he didn't want to think about the 'big' punishment they would mete out to him.

The next day when Mary came in as usual, Lonnie was at the counter to meet her. Jim was in the back and not inclined to confront Lonnie after his threat. Lonnie called her by name and asked how she was doing. She was startled that he knew her name and questions raced through her mind, 'How did he know her name? What did he want? Was he an INS agent in disguise?' She hadn't heard from them since she left Norman. 'Had they found her? Were they still after her to have Alan deported?' She looked first at him and then outside for some sign that she was being watched.

"Are you all right, Mary?"

"What do you want?" she managed to gasp, still on edge, her adrenaline pumping.

"Nothing, I just thought maybe we could go to dinner or something," he said, dejectedly. "You seem very nervous. Is something wrong?"

"Not really, I'm just surprised you know my name." As she began to calm down, her imagination of his status as an INS agent faded.

"I asked Jackie who you were so I could ask you out," he said as he handed her the dry cleaning. "I think you are wonderful and I would like to take you out, that's all."

Mary thought it might be good to go out to dinner and she felt badly about her earlier reaction to him.

"Just say 'when' and we'll go to a nice place, I promise," he said as she walked out onto the step in front of the store.

Mary promised to let him know when and left. Her thoughts returned to the INS. She had been dealing with them before she left New Pass; they wanted her to obtain a permanent visa for Alan. In fact, she had met with the Presiding Inspector for INS in New Pass Mine, Nevada, on February 15, 1948. She easily recalled that occasion and replayed the scenario in her mind.

"What is your full and correct name?" he asked her with little or no emotion in his voice. He had asked so many people these same questions that he no longer cared about them as human beings.

"Winifred Mary Cooper," she responded. She remembered the long wait before her appearance and then the stress of the questions. Alan was only four years old then and they wanted to send him back to Australia because he didn't have a visa. She had tried to get a visa, but was hampered by the 'Australian quota'. She also remembered the agent in San Francisco and thought maybe he was just being nice or didn't know what he was doing. She had completed many forms: I-256,

I-55, I-25, the list went on and on. She prepared them in triplicate and handed them to the person she had been told was the proper authority, but it seemed as though all her efforts had been in vain. She shook off the old memories and went home to find Rita there, as usual, cooking up a storm.

"What are you cooking that smells so good?"

"Just a little recipe my mother gave me before she passed. God rest her soul." Aunt Rita always said that when she spoke of someone who had died.

I can remember that day as clear as it were yesterday. Mom seemed changed; somehow she acted hopeful that everything was going to work out. She went to where Bill was lying in the makeshift crib and picked him up.

"I think we will be on a new road after today, I think we are going to be all right." This new feeling was not due to Lonnie; he was merely the instrument that reminded her that it had been a long time since she had contact with the INS.

She sat down with Bill in her arms and said to Rita, "Today, I realize that I haven't heard from the INS since May of 1948; likely they have forgotten about me." Her last real contact with them was just after she came to Reno. Mary was hoping she would be able to get the right papers this time for Alan's permanent visa, but she had been so involved in eeking out the day-to-day existence, she had not done anything concrete. There was nothing on record. Rita knew they had not forgotten Mom, since they had been to the house on several occasions to check on Mom's progress and instructed Rita not to tell Mary. Rita couldn't tell Mom, even though she wanted to, she knew that the government was all-powerful. She was hiding something from her own past...something she didn't want uncovered.

We all sat down and ate the mystery recipe that Rita had prepared. To this day, I don't have any idea what most of the things she cooked were, but they all tasted good. The next few days passed in much the same way. I watched as Mom went to work, came home, and listened to the others tell of the day they had. They shared a common problem about the difficulty of surviving on the wages and tips they earned.

"This is really bad, the harder we work, the farther behind we get. I don't see any future in this," Mary said to Jackie, as they were sitting around after dinner one night.

"You're right, Mary, it seems we earn just enough to be trapped in this job forever, unless you're lucky enough to marry your way out."

"I don't want to get married again! The previous two times were a disaster," Mom responded as she looked over to Bill and me sitting on the couch. I didn't know if she was referring to us as the problem or if she just felt lost about what to do for us.

"You know, Mary, I was talking to one of the other girls at work yesterday. She said that she and some of her friends were invited to a party where she made a lot of money," Jackie said, ignoring the others in the room.

"What do you mean?"

"She just said she made a lot of money and the people who gave the party wished other girls would come," Jackie said, now moving closer to Mom so the others would not hear.

"What kind of party was it?" Mom asked her, becoming more interested.

"Oh, you know! Typical drinking and socializing."

"Oh, but how does that make any money?"

"Just by being there, I suppose. She didn't really have time to say, she had to go back to work. I think that you dance with the guys and pretend to be interested in what they are saying."

"I don't know! It sounds too easy to me; there must be more to it."

Mary and Jackie were speaking very softly, so no one else was paying any attention to what they were saying. The whole room was buzzing with everyone talking at once about their own issues, but Mary and Jackie were in a serious conversation about how to make more money and, perhaps, ease on out of the financial situation they were in. Mary was somewhat burned out by the concept of marriage and had no desire to return. Both of her marriages could be termed disasters, at best; but she still harbored some latent feeling for her first love, John. Even now, she loved him, realizing full well how badly he had used and abused her love for him.

"How do we get invited to these parties?" Mary asked Jackie.

"I don't really know, but I can find out."

"Okay, find out all you can and let me know."

Jackie was ready to leave, after promising to let Mary know. "Where are you going?" Mary asked, still wanting to learn more about the interesting subject.

"That's all I know right now, I will tell you more after tomorrow. I need to get to bed, as tomorrow will be a long day. I'll see you later."

Mary pondered the idea of having more financial security in the future, particularly since she didn't want to go back to Australia to face Winifred.

Winfred would never understand the divorces and would not be able to forgive Mary. Marriage was a sacred institution to her and marriage meant you were bound to that person forever. She never married again after George died; there could never be anyone to replace him. She thought of him often with a smile on her face that made her glow from within.

Mary, on the other hand, had had two bad experiences and would always be very leery about the motives of men. These experiences set the stage for her entry into a new way of life. The first step was already taken. Mary felt this might give her the financial advantage she needed to complete the fight to stay in the States. This would give her an opportunity to go to Canada and wait for the quota to be increased so she could file the papers and once and for all get shed of the INS. These thoughts ran through her mind as she weighted the opportunity and the present job she had. She had no idea the parties were nothing more than a way of recruiting prostitutes to fill the legal brothels in the state. They would be judged on appearance and their impression on the clientele. If they were presentable and passed the 'test', they would be

approached for work in the hotels and the brothels. The hotels would use
them to entertain high rollers and other clients from back east. The ones
who made the top grade would become hotel girls and the others would
go straight to the brothels. This was done on a voluntary basis, but the
offer of more money was usually all the incentive the girls needed to
make the transition.

The next day Jackie told Mary that a party was being planned for
that night and she was to be invited. When she opened her locker, an
envelope with a note inside stated the she was invited to a party at 7:30
and gave an address and expected attire. She was told to bring the note
with her. Mary knew the place; it was just off the main casino row on
Virginia Street and would not be a long walk. She went home to find
Rita was already aware of the party and was available to watch the
kids.

"Now, you be careful what you're getting into. This party may not
be what you think."

"What do you mean not what I think?"

"Jest trust me, I knows what I'm saying and you needs to be careful.
Now go on, get yourself ready and don't worry about the boys."

"Wait, Rita! What do you know that you're not telling me?" Mary,
half-dressed, called to her.

"I was at one of the 'parties' when I was young, in Chicago during
the Capone days; it turned out to be a lot more than what I thought.
So, you jest watch yourself," Rita stopped at that and went on about
her business.

Mary looked at Rita's back as she went on out to the porch with a
basket of clothes to hang. She thought, 'what could be so wrong about
these parties? All Jackie said was to be nice to the clients and I would
be paid.'

Time waits for no one. It was 7:00 pm and she was not ready, but
Jackie was there and kept telling her "Mary, we've got to go if we want
to be invited again! The note said not to be late. We should be early, if
possible."

"I'm hurrying, but I'm a bit nervous about this---'party'! Did you know Rita had been to one in Chicago and it isn't what we think."

"Ah, Mary, you know how Rita is! She thinks the mob is everywhere and they control the gaming and you know that's not true."

"I don't know what you mean, the mob?"

"You know the Mafia, Al Capone, Bugsey, and all those other gangsters in New York and Chicago. C'mon, Mary, let's go."

"Okay, I'm ready, what do you think?"

"Yeah, you look great; let's go." Jackie said.

"You'll knock 'em out."

Mary and Jackie wore semi-low cut shifts that rode high on their knees revealing some, but not all their beauty. They had small handbags to carry only the vital necessities; lipstick, perfume, etc. Their high-heeled pumps, that seemed to fit nicely on their nylon covered feet, were accented with a touch of glitter across the toe to make them noticeable, but not. They both looked as if they had just stepped out of a fashion magazine.

The party was just beginning when they arrived and she could see another girl from the club near the back of the room talking to an older man who had his arm around her. Mary half-waved to her as she gave her note to the man at the door. "Where have you broads been?" the man at the door asked as he let them in. "You're almost late, and I close the door at 7:30 sharp. You should go to the bar at the far end of the room and check in with the bartender. He'll tell you what to do."

"Okay, so the bartender will let me know what to do?" Mary repeated, somewhat nervously.

"That's what I said," he growled, pointing in the direction of the bar.

'This doesn't seem like a very good time thus far,' she thought, moving past him toward the bar at the back of the room.

"I see you finally made it!" the bartender said, handing her a cocktail.

"How did you know what I like to drink?" she asked, as she realized that the drink was her favorite, a Manhattan.

"You just look to me like a big city girl. Wait here until I finish serving this drink and I will give you the whole low-down."

While she waited, she looked around the room to see if she recognized any of the other patrons. He returned to her and began to explain that she was expected to mingle with the men and act as if she enjoyed their company and was interested in what they were saying. "Do you understand?"

"Yes, I think so," she answered, somewhat reservedly. "What will this involve? You know, what else?"

"I am guessing that you are wondering about payment."

"Well, yes...is there anything else I should know?"

"Well, sweetheart, that is up to you, isn't it? Now get out there and see if you can earn some money for the sponsors. Maybe you'll be invited back again sometime...If you're lucky!"

This sudden change of attitude was a shock to her; he had been so pleasant before and now he seemed so indifferent.

The party was just as Rita had said... something more than what was advertised. The men were well dressed, in their early fifties and considered to be high rollers looking for a good time (this meant more than dancing and listening to them talk about what interested them). Mary soon found herself in a situation that would make her decide if this was the life for her or not.

"Do you live around here?" a guy asked as he stroked her bare leg up to her thigh.

"Yes, I do," she said, as she moved her dress back down to her knee.

"I'm from Chicago, do you know where that is?"

"Back east, in Illinois, I think," she answered as he began to move her dress back up.

"Is this your first party?'

"Yes, it is."

"Then maybe you don't know the rules yet."

"No, I don't! Could you explain them?"

"Sure," he said with a knowing smile that Mary would become accustomed to seeing over the next few years. "If I like you and you agree, we go to one of the rooms upstairs and become better acquainted, if you get my drift." Mary got his 'drift', now understanding what Rita had said. These parties were not what they seemed on the surface.

"So, let's be clear on this... you and I will go upstairs and have sex, if we agree. I can expect to be paid for this."

"Yes, that's the idea, if you agree! Of course, I don't want you to do anything you don't want to."

"What would be the pay? Will it be worth my while? Will I be allowed to leave here with it?"

"Of course, we're not savages! Actually, this could be the beginning of a new career."

"What do you mean?" she asked with some interest.

"Well, you could become one of the hotel girls and would be expected to 'entertain' guests."

He began to explain and told her of the 'Program' she would be party to. He explained the whole 'program' as it was known then, from the hotel girls, brothels, and the State's part of regular physicals and health records. Hotel girls were the top of the line, so to speak. They would become very important to the 'sponsors' and would usually retire in a few years with a good income and other benefits, such as marriage to very influential husbands. The 'brothels' in Nevada were legal houses of prostitution, legal in some counties and in the counties where they were not legal, they were tolerated. These 'houses' were a place where men could go pick out a 'girl' and have sex for a price. The State would regulate them and make sure to have the 'girls' medically checked on a regular basis so as not to spread diseases. These places were usually the last stop before walking the streets, where some, who later got into drugs and alcohol, would end their lives.

"Is this your first party?" she asked, covering his hand with hers to stop it from moving up her leg again.

"No, this is my third party," he said with pride as though this was some sort of status symbol. In order to be invited, one must be either a guest or an "entertainer". The guests were invited based on their ability to pay for the entertainment and the "entertainers" were there by virtue of their appearance and their entertainment value to the guests. He continued, "I suppose that the bartender told you what was expected."

"Yes and no," she said, just now realizing where his detailed explanation was going.

"What happens now is up to you and..." He stopped just short of finishing his sentence, sensing victory, and attempted to move his hand from her knee to her waist.

"And what?" she asked as he pulled her closer, almost toppling the stool she was perched on.

"Oh, be careful!" he said, moving quickly to break her fall. "Boy! That was close, we almost had a disaster; that would have been awful," he said, righting her stool and holding her steady. "Let's start over, before I make any more stupid moves. I'm George Wendell from Chicago here on business with the local casinos...and you are?"

"I'm Mary, here by invitation of...Well, I don't know who."

They both laughed and he began to tell her about his interests in Chicago, but he couldn't tell her much. He was involved with a group who operated a majority of the casinos and they did not encourage talk about their activities. He continued to talk and Mary listened very intently, trying to appear interested in what he was saying. She was unaware that she would be involved with these people for the rest of her life. She wanted to interrupt him several times, but he was enjoying talking about himself, so she just listened.

"Mary, are you enjoying the party?" Jackie asked as she walked up to her with her "friend". Introductions were made all around.

"Now that we're all old friends, maybe one of you boys can buy us a drink," Jackie announced.

"That's the ticket; what would you ladies like?"

Mary thought of her love affair with alcohol in the past; she could not afford to fall prey to that demon again. Her reputation in Austin as 'Whiskey Mary' flashed through her mind, vividly recalling the many nights she had spent lying on the floor in a drunken stupor at the Golden Saloon. Norman would drape her over his shoulder and haul her home, leaving her in the bathroom to throw up for the rest of the night. She thought, 'All I need to do is drink a little and I will slip back into that drunken nightmare. I will lose the ability to care for my children! If that happens, I won't be able to convince John that I am worthwhile and live the good life I still want.' She could not erase John from her mind, so she said, "I'm just going to have a Coke. Alcohol makes me ill and I won't be any fun if I'm ill." She accompanied her remarks with that smile, rendering her answer acceptable to the men. Their minds were on something other than the drinking and someone who was ill wouldn't be much suited to their purpose.

Even though Jackie's 'date' was already selected, Mary's smile and her petite beauty dazzled him. He briefly wondered about his chances of dumping Jackie and cutting George out of the picture. Instead, he ordered their drinks.

The bartender glared at Mary before he turned to get the drinks. Her failure to order a drink with alcohol in it made him wonder about her willingness to 'party'. When he brought the drinks, he motioned for her to meet him at the end of the bar. "What are you doing? You should know by now why you are here. How can you meet tonight's requirements if you are not drinking? You concern me with your attitude about this whole thing."

"Don't worry about me! I just can't get involved with alcohol. I have had a drinking problem in the past and, believe me, it will be disastrous to jump into the alcohol again."

"Okay! Just make sure these guys have a good time!"

It was at this point that Mary realized that she was standing at one of life's crossroads. This was not just a social gathering and Rita's words of warning echoed in her head. That little voice of conscience was not strong enough to deter the stronger voice of financial security for herself and her children. "How difficult could it be," the stronger voice said, "these guys will be smashed by the time anything sexual will happen. They will be passed out before they can even take off their clothes, if they can manage that."

"Mary, are you all right?" Jackie asked, as Mary returned from the end of the bar.

"Of course! What could possibly be wrong?" Mary replied in a more animated voice than Jackie had heard before. Mary had clearly made a decision about tonight's agenda. Jackie wondered if Mary's chat with the bartender was responsible for this obvious change of attitude. Although the others continued to drink, Mary kept to her plan and only ordered cola. The night wore on and the fancy hors de oeuvres that had been prepared went untouched.

"I guesh ish time to go to the nex' step!" George barely managed to say, trying to appear less drunk than he was.

"What do you mean?" Jackie pretended ignorance.

Both men indicated that they would enjoy some activity of a closer nature.

"Yes," replied Mary, forthrightly. "I think that the activity they're talking about is sexual."

"That's j—us' if you're com—fortable," George was giving them one last chance to opt out, but he was certain of success.

Mary, of course, had already come to terms with the whole object of this evening. She was not as disturbed by that end-result as one might have thought. She hadn't had intercourse for quite a while and realized that she had missed it. She didn't necessarily want to be labeled as a whore, but this partying aspect didn't seem too terribly bad. In Jackie's case, intoxication had removed the last of her possible objections.

"So, wha ya shink?" George mumbled, moving closer to Mary and leaning in to make sure no one else heard. "Ish thish all right wi' you?"

"Sure," Mary replied, looking at the bartender.

"It's upstairs," he said, handing her a key. "Bring the key back to me and only me; I will be here until the end of the 'party'. When you see me, we'll settle up." With that, Mary took the key and George's hand. He lagged behind her, stumbling. Jackie was still trying to process what was happening when the bartender called her over to the end of the bar.

"Are you ready?" he asked, placing a key in her hand.

"I--think so."

"Good." He explained the 'rules' to her also.

Jackie and her 'date' were having a bad time just maneuvering off the barstools. He caught her by the arm and they both fell to the floor, laughing hysterically. Between the laughter and their bumbling attempts to get up, it was like a slapstick comedy. The bartender came around the end of the bar and tried to help, but he wound up in the heap himself. Mary and George had reached the top of the stairs when they heard the commotion and looked down to see the complete show. They went back down the stairs to help everyone else get up. The floor was wet from spilled drinks and they fell down as well. The whole room was laughing; fortunately, no one was hurt. All these crazy antics eased any remaining tension, especially for the two novices to the party scene. They finally managed to pick themselves up and make it up the stairs, still laughing and holding on to each other. When Mary opened the door, her date was so unsteady that he almost fell through the doorway. After several fumbling attempts, they were undressed and in the bed, but there were problems in that location, too. George had fallen prey to that sexual dysfunction that men refuse to discuss. He was so drunk that he couldn't do anything but fall asleep. Mary arose, covered him up, and dressed herself, placing a light kiss on his cheek. She was very glad nothing had happened; she was pleased she didn't have to face that issue tonight. In a strange way, she was a bit disappointed; he was a nice man and she felt she had cheated him. She didn't stop to think that it was at least an even bet that he would have some great story to tell his friends the next day. Though his story would not be supported by the facts; in his own mind, his performance had been magnificent. Mary went down to the bartender to settle up. The amount of money had not been discussed, so she had no idea how much to expect; but she felt sure that some amount would be deducted from her pay because of what had happened or, rather, what *hadn't* happened. The bartender would probably question her about how things went and she didn't want to get caught in a lie.

"I see you are through; did everything go okay?"

"I think so; he is asleep."

"Did he have a good time?"

"Well, yes, I would guess so; he didn't complain," she said to diffuse further questions. She had an inner sense about protecting men's rather fragile egos that caused her to pretend everything went well. They proceeded to the issue of payment for services rendered. The bartender counted out $200; but explained that he couldn't present her with a bonus amount, because her date was "asleep" and unable to verify his level of satisfaction. As she eyed the cash she had earned in just one night, she realized that it equaled her *weekly* earnings as a cocktail waitress. Since she had previously reconciled the moral issues in her mind, she thought that she would indicate her interest in future invitations to the 'parties'. She was so very tired of failing to make ends meet and, after all, wasn't she being paid for giving men what they all had taken from her at no cost to themselves?

Here again was that hard core of bitterness against the way she had repeatedly been misled by men. Prostitution was not legal in Washoe County, but there was a high degree of toleration because the high rollers and entertainers needed "recreation". The casinos were all involved in this activity in a very hush-hush way, even though these 'parties' were sponsored by them, from behind-the-scenes.

"Thank you," Mary said, politely. "Do you know when the next 'party' is and if I will be invited?"

"If you are, there will be a note in your locker same as before. We will see about your level of participation as we go along."

"Okay, I will look forward to seeing a note and the possibility of 'moving-up,' if that's the correct term?" she said determinedly, as she walked through the now-empty room.

When Mary got home, she heard the clock strike 4:00 am. Everyone else was asleep. Lonely and alone, she sat in the living room and contemplated her future.

Predictably, Mary was in demand and progressed to 'hotel girl'. She became very popular with the

'Clients', not only for her performance, but also for her charm and good sense. She cultivated a reputation as a good listener with an unusual sense of humor. She was adjusting to a new life-style that would be both a bane and a blessing in the years to come. She went on for months in this manner and she made a good living at it. Rita looked after Bill and me and, strange as it may seem, Mom began a relationship with Lonnie. He didn't seem to mind about how she earned a living; she didn't downplay the issue, but did nothing to call attention to it.

Physically, Lonnie was a small and wiry man. Emotionally, he was easy-going and low-key. If someone asked me to identify his personality, I would have said that he was not moral or amoral, but somewhere in between... and was easily influenced by stronger personality types. He was doing well at the dry cleaners, but he had a desire to do better and, someday, to be his own boss. That was the American dream, then as it is now. It is strange how fate intervenes; sometimes our lives are going well, but we want something more and pay the price. The fact was that Lonnie would have been ill suited to own a business and he was certainly incapable of leading others.

It was late November of 1949 when Mary made a mistake that would haunt her for the rest of her life. She still continued her cocktail waitress job and, while on the way home from that, she was solicited by a gentleman on the sidewalk. He seemed like an average guy and she thought that the extra money wouldn't hurt. In the future, when she recalled that fateful evening, she replayed her regrets, chastising herself for her stupidity. The man began by asking how she was and commenting on the weather as he walked beside her. He paused, rather expectantly, and she asked him if he was looking for a 'date'.

"What do you mean...a 'date'?" he said, turning to face her. She stopped walking and looked at him.

"You know...a 'date'," she repeated, as he moved closer to her. She should have been alerted by the direction the conversation was taking that something was not right. She was not very street-wise yet and conducted the conversation with him as though she was at the 'party'. "A 'date'! Where you and I enter into a contract for sex."

"I don't quite understand what you mean," he said, stepping even closer than before.

"You pay me for sex," she said, managing to portray both naivety and seductiveness.

"Are you telling me that you're a prostitute?"

"Not exactly! I provide favor for compensation."

"You just said the magic words! I'm placing you under arrest for prostitution, a violation of Reno City Ordinances." He pushed her arm behind her. He grabbed her other arm and placed handcuffs on her wrists. So it came to be that she was arrested and began a three-year downhill slide. The humiliation of the arrest would color her activities and would affect her decision-making and her self-esteem for some time to come.

She called Lonnie to come to the Police Station and post bail. He dressed and pulled some spare money from the stash in his sock drawer. He walked to the Police Station on Sierra and Court Streets.

The Station was a beehive of activity; he waited impatiently in the line to see the Desk Sergeant. Being in the Station brought back bad memories of the times when he was the one waiting for someone to post his bail. He felt very uncomfortable just being there.

"You! Yeah, you! What can I do for you?" the Desk Sergeant growled at Lonnie, who was concentrating on a group of women who had just been released to a man who was attired in very loud colors. The man was shouting and pointing his finger, saying that this was the last time he would bail them out.

"Yes, I'm Lonnie Walters, here for Mary...McLean." he said rather slowly and quietly as to not attract attention.

"Are you sure?" the sergeant growled back loudly. "We have a lot of 'Marys' in here."

Yes, I'm sure," he said, more confidently now and with a hint of defiance in his voice.

The Sergeant picked up the phone and said, "Bring Mary McLean down; someone is here with the bail." He directed Lonnie to a row of benches.

"Wait over there until I decide what the bail is. When she gets here, you can pay it."

Lonnie walked to the row of benches and sat down next to a woman who had on more makeup than any ten women should. He hoped Mary hadn't painted herself in this way to attract clients. Mary came down the stairs and was escorted through the locked door to the Desk Sergeant.

"Walters, come up here." the Desk Sergeant said, loudly. It seemed that every one in the building could hear. This commotion startled Lonnie, who jumped to his feet and moved quickly toward the desk. He stood next to Mary in front of the Sergeant and waited for him to recognize them.

"Bail is $250; do you have it?" he stated, without raising his head to look at Lonnie and Mary.

Lonnie had $750 that he had been saving to leave town. He hesitated for a moment; he was momentarily concerned about whether Mary would pay him back. Would she go to court or run? Finally, he said, "Here's the money," looking at Mary all the while and wondering if he was being foolish. She gave him a tremulous smile and that was all it took to reassure him...Boy, did she have a great smile! So, after being assigned a court appearance date, they left.

Her appearance date was set for two weeks and, after her appearance, she was placed on probation for a year. During that two-week wait, Mary and Lonnie discussed moving to Gabbs, a town in Central Nevada, where they could begin a new life.

The money to make that move was a primary consideration even though this new beginning was what they both needed. Lonnie had no experience in millwork or mining, but the company was hiring inexperienced workers. Their money situation was not ideal and, with Mary's past failed marriages, she was not anxious to repeat her mistakes. Lonnie insisted on marriage because he felt that marriage would be a stabilizing influence against a repeat performance of his criminal past. He had spent much of his life in jail and had no desire to go back. A move to Gabbs, out in the middle of nowhere, would serve as a lack of temptation to renew his life of crime.

"We don't have enough money to make a move right now. The car needs repair to the tune of $1500 and all I have saved is $750...and that's only if I get your bail money back."

"We need to make some money quickly, so we can take advantage of this opportunity." Mary paced around the room, chain-smoking, as she thought out-loud, "I have $700 put aside, but I was going to use it to go back home if things got too rough here. The soldiers who told me about how fantastic America was steered me wrong; it is the same as home or any other place, both good and bad." She walked to the dresser to get another cigarette. "I think I could get work in Fallon; I have been told there is a 'house' there. I'm already branded, especially after this arrest; so it wouldn't be much of a step-down."

"What would you do with the kids?"

"Rita will look after them for a while until I get on my feet; it wouldn't cost that much, with her own here and all."

"You're right; maybe I could help out with the kids for a month or two."

"No, you should get one of your friends to take you to Gabbs and get that job before they give them all away. We can't take that chance."

"That's a good idea! We could put the car in the shop and have them start the work on it until a $1000 is gone. That would leave us $450 to make the move and set up in Gabbs. By then, we'll have the money to pay for the rest of the repairs. The owner at the shop on Fourth and Sierra told me it would cost $1,500. Maybe we'll get lucky and his estimate was high."

So the plans were made...Bill and I became semi-permanent residents of Rita's household; Mom went to Fallon, working for a house owned by Sandy, aptly named 'Sandy's'; and Lonnie went with his friend to Gabbs, where both found jobs at Basic Mining Corporation. This rather bizarre arrangement lasted for six months. We only saw Mom in the middle of the week every other week on her days off and Lonnie would come to Reno once a month. The car was repaired for less than the estimate. Things were progressing well and we could hardly wait until we moved to this wonderful place called Gabbs.

We moved in June of 1950 to start another 'new life'. The INS still had not made an appearance and Mom thought all that rigmarole was behind her. We were disappointed in Gabbs at first; but, just like many issues in our lives, time took care of everything. We had not been in Gabbs for very long when the phone incident with Rita occurred. My worst memory of her occurred the evening she died. Mom called Rita to let her know we were fine, then she handed me the phone so I could speak. "Aunt Rita, it's me, Alan."

"Yes, I know, you little scamp." She called all of us 'little scamps'.

"How are you, I'm fine and how is everyone?" I yelled into the phone, not giving her a chance to answer. Of course, at the age of seven, telephone manners are not high on the list of priorities; plus, I loved her with great enthusiasm.

"I'm jest fine," she said, trying to talk over my rambling. Then the most awful thing happened...she began to cough and choke.

"What is it, Aunt Rita, what is it?" I screamed into the phone. Mom grabbed the phone from me and put it to her ear to see what was happening.

A different voice was heard on the other end. "Mary, is that you?"

"Yes, it is. Who is this?"

"It's me, Rose."

"What's wrong, where is Rita?" Mom asked.

"Mary, we're going to call an ambulance; I think Rita is having a heart attack! Let me call you back." Rose hung up the phone before

Mom could respond. We did not discover that Rita had died until the next day. We couldn't attend the funeral but we sent flowers and Mom composed a long eulogy to be read at the funeral. I loved Aunt Rita as if she was a very close and dear relative. I would never forget the lessons of common decency she had taught me. I would carry with me forever the one where I was witness to her final words. I will never forget her! I will always remember the many principles she shared with me...to accept people at face value, having prejudice against none.

Lonnie worked at the mill and our 'home' was an Army surplus tent by one of the pump houses below Gabbs. The tent was erected on a cement slab that, within a few weeks time, became the foundation of a house we built out of the scrap lumber from the mill. I still fondly recall all the work we put into that house. It consisted of three rooms, with a screen porch view of the valley, as well as the constant dirt heading toward us from across that same valley. The wind would stir up what looked like a wall of dirt, sagebrush, and any other portable junk it could pick up along the way, and hurl it directly at our wonderful porch.

An old Indian lived down the road in a one-room shack, with only his dog for companionship. He worked at the Mill with Lonnie and they became friends of a sort. The Indian worked hard all week; but, on his days off, he would hole-up in his shack, so drunk that he couldn't even crawl or stagger out to the outhouse. I remember one time when he was drunk and driving. He fell out of his 'Model A' while it was still moving. The 'Model A' continued down the road with him hanging there, half in and half out of the car. Eventually, the car ran over him. His companion in the passenger seat didn't even realize that he was missing until the car came to halt, running off the road and high centering itself on a mound at the side of the road.

The Indian was hospitalized for treatment of his injuries for a couple of weeks, but, before leaving for the hospital, he gave over the care of his dog to Bill and me. He told us many times what tribe he belonged to, but each time it was a different tribe. He was a funny guy; he showed us a dance that he called the "Eagle Dance". He flung out his arms and circled around as if he were flying, moving his feet to a drumbeat heard only in his head, and making bird-like calls in imitation of an eagle. When he returned from the hospital, he never was the same. He still went to work and he still got drunk, but he would never leave his shack. After several months had passed, he came to our house and said he was going back to Oklahoma. He said that if we wanted anything from his house, we had better get it now. Lonnie went to the house with him, while we stayed on the screen porch to watch them lug a few things out. They went back inside and had only been in the house for several minutes when we saw them come running out. Suddenly, the house burst into flame; he had set it on fire after he had the few things he wanted...I guess that was his way. He got in his car and drove off. We never saw him again. By the time the fire truck arrived, nothing remained of the shack. The firemen sprayed the remains with water to stop the fire from spreading across the desert, and that was the end of it.

Mom stopped working at Sandy's, but we still went into Fallon to see Sandy once in a while. She wanted Mom to come back, but Mom had decided to become a housewife. Sandy was very fond of Mom. One Christmas, she bought bicycles for Bill and me; mine was a red Schwinn and Bill's was a tricycle.

We went to J.C. Penney Company on Maine Street in Fallon to pick them up. I thought that the $100 she paid for them was the most money in the world. I rode the wheels off that bike. We were happy in Gabbs; I went to school and Bill waited until I got home and we played together until supper. Everything was great, the INS was nowhere to be seen, and we were building a future. Mom no longer thought of Australia. She seemed to be content with Lonnie. So content that she relented on the marriage issue and they were married in Fallon later that year. Lonnie appeared to have cast aside his former life and Mom settled into the daily routine of a homemaker. Bill and I found ourselves in the same kind of trouble that children usually get into and we were punished accordingly. The punishment was usually forced labor, such as walking the gravel drive to pick up nails, washing the vehicle...the usual punishment for kids everywhere. Bill's job was to clean the wheels and hubcaps until we could see our reflection in them. It was my job to clean the rest of the car because I was older and taller. We shared chores, like cleaning our room; and had separate chores too...he had to empty the garbage and I had to dry the dishes. It seems as though I was always to be tasked some phase of that duty; even now, I put them away out of the dishwasher. I remember once I was drying a large bowl; part of a set that were different sizes so they fit into each other and each size was a color...red, green, blue, and off-white. They were the first Pyrex bowls. I was holding the largest one and it slipped out of my hands and crashed to the floor, breaking into a million pieces. Before the last piece stopped spinning, Mom hit me on my behind, not waiting for my explanation of what had happened. When I complained, she said, "Well, that's for something that you did and I didn't know about". There was a smile on her face as she said it. I fondly remember that day and still smile myself when I think of her words.

Mom was a good housewife and she was sober more often than she had ever been in her adult life. We spent time together as a family, sitting on the porch after supper, spinning stories about our daily adventures. We had family outings to the hills and gathered pine nuts and went fishing in the streams at East Gate. Life was good...too good to last.

Chapter 9

"Is Lonnie around?" the huge man, with a red face and hair to match, asked as he peered out from the window of his car.

"He's at work and will be home around five," I answered hesitantly, as I looked at him and tried to see who was with him in the car.

"All right if we wait for him in the drive?" he asked, not really expecting an answer.

"Sure, I'll tell Mom you're out here," I said as I headed for the front door. It was about 4:30 and I had just come home from school. I knew it wouldn't be long before Lonnie got home, so I didn't think it would be bad if they waited. They were not dressed like the INS; you know, in suits. They were dressed like every-day, run-of–the mill people.

"Mom, someone is waiting for Lonnie to get home", I announced as I entered the house.

"Who is it?" she asked, a look of panic crossing her face.

"I don't know, just some red-headed guy and a dark-haired woman," I said, heading to the refrigerator for a soda. Mom quizzed me about these people and went to the window to see if she could recognize them; just then Lonnie came in with the two people.

"Mary, I want you to meet my friend, Red Grady, and his friend, Jackie."

"Hi, we were wondering who you were. Alan told me you were here, waiting for Lonnie," she said, apprehensively. She seemed to have an unsettled feeling as she reached to shake hands with them. Later that night, we found out who they were and what they wanted.

Red, just released from prison, was on his way to Wyoming and in need of cash to make the trip. He wanted Lonnie to help him get a stake...his only skill was robbery. Mom and Lonnie didn't want to get involved in anything illegal. They had painstakingly carved out a new life for themselves by hard work and honest dealings. Their daily discussions always centered on gratitude for all that they had achieved. Unfortunately for us, Red felt that Lonnie owed him something and constantly hammered that point home.

"All we need is a place to hide before and afterward; a place to lie low until the heat is off. Then we can go our separate ways and I will consider your debt to be paid," Red said to Lonnie. Mom looked at Lonnie, and, in a half-hearted way, nodded. I think she had real qualms about becoming involved, but Mom had a strange sense of honor about repaying a debt.

"We can knock over the Toiyabe Club here in town and when the heat is off we'll leave. You don't have to be involved, Mary, other than giving us a place to lie low. You know, Lonnie, it'll be just like old times...we can cut the power early in the morning, go in and get the money, and be out before anyone knows about it."

"I'll think about it! But in the meantime, where will you stay? It's too crowded here and money is tight. Feeding two more people would put a strain on us unless we can fill the meat locker." Lonnie directed his comments to Red. "Any suggestions?"

"We could get some beef; I saw some still on the hoof about 40 miles from here near the Gabbs turnoff." He grinned, glancing and winking at Jackie.

"Do you mean to add rustling to our many crimes?" Lonnie asked, looking to Mom for approval which was not forthcoming, but he agreed anyway. "We need to get a cow that weighs less than five hundred pounds or we won't be able to handle it." Lonnie said, as he went to get the deer rifle from under the bed. It was the most popular rifle for deer hunting...a Winchester, Model 94, lever action, 30-30. He obtained it after we moved to Gabbs to shoot the coyotes that would approach the tent we first lived in.

"Wait a second, guys! We don't have a freezer," Mom blurted out, even though she was warming to the concept of an abundance of meat, as opposed to purchasing meat from payday to payday.

"We can fix the broken freezer that the old Indian left us when he went to Oklahoma. It just needs a little work and one of the guys at work, Al Kelso, said he would fix it as a favor." Lonnie turned to Red, reminiscing about shooting rabbits from the back of his dad's pickup in Idaho. He said this type of hunting wouldn't be much different, except that cows were bigger and easier to hit. "Red, do you know how to butcher one if we get it?"

"Sure, that's what I did in the slam. I worked in the kitchen and butchered everything from chickens to cows to hogs. It's easy."

"Then it's settled! I have the weekend off and a pickup to haul it in, so we'll do it," Lonnie said, beginning to get excited.

This was the onset of a year and a half of hiding, looking over our shoulders, and being on the lam. We arose very early Saturday morning and drove the forty miles to Middle Gate. Before descending the long hill to US 50, we turned off the road and drove to one of the many dry streambeds for which Nevada is known. We were a number of miles from the ranch house on the opposite side of the highway, separated by a deep ditch running parallel to the highway, as well. Lonnie thought the rancher wouldn't hear the shots; but, even if he did, he couldn't reach us before we loaded up the beef.

"The sun won't be up for another hour. We can drive right up to these cows and, as dumb as they seem, we'll shoot one and load it in the truck bed. We'll be on our way, with none the wiser," Lonnie mumbled again, thinking out-loud. "Red, you drive slowly over to that bunch there." He pointed to some dark objects on the horizon. "I'll get in the back. Alan, you ride next to the door so you can hand me more ammunition if I miss."

We took our positions and the truck began to move toward the dark clumps in the distance. We moved closer; soon these large animals, always moving, eating, and moving again, surrounded us. One turned and stuck its head through the open window, dripping froth-like slobber onto the armrest. Red kept the truck slowly moving and everyone was quiet. Suddenly the rifle burst forth with a deafening explosion and I felt the pressure from the muzzle, the animal to the right of us fell to the ground. The truck stopped as Lonnie bent down and said, "Turn around; I'll jump out and cut its throat. You back up so we can load the cow and get the hell out of here." My ears were still ringing from the shot and could only guess what had been said based on Red's actions. He turned the truck around, backing up to Lonnie.

"This is just the right size. Get the come-along and hook it to the eye bolt in the front corner of the bed."

Red jumped out as if they had been doing this for years. They worked well together and, within fifteen minutes, we were on our way back up the dry creek bed to the pavement and home...not a moment too soon. In the distance we could see the headlights of the rancher's vehicle and a rifle-flash. Dust kicked up to the right of the pickup and again to the left. Then the lights disappeared and we rounded a bend. Almost instinctively, Red turned off the lights on the pickup, still moving forward, but at a faster pace. Red remembered the path we used to get there and, even though the sun wasn't up, seemed to see every rock, bush, and dip in our way. We were soon on the pavement and zipping down the road, still without lights. After we rounded a small hill, Red turned on the lights and we sped away as fast as the pickup could go with the heavy load in the truck-bed. This was the first of many heart-stopping experiences I would have in the next year and a half. I was scared...was this action wrong? Wouldn't we be punished?

We got back to the house just as the sun was coming up. Mom and Jackie were waiting with the tools to butcher the beef and, for the first time in a long while, I thought I saw excitement in Mom's eyes. This added to my confusion about the moral issue of what we had done. Red and Lonnie butchered the cow, while Mom and Jackie wrapped the pieces in butcher paper and put it in the newly renovated freezer. Bill and I watched, unable to tell one piece of meat from another. I really didn't care, except for the steaks, for which I had a particular fondness. One other memorable experience from this debacle was eating brains and eggs.

"Go ahead... you'll like them," Red said, as he handed me a plate with scrambled eggs and brains.

"I don't think so," I said, bravely trying them. They tasted awful and I refused to eat any more.

The weekly newspaper carried a short article about the "great beef raid", but it just related that a local rancher ran off some trespassers. It was my guess that Lonnie was right about not leaving much of a trail to be followed.

Now, the Toiyabe Club robbery planning began in earnest. Lonnie and Red would sit around the table late at night and kick around ideas about how to do this job without attracting attention.

The Club was owned by the Smith Brothers of Hawthorne and one brother lived within twenty yards of the Club. His house had the only swimming pool in town and he was kind enough to allow all the town kids to swim there. His brother lived in Hawthorne and operated their casino there, the El Capitan.

Mom and Lonnie started going to the Club on nights prior to his day off. They would stay until closing time, just to observe the schedule. Afterward, they would come home and inform Red about the closing hours. They would usually be so drunk that he would have to wait until morning for the real story. Mom began drinking heavily again and, true to form, she and Lonnie argued about everything. Lonnie's friend and co-worker, Al Kelso, became more involved in their drinking sessions. He seemed to be at these sessions at the Club more and more frequently. It was obvious to me that he was infatuated with Mom; Lonnie didn't seem to notice. He was more interested in the closing schedule and drinking. Mom noticed and seemed flattered by his attention; she hadn't lost her charm. They played the 'Juke Box' and tried to sing along with Hank, Patsy, and all the other popular country western singers of that era. Sometimes, Al and Mom would stagger around the floor in a pretense of dancing, but they were so drunk that it was only a parody of the real thing. I think Al was beyond infatuation, but he didn't reveal his true feelings. His feelings were to be useful to Mom later on.

Finally, in late December, Red and Lonnie decided it was time to hit the club. Lonnie and Mom were there, as usual, socializing; but Lonnie did not drink as much. He nursed one drink all evening and stayed sober. Red and Jackie came to the Club just before closing to take Mom home. Lonnie and Red made a great public fuss about going into Hawthorne to pick up a package early that morning and they left the Club in separate vehicles. Jackie drove Mom home, while Lonnie and Red drove down the highway to the residential part of Gabbs, which was three miles away. They turned onto the street leading to the school and then turned right and cut off the lights. They drove up the back rode to just below the Club and parked Red's car, which they were using because no one was familiar with it, and walked to the power box behind the Club. Red used bolt cutters on the main feed wire, severing power to the alarm. Earlier, Jackie had dismantled the battery connection to the alarm located near the women's toilet. With everything proceeding as planned, they entered the unlit club and made their way to the office safe. Lonnie pulled a stethoscope from his jacket and placed it on the door of the safe above the tumbler and began to turn the dial. Red held the flashlight on the dial with his hand cupped around the head of the flashlight to keep it from shining out through any opening to the street. Lonnie dialed one way and the other...soon he said, "It's open!" Then, verifying his words, the door came open to reveal the contents.

"They had a good take tonight; look at that stack of bills," Red said, reaching in to get the money.

Lonnie's hand closed over his, effectively stopping his movement. "This makes us even, right?"

"Sure it does, right after you help us get to Cody."

"What? You never said anything about Cody."

"We'll discuss it after we get back to the house."

"Okay, but we need to get square. I don't want to continue doing this; I have a good life now. I don't want to go back to the old ways."

They gathered the money and closed the safe, grabbed the bolt cutters, and walked back to the car.

The next morning, Red told Lonnie what his plans were for the help he needed to get to Cody, Wyoming. "What you need to do to make this whole job work out is go on a little vacation with us, so no one will suspect us. Out of sight, out of mind, so to speak! Jackie and I have been thinking about this part of the plan for several weeks and, if you don't help us, then we could be suspects. Think about it, Lonnie! You know yourself that if you don't finish a job off right, it will fail."

He sounded very convincing; Lonnie thought for a moment and glanced toward Mom. "You're right! We need to follow through."

"That's better. Remember, we must appear to be completely innocent. When the girls make their usual trip to the store today, they should act very surprised to hear about the robbery." Having said that, Red headed for the coffeepot.

"We'll go on Monday," Lonnie said. "I have some time built up that I need to use or lose. My request for vacation time will not be a surprise to the foreman at the mill; he has been telling me to take time off, anyway."

"That's good! We'll see this through to the finish and you'll be off the hook after we get to Cody."

Lonnie jumped up from his chair. "Good, that's what I wanted to hear! Now, *everyone* knows that Cody is the last straw; we're all here to witness what you said."

"Yes, you're right, Lonnie, we'll be even."

With that assurance, everyone resumed eating breakfast.

We left for Cody on the following Monday. No one in Gabbs suspected that Red and Lonnie had robbed the Club. Everyone claimed it must have been someone passing through and the investigation concentrated on that concept.

The trip was long and tiresome. I thought we had packed enough for a long stay, instead of just two weeks. Cody, Wyoming is named for Buffalo Bill

Cody. His museum is located there...filled with all his Wild West Show memorabilia.

We rented a house, even though we were only staying for a couple of days...just until they divided up the money. Then we would say goodbye forever to Red and Jackie. It couldn't have been soon enough for me; once again, I was in a state of nervous confusion. Lonnie's plan to leave the next day and go back to the life in Gabbs soon went the way of the 'wild goose', because, that afternoon, they began to play cards and drink. They were playing penny-ante, where you play for pennies; suddenly... out of the blue...Red jumped up and fired his pistol through a light fixture in the ceiling. Bill and I, who were playing outside, heard the noise. Then they all ran out on the front lawn where we were. Bill and I stood stock-still, unable to comprehend what was happening. Red and Jackie were almost squared off with Lonnie and Mom, facing each other.

"They know too much," Red said in a loud and garbled voice.

"What do you mean 'they know too much'?" Lonnie interjected quickly.

"They know too much and we need to get rid of them, all of them."

"Do you mean the kids, Jackie, and Mary?"

"Yeah...well, not Jackie! She has been with me from the start...she's my soul-mate, but the rest have to go."

"Wait, wait! You can't mean that. What could the boys know? They're just kids and Mary is my soul mate too. What are you raving on about?"

"Mary just has to go. I'll have to shoot her. She knows too much about our operation."

"What the hell you talking about? We don't have an operation; besides, you've probably caused the neighbors to call the law by firing that gun. Now put it away before the cops get here and we have a real problem!"

"No, we need to get rid of them! Can't you see that they could slow us down and we could end up in stir again?" Red said, drunkenly, as he waved the muzzle of the pistol at Mom, Bill, and me. Mom had moved over near us during the preceding argument between Lonnie and Red. He pointed the gun at us again, but I felt calm and relaxed. I somehow knew we would not be dying that day.

Lonnie went to Red and pushed his gun hand downward. "You need to think about this, Red! You couldn't get away...the cops would seal up all the routes. As soon as you fire the gun again, some concerned citizen will call it in. Think about this! You don't have a plan."

"I don't need a plan; just shoot them, jump in the car, and get out of here before anyone realizes what happened."

"Really! Well, look at the windows on that house across the street; those people are already thinking of calling the cops." Sure enough, someone was standing at the window, watching the entire scene. He was pointing to someone else in the house. "Think of what you'll tell the cops when they show up."

Red finally agreed to go back in the house, but he tucked the gun in the back waistband of his pants. Mom sidled closer to me and said, "If I'm dead in the morning, you will know who did it." Then she calmly re-entered the house with Lonnie right behind her.

The cops didn't show up and, the next morning, when we awakened from a nearly sleepless night, Red and Jackie were gone. We never saw them again; but they took most of the money and some of Mom's clothes. So much for "honor among thieves"!

About a week later, we did read about them in the newspaper. Red Grady and Jackie Marshall were killed in a running gunfight with the Wyoming Highway Patrol after killing one of their officers. The article said they were carrying marked bills from a robbery in Nevada.

The authorities believed that their accomplices was still 'at-large', but had no identification of the suspects. Lonnie was certain he would be implicated, so our return to

Gabbs was out of the question. He made a call to one of his co-workers in Gabbs, who had shown interest in purchasing the house we had built. They struck a deal and Lonnie told him where to send the money. So we began our year and a half campout across the western states..

We spent that time moving from town to town. After the money from the sale of the house ran out, Lonnie would rob businesses to keep us in food. Mom and Lonnie argued constantly. She told him that she could go back to work at Sandy's in Fallon until it all blew over, but he refused to let her do that. He had allowed her to work at Sandy's when they first were together and he had finally decided that he didn't like the way that made him feel. He was unable to justify to himself how he could allow his then-girlfriend and his now-wife, to have sex with other men with his full knowledge. He swore to himself then that if it were within his power, he would not allow her to do that again.

We spent some time in La Grande, Oregon, living in an apartment down the alley from a furniture store, off the main street. Lonnie went to work at a laundry and Mom tried waiting tables at a restaurant. This period of time was the longest we stayed in one place. Mom wasn't very good at her new job and was sick of being on the run. One day, while Lonnie was at work, she loaded up the car, wrote him a note, and we left for Nevada.

She drove down Highway 93 to Winnemucca, turning left toward Salt Lake on Highway 40. We arrived at a town called Wells, where she saw a sign advertising 'Donna's', across the railroad tracks to the north of town. A lady had told her about this 'house' that she owned and had tried to recruit her to work there. Dorothy Jett had assumed operation of the house from Ida

Hooliway who had, in turn, taken over from Hazel Hogan...the business itself was one of the oldest houses in continuous operation in the West. We turned down the road leading to the big red house and drove right up to the front door. After telling us to stay in the car because she would be right back, Mom got out. She had only been gone for a few minutes when she returned with Dorothy trailing behind her. "Alan, this is Dorothy and she has agreed to have me work here. You kids can stay in the back of the house until I get a place. We'll still be together; don't worry!"

That was the beginning, and at the age of ten mind you, of living life in a brothel. We stayed there for about a month. In the meantime, Lonnie was looking for Mom...he loved her and wanted to be with her. We didn't know that the INS was also looking for her... AND, for me, the "excess baggage" boy. If we were picked up by the INS, they would have to determine if I could be sent out of the country alone, or would we both be deported.

Mom worked long hours, becoming very popular with the railroad men, as well as the miners at Tungsten. One of the miners was Joseph Garetto, an old Italian who had migrated to the States after the War. He bragged constantly about his 60-acre ranch in Montana that he was working at Tungsten to pay for. He always asked for Mom when he came in and declared his love for her over and over; his attraction to her was well known.

It didn't take Lonnie very long to find Mom; he just appeared one night and they went to her room to talk. He told her he was going to move to Sacramento, where he had a good job lined up and a house ready to rent. He promised her that life would be better than in Gabbs. They talked for a long time until Dorothy became concerned about Mom's inattention to the paying customers. She knocked on the door. "Mary, you need to get out here. Time's up and we have more customers asking for you."

"Just a minute! I'll be out in a minute."

"I need you, now! He's not a paying customer and you need to make some money for the house; after all, we have a reputation for service to uphold."

"All right! I just need a minute."

"Okay, but make it snappy."

"I must go back to work, Lonnie! I have tomorrow off, so we'll talk more then, okay?"

"Sure, I'll come back tomorrow; but I want you to go to Sacramento with me. I hate you working here and I want to take you away from this."

"We'll talk tomorrow." She kissed him and he left out the back door and she went to the front where she found Joe waiting for her.

"Hello, missy, how you?" he said, as she walked across the floor toward him.

Her path was barred by another guy, who said, "Hi, are you available for the room?"

"Sure, do you think you can handle me?"

"I'm sure I can, much better than that old geezer there."

"Who you call old geezer, you wisa guy?"

"I'll show you, you old bastard. You come here from another country, can't even speak the language, and expect us to take care of you." He approached Joe with his fist doubled, raised to strike. Mom stepped between them just as his fist shot out to strike Joe. Instead the blow glanced off the side of her face and knocked her to her knees. She stayed on the floor with only her hands holding her up. Dorothy ran across the room and jumped on the guy's back while Joe, with all the strength he could muster, swung the hardest blow that he had for many years. He caught the other man straight in the face, breaking his nose and cheekbone, as well as two of his own knuckles. As Mom stood upright the whole room seemed to freeze in place for a moment as everyone watched the man crumple to the floor with Dorothy still on his back. The huge man landed right in front of Mom. His face crashed into the floor with a tremendous thud, Dorothy's extra weight added to his. Dorothy looked up at Mom just in time to catch the horrible look that altered her entire face. I've only observed this look on her face once or twice in my lifetime; but I'll never forget where I saw it first.

Her eyelids closed to only half open, there seemed to be fire in her eyes as the still look of death covered her whole face. She had that stare that could pierce steel. I had never seen her so focused, and I knew she was about to do something to this now-helpless man on the floor.

"You bloody bastard, you bloody bastard!" She screamed over and over, all the while kicking him in his side and head, until finally the other men dragged her away from him. I had no way of knowing it then; but we shared this trait...my mother and I. In certain circumstances, our faces conveyed a signal from some deep, dark place in our psyche; a signal that meant we were losing control of our actions...focused only on the total annihilation of whoever had caused that loss of self-control.

"Mary, Mary, Mary! Look at me!" Dorothy shouted right into her face. Mom seemed to be somewhere else; her face was frozen into a mask and she had a stare that seemed to be looking straight into hell. "Mary!" she repeated, as she shook her by the shoulders. "Mary, answer me, say something, are you all right?"

Finally, seeming to shake off that horrible other being, Mom said, "Yes, I'm fine! What happened?"

Dorothy breathed a great sigh of relief. "It's nothing! You just come with me and I'll clean up your face."

"Who's that on the floor, did he fall down?" Mary had no memory of her actions or anything that preceded them.

Dorothy thought, "My God! She has no idea what happened. I wonder if she has a concussion."

There is no way to explain this phenomenon Mom and I share. As I grew older and was confronted with similar situations, I would have those same moments...moments where I could not recall what had happened in the heat of a situation. I don't know if there is a scientific name for this malady, but I suffer from it to this day. Perhaps it is some familial inheritance from the volatile Scots who were our ancestors.

Someone had called the police, who arrived just as Mom and Dorothy disappeared into the back room...the same room from which I had observed the entire episode. I asked her if she was okay and she assured me that she was. She asked me if Bill and I were all right. She was always worried about Bill and me, even before her own welfare. I assured her that Bill was asleep in the back.

"And what are you doing up, young man? It's way past your bedtime."

"I couldn't sleep; then I heard you and Lonnie talking."

"That is none of your concern. I'll let you know what's happening when it does and not before. You don't need to worry about anything." She looked into the mirror to see if her face was damaged. She had a red mark extending from her nose to her ear and the beginning of a bruise under her eye. There were no cuts or tears to the skin, only the red mark and the bruise.

"You're lucky, Mary, that could have ended your career or, at the very least, marred your beauty," Dorothy remarked as she placed a cold, wet washcloth against Mom's cheek.

"I don't look at this as a career! I've told you many times that I just do this to get by for now." Mom was adamant, moving her face away from the cloth as though in pain.

"Now, don't get your skirt up with me! I know you have plans to marry Mister Right with the house and the white picket fence, but this isn't the place to meet him, in case you haven't noticed."

"I know! I'm sorry, Dorothy; but you well know that we all need to hold on to some dream." Mom went into Dorothy's arms for the comfort that only another woman might offer. They remained locked in that timeless female bond until Mom pushed back and said, "You know that Lonnie wants me to go to Sacramento with him. He has a good job and has rented a house."

"Yes, I know! Maybe you should go and forget this life."

"I don't know. We very nearly achieved a good life once; then, out of the blue, one of Lonnie's old 'friends' appeared and it all went to hell!"

"Maybe he's out of 'friends'; maybe this time will be different. You should really consider it!" They were sitting there together in total camaraderie, with the cool cloth on Mom's face, when the door burst open and revealed Joe standing in front of them with his hand bandaged.

"Joe, are you all right? Is your hand okay? Let me see it!" Mom ran to him.

"Yeah, I'm a fine; but da udda guy, he not a so good! They wanna talka you, you knowa policia." He reached out to her with his good hand.

"What do they want and why are they sending you to get her?" Dorothy asked angrily.

"I don a know! They justa aska me if I knowa whata happen and if I knowa where a you at," Joe replied apprehensively.

"You go tell them that we will be there in a minute," Dorothy said sternly. "Well, don't just stand there, get going." Joe was moving too slowly to suit her. She turned to Mom and cautioned, "All I expect is the truth and that's it. Don't add anything, no thoughts or assumptions; just stick to the incident, that's all."

"I understand," Mom said as she went to meet the police.

Dorothy knew the INS could easily locate Mom if she had to go to court to testify. She was hoping for an end to the whole incident right here tonight.

"So, what happened?" the officer asked as Mom walked toward him.

"Nothing much! This man had a little too much to drink and slipped and fell." She looked straight into his eyes, waiting for some sign that he believed her story. "I tried to stop his fall and he was just too heavy for me to hold and we both fell, but no one is hurt. We can continue on with our socializing, don't you think?" She gazed at the man she had beaten up...who decided, most prudently, to go along with the lie. He was sure his nose and cheekbone was broken-the pain was intolerable-but he didn't want to end up in jail. He would worry about medical attention when he was finally away from the place.

Mom offered him a look that indicated she would change her story in a heartbeat and he would be the worse for it. The police were most certainly affording protection to the legal brothels; and, as a consequence, accepted what the owners and girls said as gospel unless their stories were too unbelievable. The story about the fall was believable and would cause no future problem, if it could be stopped now. The incident was accepted as harmless; the man went to the emergency room and had his injuries looked after; and that was the end of it.

Mom had to decide whether to leave with Lonnie or to continue to work at 'Donna's' for some undetermined period. She mentally examined the issue; and, with Dorothy's unwitting assistance by depicting 'Donna's' as a career choice, she made up her mind. I have reflected on the wisdom of her decision, wondering what would have happened if she had made a different choice. When Lonnie appeared in the morning, he asked, "Well, what is it to be?" standing over her to reinforce his position. I doubt that he even realized that, by standing, he was assuming a position of power.

"I think we will go to Sacramento and start over. What do you think?" Mom gave him that beautiful smile that had originally won his heart. He couldn't resist; he lovingly embraced her. They both vowed a silent promise to rebuild their future.

In the meantime, Mom sold the car to one of the patrons and we were in the Lonnie's car with all our stuff. The trunk was jammed full and there was stuff stacked all around us, as we headed down the road to Nebraska, not Sacramento!

"Where are we going?" Mom asked. "We're not going in the right direction!"

"We're headed to a place just outside of Lincoln to finish up the last part of a deal I made prior to finding you."

"What kind of deal?" She remembered his previous deals and was worried it might involve some shady character, the likes of Red. We rode in silence for the rest of the trip, until we got to the ranch/farm outside of Lincoln. She was right; it was another deal of the same ilk. This guy had removed some negotiable bonds from a bank and he had an offer to unload them in Sacramento. The bonds weren't the only thing Lonnie was to transport. Guns were in the equation...machine guns, high-powered rifles, and pistols. He had made this deal to get us a stake for the Sacramento move...we were back in the criminal business.

The 'merchandise' was scheduled for delivery in three months and, in the interim, we were to stay at the extra house on the hill with Lonnie's friend and his family. Mom was very upset about this, but Lonnie promised we would stay here and he would not take any other 'jobs' before we left. He said that this was the last and final job. We settled down in the normal routine of ranch/farm life for that three months and all was well between Lonnie and Mom. For a while, we felt like a real American Midwestern family. We went to school about ten miles from the place, riding the bus every day. It was nice living there. We learned about farm and ranch animals: cows, chickens, pigs, and all sorts of wild creatures.

The day we were to leave finally dawned. We packed all our belongings (such as they were) into the car, along with the bonds and guns hidden under the seats and in the door panels, invisible to the naked eye. We were just a family moving across the country to a new home.

Someone would meet us in Sacramento to accept the merchandise and all this would be over. We traveled the scenic route through Yellowstone Park; up over the road they aptly named "The Top Of The World" to Red Lodge, Montana; and on through Bozeman to Idaho Falls; and finally, to Jerome, where Lonnie's father lived. His father wasn't happy to see him, but Lonnie wanted to reconcile their differences, so we stayed there for several hours while they talked. They continued to talk for what seemed like forever. Finally, they stood up and hugged each other as father and son. His father hugged Mom and wished us well and we went to Boise for the night.

The next morning, we were on our way to the meeting place in Sacramento. We took the back way through Alturas, through Susanville to Paradise, and through Marysville to Sacramento. When we got to

Marysville, Lonnie stopped at a liquor store and bought a six-pack of beer. This astonished me...I hadn't seen him do this before. By the time we arrived in Sacramento, he was dead drunk and the car was weaving back and forth across the two lanes of traffic on "C" Street. It was in the afternoon with light traffic, but an old "Model A" sedan pulled up beside us, and the man inside flashed a Sacramento police badge.

"Pull over! Pull over!" he shouted out the window and pointed to the curb. Lonnie was not prepared for this and was hesitant at first; he couldn't reach his pistol under the seat, so he asked Mom to get it for him.

"No, pull over! Maybe we can explain this away without getting ourselves into more trouble," she said as she turned the radio down.

"Okay, okay! Maybe I should do the talking, but get rid of the gun under the seat before he gets here," he answered angrily as he pulled the car to the curb. Mom grabbed the gun, a 38-caliber

"Police Special" with a long barrel, and handed it to ME.

"Put this down the front of your pants under your shirt. They won't search you." I took it and she helped me to get it tucked down my pants before the police officer came up to the car.

"Step out of the car, Ma'am! You and the boys, step out on the sidewalk; Sir, you step out on this side." He came up on the driver's side with his hand on his weapon. He was an off-duty detective and had been watching Lonnie weaving all over the road for about a mile before deciding to stop him. A marked patrol car pulled up from the rear and another pulled up from the opposite direction, while we stood there on the sidewalk. Three policemen came out of the two cars; one of them stayed behind talking on the radio. I could see him writing something down and looking again at his clipboard; then, he got out of the car holding a shotgun and shouted something to the others. They immediately drew their weapons and ordered Lonnie to lie down on the ground. One came over and grabbed Mom by the arm and put handcuffs on her, bending her over the hood of our car. Another policeman approached me, saying that Bill and I were to sit on the grass and wait for a policewoman to arrive.

'The gun...the gun!' I thought. I didn't know what to do about the gun, but I saw a bushy plant nearby and, when they turned their heads, I quickly tossed the gun into the bush. It slid under the leaves and disappeared from sight. The police were holding Lonnie on the ground, while Mom was handcuffed and sitting in the front seat of the car with the door open. Bill and I were still sitting on the grass with our legs straight out in front of us, watching the activity. Both of us were in a state of semi-shock; we had never imagined anything like this. I thought back to when Red held us at gunpoint; it was the same feeling. We were afraid and awed by what was happening. A crowd had gathered and the police had their hands full with crowd control. Another patrol car drove up and a man in a business suit emerged from the passenger side. He walked to the side of the car where Mom was sitting. I found out in short order that he was an INS agent. He had been tracking Lonnie and Mom since we left Gabbs; but each time he nearly had us in his grasp, we would move again which bought us more time to elude him, and caused him to repeatedly have to pick up the trail.

"Hello, Mary. It's been a long time," Agent Flynn said, standing directly in front of Mom. She was startled and uncertain about what to say, so she just lowered her head and sighed. "I've been looking for you for a long time. Is that the other alien sitting there on the grass? Who is the second youngster?" he asked as he turned to look at Bill and me.

"That's my son, William," she snapped at him, as any protective mother would do. The fire and zest had returned to her eyes...she had her spunk back. She remembered him from his trips to Austin and New Pass to check on me. He warned her then that she lacked the right papers for me and, if she didn't get them, I would be taken away from her. She always asked why they were so concerned about a four-year-old child and not as concerned about criminals who were coming to the country. Mom questioned him about the reason for his interest and she was always given the same answer...it was his job and in the national interest that he keep tabs on his charges. It was my opinion that he was fond of her and invented excuses to see her. I remember a particular conversation at New Pass when Norm was underground on his shift and Robert had arrived unexpectedly. It went like this.........

"Hello, Mary. How are my little boy and my favorite female alien today?"

"Oh, hello, Agent Flynn. How are you?"

"You can call me Robert, Mary. I would like that and we can be more informal than Agent and Mrs., don't you think?"

"I suppose that's all right, since we seem to see a lot of you."

"Yes, of course you do. If we are to resolve this small problem with Alan, I think we should handle this matter on a more personal level than we are now."

"I'm sure I don't know what you mean. You are aware of our situation and I'm sure we can solve this through the normal channels." She said this, even though she suspected his motives.

"Do you ever go to Reno for business? You know, INS business, without Norm?"

"No, I don't drive. I haven't a license."

"Perhaps you should get one."

"Perhaps I should. Would I need to go to Reno or maybe Fallon for this INS business?"

"Either place is possible, if that's what is necessary to take care of this," he said, looking satisfied with her response.

Then Norm walked in, startling Mom. She wondered why she felt so strangely guilty.

"Hi, am I interrupting anything? It doesn't seem like it's been six months since you were last here," Norm commented as he hung his jacket on the hook.

"No, not at all! I was just headed to Austin to see another one of my so-called 'charges' and thought it was the perfect time to visit you!" Robert stoutly declared as he stood up to shake Norm's hand. Norm grabbed his hand and squeezed it while he shook it; Norm had a powerful grip, with no apparent idea of its effect on others. Robert winced, trying not to show how painful the grip was, but we all could see how much it had hurt him.

"I need to get going! I'll just barely make it to Austin before sundown," he said, withdrawing his mangled hand from Norm's grip. He headed for the door, but turned and looked at Mom as if to say,

"Remember. I expect you to uphold our unspoken agreement." She fully understood his real meaning and meant to abide by it. She obtained a driver's license and was soon going to Austin by herself and, occasionally, to Fallon on business. I suspect that this situation was the origin of her trouble with drinking and using sexuality to try to manipulate men. Her beauty attracted them, but instead of giving her ultimate power over them, it led her into subservience to them. She did not receive in return as much as she gave.

But, enough of the past, here we are in Sacramento; in deep trouble... trouble the likes of which we had not seen before.

"You know you're in a substantial amount of difficulty this time, Mary. I don't think I can stop them from sending you and Alan out of the country."

"Yes, I know," Mom groaned, "but I need to have him with me and I must make sure that Bill is cared for."

"I'll see what can be done." With that vague statement, he turned on his heels and went back to the car where he talked to the other officers. We sat there for a long time; finally, the policewoman came over to us. "Come along, boys. We need to take you to the home for something to eat and a place to stay."

"What about my mum, where is she going?" I asked when she put us in the back of the patrol car.

"Don't worry, you will see her soon," she said as she closed the door. Bill started to cry. I couldn't blame him, he was four years younger and he was scared. For that matter, so was I.

We left and I could see through the rear window that Mom and Lonnie were placed in another car headed in the opposite direction. We didn't see anyone for two long days and the only thing I knew was what I read in the paper. The police had taken the car apart and found the bonds along with the guns. Lonnie and Mary were being compared to Bonnie and Clyde. They had recovered two Thompson submachine guns, three high-powered rifles, half a dozen pistols, and the sawed-off shotgun that Lonnie had made for his bank jobs. I had watched him modify this weapon. He had a double-barreled, twelve-gauge shotgun and he cut the barrel and stock to make it about sixteen inches in length. The gun had exposed hammers and resembled those toy pirate pistols that kids played with. I remember the day he carried it into a small barn at the Nebraska ranch and fired it into a garbage can. The impact tore the thirty-gallon can in half. "There," he said, "that should be a deterrent to any heroes who might come along."

I had to agree with him. The explosion was so loud I thought everyone in the world had heard it, and the smoke was so thick you could have cut it with a knife. "Can I shoot it?" I asked.

"No, this is not a toy and I don't want to see you kids anywhere near this or any of the other guns. Am I clear about this?"

"Yes! Yes! We won't go near them," I agreed, as I walked outside, but he had a twenty-two rifle that I knew he would let us shoot later.

We were in the Juvenile Detention Center for three weeks before Al Kelso showed up. "Your Mom has given me the task of getting you to Tungsten. I have some friends there that you can stay with until her trial. We'll know then if you both are going to be deported." He was addressing me from across the table in the lunchroom. Bill was sitting next to me.

"What about Bill?" I asked.

"Bill will be fine. Your mother has decided to marry Joe Garetto and Bill will be left in his care. Most probably, he will be boarded out until you and your mother can return if you are actually deported," Al said.

I knew that he was in love with Mom, but he would never presume to tell her how he felt. He would spend his whole life loving her and would always be there when she needed him. If she recognized how he felt, she didn't acknowledge it. He sat there, looking at us; finally, he said again, "She wants me to take you boys to Tungsten. You will stay with my friends until we find out what is going to happen with the INS. I hope that will be okay with you boys?"

"What do you think is going to happen?" I asked.

"I don't know, but we will go to Seattle to see your mother before we go to Tungsten. Maybe she will know more."

"Okay! I guess that will be all right with us. What do you think, Bill?"

"Is it time for lunch?" He was too young to realize what was happening to us and still equated everything to the state of his stomach.

"We'll go see Mom. Won't that be neat?"

"Yeah, that will be great! Now, let's go have some lunch."

Al got up and took Bill by the hand and headed toward the door to the cafeteria. The detention facility allowed relatives to eat there, so they must have thought he was related to us. We had chicken soup with rice and bologna sandwiches. We drank milk and Al had coffee. He always had coffee. He drank so much coffee that I often wondered if he would turn into a coffee bean.

We were packed and ready to go by nine o'clock the next day, waiting for him to arrive. He signed a lot of papers and we were released to his custody. Two days later, we were standing next to the cell where Mom was kept at the Federal Detention Center in Seattle, Washington. We were allowed to visit with her in a large room with a steel-barred door that the authorities stood behind, just out of earshot.

"Did you get it all set? Did Joe agree to the marriage?"

"Yes, he did. Now you have to get it approved by the INS."

"I talked to Robert and he said it would be taken care of if I could get Joe to agree. Did you bring the paper with his signature?"

"Here it is, are you sure this is what you want?"

"Yes, Joe has a lot of money and that will help me get back to the States. I must have someone here who can financially support my return, because Bill will still be here and I will need to return for him."

"I just want to make sure you know what is best; I, uh, uh--." He stopped in mid-sentence. I think he was about to break his long silence about how he felt about her. He would support her in everything she needed, if only she would show him some positive sign, but it was not to be.

Unnoticed and unattended, Bill was playing near the door. The next we knew, he was outside the door...he had apparently slipped through the bars and was standing outside in front of the guard.

"What are you doing, son?" he asked as he bent down to pick up Bill. "Ma'am, here's your boy. I bet you wish you could get out this easily."

"It would be nice, but you would just come after me; besides, how far do you think I'd go in this fine getup?"

"You're right; it's not very flattering. Here, take him back," he said with a chuckle, opening the door and setting Bill down. Bill ran to Mom and jumped into her arms. He always felt safe when he was with her. She held him for a moment and then beckoned for me to come to her. I went to her and she hugged us both tightly. I knew from that moment that we would always have something special between us. We three would always be connected, no matter how far apart we were. We held each other like that for a long time. We didn't know it then, but this would be the last time Bill would see Mom for three long years.

Back in Tungsten, we lived with a family and behaved as a family to the extent that was possible. We both attended school, church, and played as if we were part of that family. We had little problem adapting to a new environment; we had adapted to every type of situation that life had thrown our way for our entire short lives. We had lived with people who were strangers, we had been boarded out, lived in tents, existed out of the back of a truck, and spent time on a farm. We were accustomed to making do with whatever situation we were in at that moment. I promised myself if I ever had children of my own that they would never experience what I had gone through. I looked after Bill to the best of my somewhat limited ability...I wouldn't allow anyone to hurt him. We were there in Tungsten for almost six months...then, one day, the INS agents came. It was my old friend, Robert Flynn. He and another agent knocked on the door.

"Can I help you gentlemen?" Mrs. Sorenson asked.

"We are with the INS, here to pick up Alan to be sent to Reno for deportation. Is he here?" Robert said as he tried to look past her into the house.

"Do you have identification?" Mr. Sorenson had overheard and stepped up behind his wife. Robert flashed his badge as he must have done a thousand times, waving it in the air and snapping it back down before anyone could catch a glimpse of what it said. "I'm sorry, but I need to see that badge at a slower rate of speed. I'm not going to assume who you are until I have proof." Mr. Sorenson now moved in front of his wife. This clearly upset

Robert, but Mr. Sorenson was not one to be bullied by anyone claiming to be a government official. Robert held his badge up to the screen door, as well as the court order giving him the right to pick me up. After Mr. Sorenson carefully read the badge and the order, he invited them in. "When will you want to take him with you?"

"We will be here tomorrow around noon. He will need to bring whatever clothes and personal items he has that will fit in two suitcases."

"He will be ready at that time."

"Alan, say your goodbyes to your brother tonight, because tomorrow I will be here to take you to Reno to your mother. Do you understand what I mean?"

"Yes, but what do you mean 'goodbye'? I'm not coming back?"

"No, you and your mother will be going to Australia the following day." He said this with such finality that I will never forget the sinking feeling I suffered at that moment...another end to a way of life and the beginning of another unknown.

Chapter 10

Two days later, Mom and I were on a DC-3 aircraft headed for San Francisco and scheduled to board a four-engine Pan Am overseas flight to Australia. This was the first time I had flown and I was excited. We were not just flying, but we were flying First Class.

It was a two-day flight to reach Australia. We stopped in Hawaii and the ever-present INS agent, Robert Flynn, left the plane. Robert and Mom had talked the entire flight to Hawaii. I didn't know what they were talking about, but it seemed very intense. We flew to a spot in the middle of the Pacific Ocean called 'Canton Atoll', for refueling; then on to the Fiji Islands; and, finally, Sydney.

Flying over the ocean in this huge 'Double Decked Strato-Cruiser,' this was the designation that Pan Am had given the plane, was an adventure.

The airport in Las Vegas has one parked by one of its storage buildings today that some entrepreneur was going to use as a flying restaurant. Every time I see it I am reminded of the trip I once took. The plane was small by today's standards, but back then it was huge. The top deck had seats as far as you could see, at least to me, from the cockpit door to the tail. Two rows of three seats per side and a wide isle down the middle. Leading down from first class was a spiral staircase which led to a bar just under the first class seating, thus the name 'Double Deck'. I was only allowed to look down the staircase, but you could see the passengers bellied up to the bar drinking and having a good time. The cockpit, in those days they would take you in and show you around if you were a kid, had two seats at the front with gauges on every bit of wall space that didn't have a window. The navigator had a large bubble above him that magnified the night sky so he could get astronomical readings for navigation. There was a window that looked down to the surface of the planet for landmark navigation. You could see below the surface of the ocean when we broke cloud cover. We saw a submarine beneath the surface and the navigator said it was about 100 hundred feet deep. Back in the cabin, during the day, looking out the window you could see oil or fuel running down the wing. At night you could see a five-foot flame from the exhaust. I have often wondered, were they worried about that flame and could it have ignited the fuel.

Mom had called her brother John before we left and he was there to greet us after we went through the Australian INS officials. Mom was told she would be on a criminal watch list and if she did anything out of line it would be the prison for her. She nodded politely and agreed with them and then went to meet John. They hugged each other, then he picked me up and I think he said, "How are you lad, good to have you back?" I'm not real sure that was what it was, because they spoke with an accent that I had long forgotten.

"These people talk funny, don't they Mom?" They both looked at me, then each other and burst into laughter.

"You will be speaking like them before long," she said as she took me from John.

We headed to the next flight we would need to take to get to Melbourne. Sydney is the port of entry and we needed to get to Melbourne where John and Winifred lived. We boarded a DC-3 left over from the War and it rumbled down the runway, took flight, and we were off. The flight was the worst of my life. We flew into a storm and this is when I learned something I would never forget. Australians seemed to have no fear; they always felt it would get better, so continue on. The plane did everything but land; we were up, down, on our side into a dive, climbing toward the night sky. The lightning was everywhere, it rolled up the wings crashing into the fuselage. I needed a sick bag, and mom and John just sat there talking as if nothing was going on. I could not believe what was happening and I was scared to death.

The plane finally landed in Melbourne, which was a great relief to me. And, best of all, Winifred was waiting for us, and she hugged Mom and me until I thought I was going to be crushed. Uncle John told her how I had been sick on the plane and that only made the hug become more intense. Mom made John swear he wouldn't tell Winifred about the circumstances under which she had returned to Australia. They concocted a story that she was only on holiday and would be returning to America soon. We left the airport and drove to her house. I was so impressed…she lived in a three-story house, sitting on a large plot of land; that I estimated to be four acres. Her house was located down a lane off the main thoroughfare leading to the center of Melbourne. My Grandmum Winifred and I would go to town on the trolleys that ran on the main thoroughfare. These trolleys were heavily armored from the war and looked like land-locked submarines. Once, a lorry, an Australia three-wheeled delivery truck, was hit by a trolley and the lorry was completely destroyed, but the trolley was only knocked off the tracks. The trolley was soon placed back on the tracks going on its merry way; while the lorry was hooked on the back of a wrecker and taken to the scrap heap.

We stayed with Grandmum for two months and Mom helped out in John's restaurant; but, before long, she began to drink. She got so drunk that she was unable to make it back to the house so she would stay at John and Laurie's. Uncle John had a hard time hiding Mom's true condition from Grandmum and finally, despite everyone's best efforts, she found out. She scolded Mom and the fights about her drinking were legendary. She lectured Mom about her responsibility to herself and to me. John and Mom had a fight in which he beat her and she had a black eye and bruises on her face. They originally told me that a patron at the restaurant who had had too much to drink had attacked her. Later, I discovered that the story was a lie; I have not cared for John since that discovery. The final straw that severed the relationship between Mom and Grandmum occurred after John told her the truth about Mom's homecoming. Grandmum and Mom had final and bitter words about the lie and we left that day. I was never to see Grandmum again, a particular sadness for me because we had formed such a close bond with each other. We spent a lot of together riding the trams to go to her favorite shops downtown. I enjoyed our time together, even when she had me learning to knit while riding on the trams. We bought a model of an airplane, a Cessna made of balsa wood, and we commandeered one of the kitchen chairs to do our assembly. I had the frame pinned to the chair seat and Grandmum would apply the glue. The glue was everywhere, on the model, on the chair, even some on the floor under the chair; she was not the best at gluing. The outer skin of the aircraft was bright yellow, just like the real airplane. This time was very special to me and I thought we would be together again so we could finish it. I hoped she had put it away somewhere, so when I returned we could.

We traveled to Stanhope, where another episode in the continuous saga began. Aunt Linda and Uncle Ron met us at the bus stop. Ron was so glad to see Mom that he hugged her for a long time. They had been so close as children, with only a year's difference in their ages, and they still had many common memories. We stayed at their house where I was introduced to the wonderful world of cheese. The fabled factory, now under ownership of Jack, was running at full capacity. I remember that the buildings had large vats lining the main floor, while at the mezzanine level cheese blocks would be hung to cure. The vats contained every type of cheese imaginable. The smell left much to be desired and this smell permeated my being. Remembering an incident in Park City where Norm forced me to eat cottage cheese, being in the factory only re-enforced my dislike of it. To this day I still cannot eat cottage cheese.

We left there after two weeks and hitchhiked to Sydney, where

Mom began her quest to return to the States. She had a little money that Joe had sent her, but it was not enough. He was reluctant to send more. So…it was back on the streets, where she resumed her life as a prostitute. I spent most of my time on the roof of the hotel where we were staying, playing with the other kids whose mothers had to work. It didn't seem wrong at the time but we didn't go to school. All we did was play all day! This was to haunt me later in life, but I didn't give a care at the time. Mom heard about the big American base outside of Brisbane and we were off again to that port city.

Brisbane was nice; the climate was tropical warm and sunny most of the time. Mom found a place for me to stay, with the family of a cab driver. I stayed with them about four months and actually attended school with his children. Mom worked at the docks where the sailors came in and soon she was very popular. She could relate to the Americans because she had been there and they would like to talk of home. She made a great deal of money; enough to set aside for our trip back to the States, enough to buy several appliances for the cab driver's family. She also purchased a cab for him. They had an arrangement, in which he was to send her a percentage of the proceeds from the cab and it would, eventually, pay off his part of the cab. I don't know if that ever happened.

One day Mom came to the cabdriver's house and said, "Get your things together. We're on our way to England."

We packed what little I had, said our goodbyes, and headed for the airport where a DC-3 awaited us on the runway. The pilot, Mike, sat behind the wheel, dressed in a leather bomber jacket with an earphone around his neck.

"Get yourselves strapped in and we'll be off in a moment." He pushed the throttles on the console, bringing the engines to a roar. We were strapped in and the plane lunged forward after a slight hesitation; then we were pushed back in the seats as the plane made a loping movement down the runway and, finally we were airborne.

We flew to Darwin, where we were refueled and Mike told the

authorities we were flying to an eastern part of Australia; when we were, in fact, headed for Singapore. We were flying so low over the waves, which sometimes appeared to splash over the windshield, that Mom would go to the cockpit, look out the window and then back at Mike, shaking her head.

"Are you sure we will make it to Singapore?"

"No worries, I've flown this route many times."

"I know that, but will we make it?" she would ask him over and over again, and he responded in the same way, "No worries, I've flown this many times."

It always has amazed me (and I have mentioned this before) that the Aussies never seem to worry about anything and always feel they will be all right.

We made it to the airport at Singapore, where I was glad to take our leave of Mike, and boarded a commercial aircraft to London, England. This was a much better flight; we were higher in the air and water spray on the windshield did not seem to be an issue. The plane landed in several places along the way: Calcutta, Ceylon, Karachi, Cairo; and Rome, where we stayed for two days. All the other landings were for one day but we were allowed to go on tours to see all the sights. In Rome, we stayed at one of the finest hotels I had ever seen. It had marble everywhere; even the bathtub was marble with a lion's head spouting water. The stairs leading to the rooms were marble with a large marble lion on the three-foot wide banister guarding the entrance at the base of the staircase. The dining room had large marble tables with sculptures every four feet down the center. The silverware at each place setting seemed, to young or old eyes, to be for at least three people. The waiters served the food in covered plates and each portion had a different utensil for it. The hotel was the very epitome of luxury…it was very grand. We arrived late in the day and went directly to the hotel; the next day we toured the city.

Some of my strongest memories are of the wild rides around the city. The Italians are wonderful people, except when they get behind the wheel of an automobile. They become the most aggressive drivers in the world, second only to the French. At the intersections, it's 'balls to the wall' and whoever has the biggest and brassiest ego went first. If I were a betting man, I would have backed our tour driver as the 'ballsiest' of them all. We would zip down the narrow streets, wide enough for only one vehicle, at eighty miles an hour and turn 90 degrees onto another street…all without the driver removing his foot one scintilla from the gas pedal. The only warning to others that we were careening along would be to lay on the horn about halfway down the street until we turned onto another. I will never forget that horn, 'dah dah-dah dah', over and over as we slid around the corner and raced to the next stop. Most of the people on the tour were happy to drink the wine at lunch as an anesthetic against their fear. The tour was great; we saw all the sights and walked around St. Peter's Square. This was truly a magnificent city.

The next day, we were on our way to London. We were able to travel throughout the British Empire without a passport, as British subjects; it was an easy trip to England. Most of the other countries didn't check too closely either. We arrived at Heathrow in a blinding snowstorm and our first impression of London was cold, wet, and miserable. Money was running low and Mom was faced with financial difficulty…we did not have enough to return to the States. So, once again, she began to work the streets. This life must have been very hard on her. She had me to drag around and she had to portray herself in an attractive manner to appeal to her customers. I have often wondered whether she consciously chose this line of work or whether it had chosen her. What kind of mindset would she have had to adopt for her to do what she felt she had to do to survive? She still had Bill back in the States and her drive was to unite the family, along with her ineffectual love of John Reese. She worked the streets and I stayed at the flat, which was the base of operation. I would have to leave when she brought someone back; that was the way it was for the six months we stayed in London. She soon had enough to get us to Jamaica. She had met some people from there who said it was easier to enter the States from there…so we were on our way to Jamaica. We took a passenger/cargo ship, traveling at 10 knots, to Kingston. The trip was fun for me as I had the run of the ship. I would play cricket with the sailors in their off-duty time. It was my job to construct the cricket balls…a never-ending task because most of them were hit overboard during the games. They were easy to make, a simple matter of tying hemp string to a fixed point and rolling the string into a ball then wrapping tape around it. I must have made two-dozen of these balls on the weeklong trip to Kingston. The ship docked in Kingston and we went immediately to the house of relatives of our London friends. They knew we were coming and welcomed us into their house. They had been told what 'business' Mom was in and, subsequently, introduced her to a woman with connections to a 'house' just outside of town. We stayed with them for two days and then went to the 'house'.

It was a grand house from another era that stood two stories high, with a large veranda that encircled half of the lower floor. There was a large overhanging porch extending over the front part of the house to cover the veranda on the lower floor. The large living room in front was the area where the 'clients' gathered to socialize with the 'ladies'. This room covered the whole front portion of the building, with a bar at one end and at the other end, couches and chairs of various sizes and types were scattered about, forming a mosaic of color and an eclectic style. The staircase leading to the second floor covered the back center and effectively hid the doors to the back rooms and kitchen. A small dance floor was located at one end of the bar and an ornate grandfather clock stood at the other end. Behind the bar, a large mirror reflected the whole room creating the impression the room was twice its size. The 'clients' would stand at the bar and look at the mirror to select the girl of their choice. It was less obvious that way and lent an air of gentility to the whole process. The bartender was a large black woman, Camille, who reminded me of Rita. She was about the same size and demeanor as Rita, but she had more bounce to her step and was not hesitant to speak her mind. I hadn't been there long before I saw living proof of this.

"Now, don' ya' be tellin' me I didn't see what I saw! Ya' will stop and behave right now," she told one drunken sailor who was handling one of the girls roughly.

"Who do you think you are, missy?" he retorted, and before he could speak another word, he found himself on the floor, dazedly looking up at an angry woman with a large stick in her hand.

"I suggest ya' be getting yourself up and out of here before I get real opset".

"And what are you going to do if I don't?

When Camille heard that the stick in her hand seemed to take on a life of its own, striking him more rapidly and furiously than anything I had ever seen. The only thing the sailor could do was hold his head and try to dodge the strokes. He tried to get up and was hit again, just before Justin, the house bouncer came at him from the back, grabbing and securing him by his arms. Quick as lightning, he was tossed into the front yard, headfirst, with Camille staring directly in his face.

"Ya' were sayin?" she asked. Obviously, even in his drunken state, he realized he had stepped over the line with her.

"Nothing, nothing Ma'am," he answered, lowering his head in submission.

"I think it's best ya' go on home and maybe get summa' ya' senses back."

"Yes, Ma'am! That would be the best thing for me; good night to you, Ma'am." Then he reeled down the drive to the road leading to the base to sleep off a bad experience. Camille looked at Justin and she had to look up, because Justin was the biggest man I had ever seen. He stood about six feet, six inches and weighed about 240 lbs. His arms were as big as most men's thighs and his chest was much larger than his waist. His job at the 'house' was primarily and ostensibly to maintain the yards and fix things. His other job (unstated, but clearly understood) was to protect the house from unruly customers. It was my impression that Camille really didn't needed any help in that department; she kept everything in line most of the time.

The owner, Raul Medina, only came to the 'house' once a week, every Tuesday, to collect the money. He knew the 'house' was in trusted hands. He sat at the bar and talk to Camille; joking and laughing with her, stopping only to make sure that no one noticed their camaraderie. He relied on her to tell him how things were going, if she wanted to make any changes or improvements, or if she needed anything for her children. He seemed concerned about everyone who worked for him, and would ask about the girls, their welfare. He always made sure that their clothes were in good condition; he ran a good place and had a strange sense of honor about his reputation. I hid under the staircase with my new friend and watched and listened to them talk. My friend was a Jamaican named 'Blue'. I didn't know how or why he had that name; most of my previous experiences had taught me to accept people at face value. Blue and I were the best of friends; we had the run of the house and of the island. Raul knew we were under the staircase, but he never did let on to Camille. He would look at us and wink. We thought she would hit both of us with her stick if she had known. She told me later, after I was an adult, that she knew we were there. She had many a chuckle about how she had fooled us, and, Raul, too. Raul would come each and every week, and every week it was the same thing; we would hide, and they would talk and laugh. This went on for a months. Then it happened…Raul saw Mom in the mirror; he was so stunned that he stopped in mid-sentence and just stared. She walked over to the bar and began to talk to Camille about one of the clients, completely oblivious to Raul, who continued to sit and stare. Camille stopped Mary and said, "Mary, I would like ya' ta meet Raul, he's…"

"I know, another client with a special pass and you want me to entertain him! Not today! I haven't slept and I'm just too damn tired." Mary said this as she turned to go to her room to sleep.

"Mary, it's not that…" Camille started to say.

Calmly Raul interrupted her. "It's all right, Camille. I'll come back another time." Mom ascended the staircase and went up to her room. Raul watched her as she walked up the stairs; then turned to Camille, who stood there with her mouth agape. "I would like to have that girl, Mary, up to the other house next Friday. Will you arrange it? Get her a real nice floor length dress and I will send the car to pick her up."

"Oh, sure I can, Boss! Ya' wan' me ta tell her who she just snubbed?"

"No, don't let on who I am or what is going on. I am having a party for some of the 'Dignitaries', if you know who I mean, and I need an escort."

"Ya' mean a date?"

"Yes, for dinner and socializing, that's it! I will have her back before midnight, Mom." He laughed and he patted her on the shoulder. His first glimpse of Mom and the feelings she incited in him would only intensify with time.

"Mary, I will be needin' ya' ta do something for me next Friday; can ya' do it?" Camille said.

"I guess so, what is it?"

"First, ya' will go ta town w' Justin and get a long party dress and shoes ta match. Then Friday morning Justin will take ya' ta the beauty parlor for a complete do over."

"Wait a minute! What is all this…how much is this going to cost me?"

"Why, nothin'. Ya' are goin' ta a party and I want ya' ta look your best." At that point, Mom sat down and began to listen to Camille's plan. She was to be ready at 7:00 pm, when the car would arrive to take her to the party. Mom remembered the 'Parties' in Reno and thought it would be more of the same.

As she stepped into the car with Justin to go get the dress she was thinking 'I don't want to get involved with this again, it will only lead to me having to step up my move to the States. I can't become a party girl and expect to save for the trip, because I will have to purchase more expensive clothes and that will cut into my travel funds. I guess I'll go to see what it's about, but I think I need to start planning for the trip.'

"Ya' sure be the pretty one at the party! I know ya' will have a good time, there is always a good time at Mister Medina's place," Justin said as he drove the two miles to town. Mary sat alongside Justin in the front seat where he occupied most of the seat while she had to squeeze close to the door. He talked the whole time; but, deep in thought, Mary didn't hear a word he said. Her thoughts were occupied by her plans to go back to the States.

The market was an open-air market with many booths and stands selling everything imaginable. Justin parked the car and took Mary by the hand, leading her past the fruits, vegetables, fish, pork, and trinkets, to the center of the market. The center contained the choicest stands. He stopped at one of the stands displaying the most beautiful dresses Mary had ever seen.

"How can I help you, Justin?" asked Marcy, the girl at the stand.

"I need a dress for a party," Justin responded.

"I don't think I have one in your size, Justin." She giggled.

"It's not for me; it's for this nice lady."

"Oh, Justin, you're just too serious about everything! I knew what you meant, but if you don't laugh once in a while, your frowns will be stamped on your face for all eternity." She reached up to press the frown lines smooth. Mary laughed out loud, she and Marcy hugged each other, and they both looked at Justin as he made an attempt to smile. "Well tell me what you need the dress for?" Marcy asked as she let go of Mary.

"It's for a party on Friday night, and I need to look very nice."

"I have just the dress for you," as she disappeared into the maze of dresses. Marcy was gone for several minutes. Long enough for Mary to begin to feel uncomfortable with Justin standing there, looking as if he wished he was anywhere but there.

"Justin, what is wrong; are you bored?" she asked.

He stood silently looking at her with his coal black eyes; then, he gave her a pearly-white smile that lit up his face and said, "I'm not bored when I'm with ya', but I should be back at the house working, not just bein' an errand boy. I like bein' with ya'- it makes me feel good...too good," he said wistfully.

"I like you, too, Justin; but you know how it is! I am what I am and you are what you are…and the times are…." Justin smiled at her and gave her a pat on her arm to show he understood her words.

Marcy reappeared out of the rows of clothes and on her arm was a long dress that was both flattering and revealing. When Mary tried it on, it reached nearly to the ground, with just enough flip at the bottom hem to show her shoes. The dress was bright white with a touch of gold woven throughout the fabric. The neckline had a deep plunge in the front and revealed the area between her breasts, while over the shoulders it was narrow and dipped again to the middle of her back. Marcy had miraculously produced black shoes with gold stripes across the toe area and only a small strap across the heel.

"This should give them something to talk about," Marcy said as she tied the sash around Mary's waist. "What are you looking at, Boy?" she asked Justin as he stood there with eyes glued to Mary.

"Nothing---nothing," he stuttered as he tried to turn away.

"That's all right, Justin, I see it pleases you," Mary said, placing her hand on his arm.

"Jus' seein' ya' lookin' so good makes me feel better about the party."

Mary and Justin were good friends, so he tended to watch over her and make sure no one hurt her. He did this because he felt she had no prejudice against him or anyone else. Mary changed out of the dress and Marcy carefully folded it into a large flat box. She placed some coordinating under garments in a bag.

"Put it on Mister M's bill," Justin said to Marcy as he picked up the purchases and motioned for Mary to leave. He held the door for Mary to get into the car and closed it behind her. Then he went around the front to his side of the car and got in. They were quiet on the way back to the house; Mary sat looking out the side window, wondering about who Mister M was. She did not remember hearing that name. When they arrived at the 'house,' Justin stopped the car at the side entrance and started to get out.

"Justin, who is Mister M?"

"I can' say! I was told it would be a surprise, so please don' ask me."

"Maybe I won't go to the party if I don't know who it is," Mary lashed out angrily.

"Now, don' be that way; I can' say! Please trust me that it will be all right and ya' will be very surprised."

"Okay, I will trust you, but if it turns out badly I will come back and hit you right in the heart."

"Ya' go on in. I'll get everythin' and bring it to ya.' Don' argue, I know what's best," he said as he marched to the door and opened it. Mary went to her room, took off her shoes, and fell face down on the bed.

'What have I gotten into? I don't even know who this Mister M is and I'm not sure that I will like the party. Camille hasn't told me any details and I'm not sure what I have to do.' These thoughts kept rolling through her mind. She wondered why she had been selected, and if the other girls knew anything.

"Should I hang these in the closet?" Camille asked, as she entered the room behind Justin who was carrying everything.

"That would be fine! Justin won't tell me anything about this thing on Friday. Do you know anything?" she wailed.

"Yes, but I can' say! I have orders not ta tell ya' anything, except it will be an op front party, no hanky-panky, so ya' need not worry so."

"Are you sure?"

"Yes, just dinner and cocktails, trust me." Mary recalled hearing those very words from John Reese and look what happened then. Now she was more nervous than ever. She spent the next two days resting after her shift at night. She wanted to be alert and lively at the party.

Just as planned, on Friday Justin brought the car around to the side door and Mom quickly entered the car. She had spent the last two hours getting her hair done, and with the help of the other girls, was ready. They had been told about the invitation and were more excited than Mom. The 'Sisterhood', as they referred to themselves, was the first to help and assist a fellow 'sister' along in her 'career'. They fought among themselves, but they were always first in line to help each other out. I learned that about 'Ladies of the Evening' very early on; for, even in all the other places Mom had worked, there was this sense of camaraderie that was never articulated, but simply there. Mom was off to the house on the hill and Blue and I were back in the kitchen, raiding the icebox. This was a true icebox in every sense of the word. Ice was placed on the upper level every day or the food would spoil. There were several models of these iceboxes; we had the largest model at the 'house'.

Mary arrived at her destination. To her surprise it was the very house on the hill that we often stared at, wondering who lived there. A small man in a butler uniform, tails and all, met her at the door. He held her hand lightly, as she passed into the house.

"Good evening, Madam," he said in precise English.

"May I take your wrap?" He whisked off her shawl in the blink of an eye.

"Yes, thank you," she responded. When the butler heard her Australian accent, he stepped back to take a second look. For a moment, he abandoned his butler's persona. He had never heard the accent before and so he asked, "Where do you hail from? I don't believe I've ever heard anyone speak like you."

"I'm from Australia," she said proudly.

"Very good," he said. "Please follow me." And he resumed his staid and proper English demeanor.

Mom later described to me her impression of the house. The room off the foyer was very large… almost three times the size of the main room of the 'house'. It had many occasional tables, divans, and chairs arranged in small groupings around the perimeter of the room. There was a bar in one corner and a large window, adjacent to a veranda overlooking the sea. The veranda had marble tiles and an ornate marble wall with seats carved into the railing, where one could sit and watch the sunset. Below the veranda, and slightly indented under it, was a large swimming pool edged with marble benches surrounding marble tables sporting decorative umbrellas. A long marble wall with

Roman carvings concealed all this from the view of the veranda. The house and the surrounding gardens were very similar to an advertisement for a vacation spot that one might label 'Roman Villa'. You could see the ocean from almost every spot on the front of the house. The back of the house was a grassy plain as far as the eye could see, and the gardens to either side were so beautiful they seemed almost surreal.

Mom was guided gently to the center of the room where a tall, well-dressed man had his back to her. The butler tapped him on the shoulder and said,

"Mister M, allow me to present Mary from Australia."

He turned slowly around to face her and she recognized him as the 'client' to whom she had been rude at the 'house'.

"How are you tonight; not tired, I hope?"

"No…No, not really. I'm sorry for the other day, you must think I'm a twit."

"Not at all, I admire a woman who can stand up for herself."

"I'm glad. I am really sorry."

"Enough said! Let's forget about that unfortunate incident and move on to bigger and better things."

"Alright! This is the last time I will ever mention it."

"Are you hungry?" he asked, taking her hand.

"Yes, I am…a little! We don't eat much at the house. We must keep our weight down, you know."

"Yes, I understand; but let's not talk about work tonight. I brought you here to have a nice time and not to work."

Mary was puzzled why a man of his stature would want to socialize with a whore, especially when he could have anyone he wanted at any time. "Okay, I will have a good time if you will."

She looked him straight in the eyes, gauging his reaction. She told me that it is easy to tell what a person is thinking if you can catch their eyes at the very moment of a question and she had become very skilled at it. His reaction presented an inherent honesty and kindness not seen by her since before her beloved father's death so many years before. It was by looking into her father's eyes that she first realized that a person's eyes were a window to their soul.

"Yes, I think we will have a great time." Mary suddenly was aware that he had never let go of her hand from the moment of introduction.

"Would you like a drink and maybe a shrimp cocktail? They are very good."

"Yes, I would, thank you! And I'd like a Manhattan to drink, please."

Raul spent much of the evening with her exclusively, except when he was called away to greet some men who looked as if they were out of a Hollywood gangster movie. They would briefly retire to a room just off the main room. He would later return directly to Mom and pick up the conversation as though he had never left. When Raul was absent, a beefy man stayed by her and intercepted anyone else who approached her. I didn't know who this man was or what his role in my life would be until much later. The only information I was privy to for a long time was that his name was Joe and that he had come from Cuba with Raul.

Raul was a tall man, about 6'2", and well built. He must have spent a number of years working out in a gym. His father worked for Batista in Cuba and was involved with the 'Families' from New York and Chicago who were in the rum and sugar trade...trade that later evolved into money laundering and drugs. His father had a position in the Army that allowed him to travel to the different Caribbean Islands, establishing routes for the rum trade. He came to Jamaica and, while there, found and married a lovely woman, thus producing Raul. Raul was half-Cuban and half-Jamaican, which was quite a combination. His features were such that he could travel very comfortably between locations and be accepted in both places. His father was the liaison between Batista and the 'Families.' This relationship offered Raul the opportunity to go to an American University and receive an excellent education. He majored in business and when not in school he was able to learn the 'family business.' The 'Families' trusted Raul and gave him an important position in the organization. He became the Jamaican link in the 'circle'. The 'circle' as it was referred to, involved shipping money from Chicago through New York and Jamaica to South America to buy drugs, and then the drugs were shipped from South America through Jamaica to the East Coast. The money was sent to banks in Europe to be returned to the East Coast as 'clean money' for investment in legitimate businesses. The drugs sent to the East Coast were distributed to various areas throughout the United States. Raul was responsible for the even distribution of assets through Jamaica. Other enterprises he supervised also entered into the operational equation but, more nefariously, they were utilized to funnel bribes and kickbacks to the authorities. The party Mom attended was a part of that equation; it was used to blend the two factions together in a social setting. The purpose of the introductions was to make every member of the 'circle' aware of the others so favors were easy to grant. The whole system worked very well and everyone in the circle made a tremendous amount of money. Raul lived the life of a medieval lord and, even though his father had retired, his parents were living according to the same standard. All his father did was play golf with the elite of the Batista Regime and his mother attended afternoon teas and social functions. This era was good for the Medinas and Mom was about to become a part of that lifestyle.

Again, I have digressed…that first party lasted well into the night. Mom discovered that she liked the company and didn't feel socially inferior. After all, she had attended good schools in Melbourne and was a quick study for the rest of the social graces. Raul was always by her side and, not surprisingly, so was Joe. She was soon known to all as Raul's girl and an important part of his life.

"Are you having a good time?" he asked Mary, as he bade good night to the last guest.

"Yes, I am," she answered, placing her head on his chest.

"I did too, but let me get Joe to take you back. May I call on you tomorrow?"

She was somewhat surprised by his question and asked "Don't you want me to stay?"

"Yes, I do; but that would be cheap and I don't want our relationship to be cheapened. I'll call you tomorrow and we'll go for a ride in the country. Then, I will tell you what I have been thinking of since I first saw you last week."

"I will be waiting for tomorrow," she replied, still reacting with surprise about being treated in this gentlemanly manner.

"Until tomorrow, then," he said as he embraced her, placing a soft kiss on her cheek. He held her in his arms with the gentle touch of subtle strength and she felt safe and warm for that moment. She felt something more than just his closeness and touch. She sensed caring and kindness and that felt very good. He helped her into the car and closed the door. The car moved down the drive and she watched him watching her disappear into the night. She sat, almost bemused by the wonderful night…it was almost like a fairytale and she was the princess. She daydreamed about future possibilities. Of course, she would have to tell Raul about me, and about Bill. She would explain how she had come to Jamaica with the intent of returning to the States and reuniting her family.

"Here we are, Miss." Joe's New York accent broke through her reverie. He came around to open the door but she was already out, and about to close the door.

"From now on I will get the door for you," he said, taking her by the hand and guiding her up the steps to the front door of the 'House'. She stood inside the parlor and wondered about Joe. He seemed very gruff with her, but his hand had held hers with respect…respect she had never felt from a stranger.

"I guess that is his way, or maybe I should ask Raul tomorrow when we're riding," she thought as she went to her room and found me asleep on the bed.

"Get up, get up!" she said, shaking me awake, "You're not to be here, you need to be at the other place. You know what will happen. I'll lose my position." She was in a small panic because relatives were not to be at the 'House' late at night. It was bad for business.

"It's okay, Mom, Camille told me to wait for you here."

"Why would she do that?"

"I don't know, she just said wait here. Then I got tired and fell asleep."

"We'll talk more about this in the morning; now go to sleep."

In spite of her admonition to me, she didn't sleep well…she was awake more than asleep for the rest of the night. She spent much of the time sitting in the chair by the window. She would look out the window, then back at me, still sound asleep and in my clothes. She relived the night she had spent at a glorious party, where she was not required to 'entertain' anyone, was pampered by the host, then sent home with the promise of an adventure the next day. This was almost too much for her to comprehend. Coupled with her usual lack of luck, she was distrustful of the whole situation. "I don't know what's going to happen; I don't know much about Raul Medina and I'm not sure I want to; but he treats me as though I'm very special." She continued to look out the window; then back to me. "I can't understand why Camille would allow Alan to be here. It's against the rules so why is it different now? Did Raul tell her it was okay? I just don't understand." She finally gave in to sleep with her head resting back against the chair, and she remained asleep until the door opened and Camille came in.

"Mary, it's 9:00am and Mister M will be here any minute, why are ya' not ready?"

"Ready? Ready for what?" Mom asked, surprised by the fact that she had fallen asleep in the chair. "Camille, I can't move my head; my neck hurts."

"Now, don' ya' be concerned, I will fix it for ya'." Camille rubbed Mom's neck and shoulders to loosen the muscles, as she ordered the maid to run the bath. "I will bring her in, in just a moment. Boy! ya' need to go ta the kitchen and get some breakfast, now go." Soon we were all in the places to which she had directed us. In no time at all, Mom was down at the table drinking her morning coffee and waiting for Raul to arrive.

"I had a picnic fixed for ya' and Mister M. I know ya' will be at a picnic place by this afternoon and I don' want ya' back here hungry, so eat at the picnic or---." Just then, Camille heard the car pull up so she headed for the back door, opening it to see Joe.

"Joe, what are ya' doin' here? Where is Mister M?"

"He's in the car. I'm to get Miss Mary and take her to the car. Is she ready?"

Mom spoke up, "Yes, I am. I thought just Raul and I were going." She looked out the doorway at a long black sedan; it was the biggest car she had ever seen. Joe took the lunch in one hand and Mary by the arm with the other, and they were gone. Mary and Raul sat in the back, while Joe drove the car, but some unknown person was in the front passenger seat. She started to say something, but Raul indicated she should wait; he motioned to Joe and a window dividing the driver from the passengers rolled up.

"Sorry for that, but I thought we should have a little privacy. Joe doesn't need to know what we are talking about, in fact, I'm sure he really doesn't want to know," he said, using the same gentle voice she had remembered from last night. "I must apologize for how gruff Joe seems, but the people from New York do seem very abrupt to us."

"I was going to ask you about him, but now I understand."

"I'm not sure you do, but this is what this outing is about. I'll try to explain, and even though I will be very vague about a lot of things, I want you to trust me."

"I don't have any reason not to trust you now, but that could change."

He laughed and told her that her ground rules were fine with him. Then he asked, "If I were to make it possible, would you be interested in moving from the house at the bottom of the hill to the one on top?"

"I have a son to consider. Would that include him in this package deal?"

"Yes, of course! He would come also, and would go to school. You would be my girl and be accorded all the benefits that go along with that: the run of the house, the respect of my employees, and my devotion to you."

She just sat there in a daze...this was too much for her to absorb.

"Mary the strength of my devotion to you in just this brief time astounds me too. Let's just see where this takes us for now. You are the most precious thing in my world. Please give me a chance to prove that to you."

"I don't know! I have some problems that could--." He stopped her in mid-sentence and caressed her hand.

"Mary, your problems belong to me now. Don't tell me that you do not believe me?" She finally understood the sincerity with which he spoke and took comfort from that understanding. As she lay her head on his chest he cradled it as if she were a child. Only the roughness of the bumpy road that Joe turned onto brought her back to reality, and she wondered out loud where were they going.

"I have a place up here, from which the entire island can be seen."

"You have more places than I can keep track of. Exactly what is it that you do?"

He answered her immediately and she watched the expression on his face change, and his eyes became flat and hollow looking. Then, in a very controlled voice, he said, "I have told you as much as I can, but you must trust me, trust me as you would your mother."

She looked at him and, in that very instant, she saw the face of her mother...that stern but soothing, "I love you but I won't brook any nonsense" look that her mother constantly wore.

Without even hesitating, she blurted out that she trusted him and the depth of that trust convinced Raul that her words were true and heart-felt.

"You probably wondered what I was doing when I had to leave you occasionally at the party to greet those other people. Those so-called 'dignitaries' were from many different parts of many different countries. Some were from Chicago, New York, Miami, and San Francisco in the U.S.; Cuba; and South America; as well as our own politicians here in

Jamaica. For them and for me that was not a party per se, but a meeting. You may have noticed that I had to keep leaving you and meeting with them." Mary nodded her head and indicated that he should continue. "I was meeting with representatives from these places to establish some new business and that's all I will tell you. It is best for us both that you don't know more than that."

She agreed with him and told him that she wanted to give their relationship a chance to grow into something better and brighter. When Raul heard her words, he wrapped her in his strong arms and kissed her. The heady combination of strength and passion in his kiss made Mary lose any lingering doubts she might have had, and she surprised both of them with the passion in her own response. The car came to a stop and Joe extended his hand to Mary to help her out of the car, with Raul and the unidentified man following. Joe took the lunch and led them into a small house and through to the back porch where the view was breathtaking.

"Oh, this is beautiful! You were right, you *can* see everything! Thank you for bringing me to see this," Mary said exuberantly, swinging on the rail at the edge of the porch. The house was a four-room structure: just a bedroom, living room, kitchen, and bathroom. It was small, but was just as functional as the large house. It had running water, electric lights, and the grounds were well groomed. Raul came up behind her and they embraced and kissed again. Joe and the other man returned to the car and drove it down to another house just barely out of sight.

"It seems we're alone," he said as he led her into the kitchen where Joe had set the lunch before he left.

As she sat down at the table, Mary lost a bit of her exuberance, and somberly said, "I have one question, and I will never ask again, but I need to know."

Raul began to serve lunch and told her to go ahead and ask away.

"Why didn't we come up here alone? Why are Joe and the other man with us?"

"It is a dangerous business that I am involved in. I need these people around to protect my interests," he said, emotionlessly.

"What do you mean dangerous?"

"The competition is very keen and we sometimes need to do certain things that we don't like, but find necessary."

"I noticed that Joe has a gun and I'm sure the other man has one also. Will my son and I be under the same protection when I move to your house?" Mary was very concerned.

"Now I've been given two questions, both of which I will answer "yes" to. Are you reconsidering our relationship?"

Mary again reassured him that she just needed to know what to expect. Her own safety was one issue, but her son's safety was of paramount importance to her.

"You and your son will be under my protection, and believe me that protection will be the same as it is for me. You should get used to it because Joe and Mark are very professional and half the time you won't even see them," he said with a smile that gave a glow to his face as he poured the wine.

"That's all I need to know. I won't ask you about your business again." She was true to her word and she made sure I honored the vow also; it was never discussed again. They sat and talked about what they were to embark on over the next few days. They ate and drank, laughed and held hands until sun down. They stood together on the porch and watched the sun set into the ocean. It was a beautiful sight, and he held her and she laid her head on his shoulder.

A knock at the door announced Joe and Mark.

"You ready to go boss?" Joe said as he came into house. He stopped at the edge of the table and waited for Raul to respond.

"Yes, I think that would be good. We're just going to the big house. Tomorrow go get Mary's and her son's things. They will be staying there from now on," he said with a casual wave of his hand that was hardly noticed by Mary.

Mary could feel the respect in the room as Joe and Mark went about cleaning up of the lunch and packed the leftovers into the basket. Joe and Mark were from the 'families' in Chicago and were there to protect their interests. They were both originally from New York and had worked their way up through the system. Mary would become very familiar with Joe and his position over the next few months; he never seemed to be very far from her and was ever vigil. Mary would learn that he was to protect her from anything and was to give his life if necessary. The tie between them became very close, and Joe would show nothing but respect for her and he would tend to her with a respect she had never known. Mary had moved from a Lower House prostitute to Raul's lady and no one would ever say or do anything to show disrespect. She was very gracious with everyone and was well liked by all the staff at the big house. She spent a lot of time with the staff in the kitchen and they enjoyed her stories. Raul spent a lot of time out of the country because the revolution in Cuba was not going well for Batista and it seemed as though the revolutionaries were going to win. This would not be good for the 'Families' or Raul's interest.

Life was good for us now that we were living at a higher level and I went to a school with the social elite of the island. We were pampered at the house and it seemed everything was at our command. Raul, when he was home, would pamper Mary as if she were a queen. He loved her and anything she wanted was hers. She didn't ask for much because I think she loved him as he did her. I spent my time with Joe and Mark; they had so many stories to tell. Joe told me one that stuck in my mind until this day.

There was a singer in Chicago, a Puerto Rican, who went by the name of "Bobby P, P was for his middle name "Patrick" which he hated. He had an up and coming career with the help of Joe's employers and some of the other 'Family' representatives that had ties with the entertainment industry. They had sponsored him with contracts and money and they expected some 'favors' in return. Apparently the 'favors' were that he would perform at their clubs for free, and at any time they would 'request'. They just wanted their investment back and felt they were entitled to that portion of his career. The arrangement was never written down and after a while he felt they were not binding. His career began to take off and he decided he didn't need them anymore.

This is when Joe became a part of his life, a tragic part. Joe's eyes became cold and blank as he began to tell me the story. His face lost all expression; I could see only black eyes that looked through me. He began with a slow monotone voice. The room seemed to move from color to black and white. It gave me a cold feeling that I would one day learn to imitate.

"I will tell you this, but it will never be repeated," he said as he looked directly into my soul. "Bobby P disrespected his friends and they asked me to get that respect back. I spoke to him and he told me his obligation was over, but as you will learn, your obligation is never over until it is granted by the one who gives you that obligation."

"What do you mean, Joe?" I asked. His hand motioned to listen and he went on.

"I spoke to him for a while and I only heard arrogance in his answers. He thought he had become too important to associate with his benefactors and he was no longer obligated. This was a big mistake. I told him he should rethink his position, but he began to call me and my 'associates' names and told me to get out." He paused for a moment to form his words so as not to give me any specific person's name or any location I might know. Then he began again. "I reported back about the meeting we had and I was told to take care of the problem. I was told I would be transferred here after the problem was solved. I went to Bobby P and I cut his vocal cords so he would never sing again and now he is an insurance salesman on the West Coast. I was transferred here to look after their interests and Mister M."

I looked at Joe as he finished, and wondered if it would ever come to that with Mister M. I would never forget these stories, even though it didn't really seem real when he told me because of my age. I was fifteen and still at that age where I was indestructible and everything was just that, stories. He seemed so dedicated to Mister M and all of us. He was

ever-present in the household but invisible; he was part of the furniture
and part of the grounds; sometimes he would fade into the background
and disappear; but he was always there. He would always finish with,
"This is between you and me, not a word will be repeated." I knew what
that meant and I would never repeat anything. Even when 'Blue' and I
were running around after school I wouldn't answer his inquiries about
what went on in the house on the hill.

Mary became bored with Raul gone much of the time. She began
to drink and drugs became a part of her life. The parties were often and
she would become so drunk Raul would have Joe take her to the cabin
in the hills to sober her up. She would sometimes spend a week there
and when she came back she was fine for weeks. Then the cycle would
happen again. The local officials were beginning to question Raul about
her behavior and if he would take care of the situation before it became
a real problem for business. I really didn't know what they meant by
'take care of it' until one evening when I was in the back of the large
office where Raul met important people from the East Coast when they
came to visit. I was doing my homework when I heard them coming up
the stairs and I didn't have time to get out the back so I hid behind the
large bookshelf in the back of the room. I was well out of sight; it was
probably the first time Joe didn't look everywhere in the room before he
shut the door so they could be alone for their meeting.

"Stand by the door, Joe," Raul said as he looked at the rest of the
men. "What is it you need to talk about on such short notice?" he asked
with some anger in his voice.

One of them began, with apprehension in his voice, but also with
some authority. "You know how our operation must be invisible to the
island and to American authorities, so our associates will not stop the
flow of money to our bank accounts."

"Yes I understand."

"Well, it has come to the attention of some of us that Mary and
her activities are calling too much attention on you and maybe it is
compromising the operation."

"Have you heard anything for the East Coast about this?"

"No, and we don't want too."

With that Raul looked directly at him and then to Joe. "I suppose you want me to do something. What is it?"

"We think a boat ride would be the answer."

When I heard that, I knew what it meant. I slumped to the floor. The room became deathly quiet and I thought they had heard me!

"What you are asking is not what I am willing to do. You must think this over and get back to me with a better solution," Raul said as he motioned Joe to open the door to let them out.

The spokesman for the group turned to go and then turned back to Raul. "I think it's you who should come up with a solution and not us. It is your problem and I think it would be wise for you to consider adding the boy to that solution." He turned and went to the door. Passing Joe, I think he could feel his cold stare and moved away from him to the other side of the opening as he walked through. Joe closed the door, moved toward Raul, and sat across the desk from him as Raul slumped down in his chair with a look of disbelief and anger in his eyes.

"Joe, has anyone from the East said anything to you?"

"I had a call from Chicago, an inquiry, nothing more, I told them it was handled, and they are having their own problems with New York anyway."

"I know they are about to split and when I was in Chicago they asked me to get a courier and not to have me bring them news from here. They said it was getting too dangerous for me and I should find someone, and have them use a new route."

"That could be your answer to this problem, you know the problem with Mary and those in town," Joe said in passing, not really knowing if that would get through to Raul.

Raul was looking out the window in deep thought about all the problems he was facing. It seemed he was a target now and he would have to make a decision. He had been approached by the New York group and they had given him information, information he thought would be vital to the operation, he wanted to tell Joe but he knew Joe would report to Chicago. Raul had loyalty to Chicago, but he knew he would have to deal with New York if they were to win in this compromise of control. He also had to protect his people on the island and make sure they would not feel the fallout if a war was to begin with the two factions on the east coast. There were some very tough decisions to be made so he really didn't hear what Joe had said.

"Joe, I need to see Mary, is she here?"

"No, she's at the hill house with Mark. I can take you up there. Did you want to go?"

"Yes, and find the boy. I want them both there."

"Did you hear me when I said two of your problems could be solved with her?"

"No, tell me on the way. I'll ride in front and Alan can ride in back so we can talk. Get the car."

Joe nodded and left the room to get the car and look for me. I didn't know how I was going to get out of the room and be somewhere else so Joe could find me. Raul just sat in the chair and waited for

Joe to come back. I sat behind the bookcase waiting for the next move or for Joe to find me and I knew if he found me there it would be the end. Time stopped and it seemed I was there for hours. I was scared and I really didn't know how it would turn out. I thought he would come back and they would look behind the bookcase and there I would be. Then the boat ride would take affect and Mom and I would be chum. I heard a knock on the door and Raul answered. "Enter." One of the house staff came in and said something in Spanish and they left. The door closed behind them and I moved quickly to the rear door and left.

I went down the hall and stepped outside just as Joe was entering. We both had turned the doorknob at the same time, and he pushed the door open as I pulled.

"I've been looking for you. Where have you been?" That is when I began my career of the blank stare I had seen so many times on his face; I was no longer the student.

"I was out in the front and I had just come in to go to the back. Is Mister M. back on the island?"

"Yes, we're going to see you mother," he said as he held my arm and moved me to the car; he opened the back door and started to push me inside.

"Am I riding in the back? I usually ride with you," I said as I held my ground at the door.

"Yes, Mister M. and I need to talk." He pushed me inside and closed the door. I had never been in the back before. It was large with seats facing both forward and back, a bar to one side, and all kinds of buttons for the radio, side windows and the front window between the driver and passengers.

Joe locked that dividing window as he and Raul talked. I could barely make out their faces through the dark window, but they were in deep conversation. Raul would always listen to what Joe had to say because of his experience on the East Coast. He would listen and then make a decision, and his decisions were often as Joe had told him. The trip to the hill house was long and I fell asleep from boredom.

We arrived late that afternoon and Mom came out to greet us.

"Where have you been I thought you would be here sooner?" she said as she leaped into Raul's waiting arms. He had a smile on his face, but she knew him well now and could see the concern. "What's the matter?"

"Nothing, but I want to talk to you, so let's go inside. Joe, park the car and take Alan down to the other place for a while. I think you had a good idea. I'll let you know." He took Mom by the hand and they disappeared into the house. We went on down the road to the other place where Mark was standing, and the car stopped. He opened the door and I got out and started to go back up the hill to see Mom.

"You wait here with us. We'll go up to see your Mom when they call us," Joe said with a half-smile, half-serious look on his face. I knew he meant what he said and I followed them into house. Mark had fixed some Jamaican coffee and he offered us a cup. If you had never tried this coffee you probably would think it was very strong and wouldn't like it. It is ground almost to a powder and is deep black with a somewhat bitter taste, but after you get used to it, it's quite good.

We didn't hear from the other house until the next day when Raul called down to Joe and told him to come up. "Bring Alan with you," I heard him say as an after thought.

We went up and found he and Mom sitting on the veranda overlooking the ocean view.

"Sit down. We have something to tell you both and it will not leave this house."

"Ok, should I get Mark?" Joe asked.

"Well, yes, or what do you think Joe?"

"He and I are on the same page with you Mister M. You know we are your friends as well as co-workers. You've always known that."

"You're right, I should have understood that. I'm sorry. Please call him."

Joe went to the front of the house and motioned to Mark. We soon were all sitting on the veranda drinking coffee and Raul began.

"I will tell you this now and I hope you will understand what I am about to propose." He paused to look at Mom and me as if to get an Ok to proceed.

Mom nodded her approval and he looked to me. This was the end of my childhood. I would no longer be a fifteen-year-old. Now I was an adult in a child's body. I nodded and he looked to Joe and Mark. They also nodded their approval.

"As you may or may not know I have been instructed to get rid of you both." He looked at Mom and me. He had told Mom, not me, last night, but I already knew. Mom looked at me and gave me an indication everything was all right.

"Joe and I," he continued, "have come up with a plan that will benefit everyone, but we must do some things to make it happen. There is a problem between New York and Chicago. We could benefit from either no matter who wins, but Joe and I think it would be better if

Chicago wins. So this is what we have decided, but if you have any other ideas now would be the time." He stopped and looked at Mark.

"Let me hear what it is then I will tell you if I have a better plan or not," Mark said as he looked over at Joe. That was only about the third time I had ever heard Mark say anything. He mostly only answered with a yes or no.

Raul went on to tell us that we would be deported from Jamaica back to England where we would stay for a short while, then on to Mexico, Veracruz, and then to El Paso. I didn't know at the time, but Mom would have a message she had to take to Chicago; so New York would become less of a partner in the circle, but they would also benefit almost as much as before, so with this deal the problem could be resolved. Raul would let them know he had a new courier, so he would not be at risk as both factions indicated they wanted. This move brought us, Mom and me, further into the workings of the circle. This was also a chance for Mom to get Bill.

We were deported and that satisfied the local authorities. Raul told them it would be in the best interest of the organization that it happened this way and they agreed.

We were placed on a passenger/cargo vessel in Montego Bay. I watched as they loaded green bananas in six-foot stalks. The dockworkers would carry the stalks on their heads and go by the tallyman as he counted how many each worker loaded. They were paid a meager price for each one, and at the end of the day the ship was ready for the tide in the morning. We sailed to England, docked at South Hampton then went by train to Liverpool.

Mom set up residence on Parliament Street and began to ply her trade again, so as not to attract attention. I attended Granby Street School and everything seemed to fit into place.

We spent the next three months there, and then one day Mom said we are ready to go. We took the train to London. There she went to the shipping office and we were on another ship headed across the Atlantic to New York. We traveled in steerage for the first two days then somehow we moved to first class. The Sergeant of Arms came to her and told her he had been instructed to move us to a cabin on the upper deck. I think Raul had something to do with it. The ship, I don't remember its name, was Italian, and Raul had some contacts in Italy. It was a very large ship for its day. We docked in New York along side the Queen Mary and it was just as large. While there we stayed on board. The next stop was Havana, where a rotund short man in a white suit and straw hat met us. He never gave us his name; just took us to a location outside the city where we were met by another similarly dress man. He gave Mom a large package and envelope saying "Take this to Chicago when you get to the States, the address is in this envelope, there should be enough money for you to make the trip to Ogden." We got back in the car with the first man and went back to the ship. Two days later the ship docked in Veracruz. We were led down the gangway to the dock, around customs, and met by a taxi driver. The Sergeant at Arms bid us goodbye and the taxi driver took us to a villa on the beach south of Veracruz. We stayed there for two weeks, inside the walls of the villa. Mom received a phone call and we were on our way to El Paso. We took the bus and sat in the back so the inspectors that stopped the bus at every town would not notice us. But they never came on board. The driver spoke to them, something changed hands, and we were on our way again.

We arrived late in the afternoon on the second day at Ciudad Juarez just across the border from El Paso. We were met again by a taxi driver and taken to a hotel owned by the Roja family where we were set up in one of the top floor rooms, and later taken to their house for dinner and some conversation between Mr. Roja and Mom.

We stayed there for a few days and the routine was much the same every day. We would go eat at their house, Mom and Mr. Roja would talk, and I would watch television.

It was Saturday morning and the taxi driver came to the door and said we were to go to El Paso. We loaded our luggage into the taxi and headed for the bridge over the Rio Grande, drove across, and were asked by the border patrol, "Were we Americans?" In flawless American, with a Texas accent, Mom answered. "Yes, and it's good to be back from vacation, how are you?"

We were in the States again, and later the next day we would be on our way to Ogden, Utah. Or, more precisely, it was a small town outside Ogden called Roy. We stayed at a place that was run down and basically in the slum portion of El Paso. A man met us at the door and said to Mom, "Your late, you were to be here yesterday." Then he took our bags and led us down a dark hall to an old wooden door. He opened the door and, to my surprise, inside a large well-furnished apartment met our eyes. I couldn't believe how run down and dilapidated the building looked from the outside and how modern and very well kept it was beyond the wooden door. A lady appeared from the kitchen and said something to the man in Spanish. I thought it might be something about a meal being served but my Spanish wasn't very good and she spoke very fast and very low.

"Come on and get something to eat while I tell you about what Raul sent to the drop off point in Utah." I was right, Mom was on a mission and only Raul knew this. He told me several times during our stay in Jamaica, "Never tell all to one, give only pieces that will get the result you want." He would continue, "And never trust everyone in the chain, give each link just enough to feel they are a part." This was how it was with the trip we were on, each piece was given to Mom at a different time and place, and she wouldn't see the whole picture until Chicago. He must have trusted her more than I thought. The whole deportation and Mom being into drugs were a deception from the start. I was beginning to see it first hand.

The next morning we were taken to the bus depot and she was given some instructions about our destination and who she was to meet. I would be left at our destination in Utah and she would go on to Chicago alone.

We road the bus again and to this day I hate riding the bus. Two days on a bus will make you hate it, you stop at every town or gas station to deliver mail, pick up a passenger, or drop them off. The ride was rough because in 1957 the roads were not the freeways you see today. They were in good repair, but it was a never-ending battle with the trucks that rolled up and down these highways day and night. They were very heavy and would take out big chunks of the roadway, creating a pothole. Then other vehicles bouncing through them would cave in the sides of the hole. We arrived two days later at the bus stop in Roy and were greeted by Al Kelso, mom's friend from her days in Nevada. "Hi Mary how are you?" he asked as he gave her a hug and kissed her cheek.

"I'm good. How are you? Did you see your brother?" she asked as she hugged him back.

Al looked at me and said, "You must be Alan, you've grown since I last saw you" and then he looked back to Mom replying, "Yes I saw him yesterday and everything is set." He picked up the bags and we went into the 'Deseret Lounge' just off the main street where the bus had let us out. We entered the lounge and had to stand in the doorway for a moment to get our eyes accustomed the darkness. Al motioned us to the back where families were allowed to sit and have sandwiches, pizza, and soft drinks. He set the bags down and moved Mom's chair out so she could sit then slid it under her as she sat down. He motioned to me to sit on the other side of the table and he sat down next to her. We ordered and I ate as they talked. He gave me some nickels and pointed to the pinball machines against the wall. I went over and played until the nickels ran out, then it was time to go.

He picked up the bags and we went out the back to where his car was parked, got in, and drove to his bother's house. The house was on a wide street that went down a hill. The lot had been leveled and this made the house look small because of the hillside that dropped off from the lot next to it. The house was the typical two stories with a basement that the people of Utah build around the

Salt Lake City area. It had something to do with the Mormon religion, something about saving food stores and the basement was the best place. They had rows of canned goods stacked to the ceiling and large metal cans with several different types of grains. Bottles of water stored in rows around the wall of the room.

"How are you, Robert?" asked Al, as we entered the front door.

"I'm fine and you? Who is this?"

"Robert, meet Mary and Alan. They're the ones I told you about."

"Yes, I figured. This is my wife Myrtle, and my two kids, Bob and Jean. How are you?"

"Very well, thank you," Mom answered as she moved to take Robert's hand. She then turned to Myrtle and said, "You have a very lovely home and I'm so pleased you will take Alan while I'm gone to Chicago for a few days."

"Al told us all about you and we are happy to have you here," Myrtle replied as she held Mom by the hand. Al really had no idea what Mom was doing and had told them she had been sent back to pick up Bill, because he was to be sent to Norman. They thought the INS knew of her being here. They were the most law-abiding people I ever knew. Al knew we had come across the border illegally, but knew nothing of the Chicago trip. He looked at her when she said she was to go to Chicago, because he knew Bill was in Winnemucca, Nevada. She saw his expression and said, "I need to go to Chicago to take care of some business before I can transfer custody of Bill to Norman."

"You didn't mention this before. What kind of business, something I could help you with?"

"No, it won't take long and you need to find where Norman is anyway."

"Yes, you're right, I do need to find him."

"Well, let's get you settled, Alan," Myrtle said as she took my hand and led me to a bedroom on the second floor of the house.

Mom, Al, Robert and Myrtle were up very late talking and the next morning, I watched television with Bob and Jean in the front room until they came down. This was the first television I had seen and I was fascinated with the cartoons.

"Alan, come here a moment, I need to talk to you," Mom said as she cleared the last step. "I will be going to Chicago and you will stay here with Robert and Myrtle until I return. Also, Bill will be here in a few days and we will go to Ely with Al when I get back." She put her hands on my shoulders and looked into my eyes to make sure I understood.

"I understand, and Bill and I will be ready when you come back."

"Good. You will go to school with Bob and Jean while I'm gone. I know you haven't been for a while, but I'm sure they will place you in the right class, or is it grade here?" she asked as she looked to Myrtle for the answer.

"Yes Mary, it is grade and he will go to church with us also."

In only a few minutes it was settled that I would be signed up for school and church. I hadn't been to either since Liverpool.

The Church of England oversaw the school system and you were required to attend, and march to church from the school on religious holidays or any time the teachers decided you needed religion. I could remember one instructor, Mr. Lancaster; he seemed to have a special interest in my unruly friends and me. He would always be there when we made dumb mistakes and would administer the punishment. The schools in England had a nasty habit in those days of 'caning' students. "What hand do you use to write?" he would ask.

We tried to fool him but it never worked. I would say, "This one" and put out my left hand.

"Open your hand, palm up" he would say. The cane would come from out of nowhere across the palm and your hand would be useless for hours. He would then have you write: "I will not do 'whatever it was you had done'" one hundred times before you could go home. I got away with giving him the wrong hand only once; he could not only remember your name, grade, classroom, he could also remember which hand you used to write. "Wrong", he would say, "hold out the other."

I told him once I was not a member of the Church of England, therefore I did not have to march to the church.

"It makes no difference of what religion you are, and you need the discipline of the church," he would respond as he lined us up to march the three blocks to the church. I hoped the schools here would not have the 'cane' and the church was not as regimented as the Church of England.

The next morning Mom was gone along with Al Kelso. He went to Ely where he lived and worked in McGill fourteen miles north of Ely at the copper mill; she to Chicago. Bob, Jean, Myrtle, and I went to school where I was to be registered as Alan Kelso, son of Al Kelso.

They somehow had paper to legitimize the claim, thus I entered school for the first time in awhile. I was placed a grade below what I would have been if I had been in school on a regular basis. I had been kept up to this level by Mom having me read and study mathematics while we were in Jamaica and on board ship as we traveled about the world; plus the short period I attended in Jamaica.

About a month passed and Bill arrived from Winnemucca with Al, and he was enrolled in school as well. We settled down to a normal life and spent the weekdays at school and afterwards doing chores. I have dried dishes my entire life and wouldn't know what to do without that chore. Every Sunday we spent at Church. I can't remember but it seems the Church's nickname was "Holy Rollers". Once a lady sitting next to Bill jumped up and began to thrash around shouting, "Yes Jesus, yes Jesus". Over and over she shouted this as loud as she could, and then she collapsed on the floor. This action scared the hell out of Bill and he ran to Myrtle crying and screaming. Of course, the rest of us began to laugh at him until Myrtle turned and gave us the look of death. She was a slight woman, maybe one hundred pounds if she had on those heavy shoes she wore, but she was in charge and everyone knew it, even her husband.

Robert was a hard working quiet person and he didn't have much to do with the domestic activities of the household. He went to work, came home, had supper and sat down to read the paper. On the weekend he did things around the house to keep up the yard and the buildings, and went to Church on Sunday. Myrtle ran the house and set out the chores to be done and if any punishment was to be administered, she did that. We lived this way for the next three months after Bill arrived.

One Saturday Al arrived and with him was Mom. They had just come from Ely, and she had been there for about a week. She had completed her trip to Chicago and gone back to Ely to pick up Al. She was just ahead of the INS and we had to pack and leave that day. It was always like that, no goodbyes. We would just be gone the next day and no one would see us again.

We went to Ely, about five hundred miles from Roy, and set up residence in the Plaza Hotel. The hotel was small and it was typical of small town hotels. It had a small bar, maybe five stools, two tables, and a half wall separated the lobby from the bar. It was on the corner of the main street facing a park and across Main Street from the high school. The Plaza was closed and now part of Raul's holdings, a place to hide.

We stayed there for two weeks while Al looked for Norman. Al knew the INS was closing in and had to find Norman so Mom could give Bill and me to him before she was deported again.

Sixty miles from Ely, Current Creek then another thirty south in Railroad Valley to Nyala and up a canyon to the tungsten mine, he finally found him. Norman had a mine contract with a cotton farmer out of Arizona for tax purposes. They sank thousands of dollars into the mine and wrote it off as a tax loss. It was a good deal for both sides, Norman made a good living and the farmer received a smaller tax bill.

We left Ely early on a Saturday and drove for what seemed like days, Al drove at a blazing forty-five miles an hour, even though there was no speed limit in Nevada. Rounding a bend just before we got to Current Creek one of the hubcaps spun off into the brush. Al stopped the truck within seconds as we watched the hubcap sail into the tall sagebrush alongside the road. He jumped out of the truck and headed to the spot where it had left the rode. He stopped and looked into the brush and turned to say, "We need to find the hubcap before we go on, because they are hard to replace and will cost two dollars or more if I can even get one." I remember that to this day and the time we spent looking for that hubcap. We never found it and he complained the rest of the way to the mine. I didn't realize it then, but the reason Mom never married him was because he was so cheap. He needed every nickel he had to support a heroin habit. He drove so slowly because he couldn't see more than two hundred feet in front of himself. He hid his habit very well and I didn't learn about it until much later from Mom.

The mine was up a narrow canyon that opened into a large meadow with rolling hills to the right and steep cliffs to the left. The camp, as it was called, was on the far end of the meadow with the mine tunnel up to the left just beyond the mill. The camp consisted of one large square house which had a kitchen, an open room, and a bedroom; just to the left and ahead was a camp trailer; beyond that a tool and workshop. Norman had built all these buildings and they were very rough-hewn; he used rough lumber and timber as though they were to stand for the duration. He had a large pond just up to the right and behind the house, for the water supply, and in the pond, trout that he and his wife Neva had caught. A road circled behind the pond up to the tracks between the tunnel and the grizzly where the raw ore was dumped into the crusher. Another track forked off to the lower part of the mill where the finished ore was put on trucks to be sent to the smelter.

We arrived that afternoon and were greeted by Norman and Neva. Norman hadn't aged much since I had seen him last. Neva was older than Norman, and she was much shorter than anyone but Bill. Her hair was just turning to a light gray from blond, and was very curly. She had a nice smile that filled her whole being and you knew her heart was good. She wore a simple dress covered by a large apron and she must have been cooking or doing something in the kitchen because she was still carrying a hand towel. They stood side by side as we got out of the truck, then Norman moved toward us as we stopped in front of the truck and he said, "Hello Mary, how are you and the boys?"

"We are fine and you?"

"Fine. This is Neva. I spoke to you about her when you called."

"Yes. How are you? And you know Al," she said as she took Neva's hand.

"Pleased to meet you, Mary. Norm has told me about you and the boys."

"Let's go inside and talk. You boys can go look around but don't go in the tunnel." Norm's words were soft but in a commanding tone and we knew not to go into the tunnel. They went into the house and Bill and I went up to the mill to look around. I knew what they were talking about because Mom had told me the day before. She was going to leave Bill and me with Norman, then turn herself in to the INS. She knew Norman would go to his lawyer and get something passed that would allow me to stay in America, and we would have a normal life. We spent the rest of the day at the mine, Bill and I exploring, and they talking. We were up at the mill when we heard Norman shout, "Bill and Alan come down here. We're going to eat."

"Ok," I shouted back as we headed down the hill.

"Did you boys find anything interesting at the mill?" he asked as we came through the door.

"What are those machines in the mill building for?" I asked.

"They're for ore processing. One machine grinds the ore and then it is moved to the shaker tables to be separated and what finally comes out is Tungsten to be used in steel to harden it," he answered as he pointed us to the sink to wash up. We all sat down and began to eat. Neva was a very good cook and the food was delicious.

"Norman and I have decided you and Bill will stay here while Al and I will go back to Ely so I can get on with what I have to do," Mom said as she looked at me, her expression reminding me that we had already discussed this arrangement.

"Ok, Mom, we will be alright but will we see you again?"

"Yes, of course. I will be gone only a short time. I have some things to do and then I will be back."

"Will we go with you then, or is this goodbye and you will only visit?" I asked this for Bill's benefit because he had no idea what we had discussed the previous day, and he looked very worried.

"I'm not sure. We'll see when I get back. I have these things to get done and then we will work out what is best for everyone." With that she stood up, went to Bill and hugged him, kissing him on the forehead, and whispered in his ear. She turned to me and I received the same.

She shook Norman and Neva's hands and turned to the door and motioned to Al, it was time to go. Al unloaded the small amount of clothing we had and they backed away from the house, turned and headed down the road to Ely.

"You boys will stay here in the trailer for tonight and we will set up better sleeping quarters tomorrow," Norman said as he picked up the clothes and headed to the trailer.

We stayed at the mine the rest of the summer, about two months, and then moved to Tonopah. We moved to a house on Charles Street and were enrolled in school. About a month went by then the INS came to the house. They had a warrant for my arrest. It was Robert Flynn who knocked on the door and Norman answered it.

"Hello, I'm here to pick up Alan McLean, for illegal entry and no visa."

"I'm Norman Cooper, and I think you will have to talk to my attorney."

"And who might that be, Mr. Cooper?" he asked as he tried to force his way into the house.

"You wait right there on the porch and I'll get my coat and we can go see him at the Court House," Norman said as he closed the door and went to get his keys and his coat.

Flynn had a look of shock on his face. He had never been told to wait on the porch. He just stood there until Norman came back and then went to his car and followed Norman to the Court House.

Up the steps into the Court House they went in a line with Norman in the lead, Flynn and his assistant close behind. The Law Office of

William P. Belton it read on the door. Norman opened the door and walked straight in followed by the INS.

"He can't see you now, he has another client," the secretary said as Norman headed for the inner door.

"I think he will, tell him I'm here with the INS."

"I don't think he will."

"Just tell him, we'll wait."

"Ok, I will," she said with a hint of hostility. She had never had to deal with rough miners until now; she had just come from school back east and had only been in Tonopah for a few weeks.

It was just a few minutes and Mr. Belton appeared at the door. "Norm, how are you?"

"Not good as you can see, they're here for Alan. I thought we had that worked out."

"Yes, we do, come in and I'll bring you up to date. You officers can come in also." With that, they went into the office. He sat behind the large desk and they sat in chairs placed in front in a semicircle. "As of now there is a Bill in congress to give Alan relief of deportation. It will be signed by the President by the seventh of this month, June 1960, so I don't see any need for you to continue with this arrest warrant."

"We haven't received any notification of this," Flynn said angrily as he began to stand.

"I suggest you call your office and check, because it won't look very good if you made an arrest while the President is signing a relief bill in the detainee's behalf."

Flynn and his assistant stood up and left. That was the last time I would see him until much later.

"It looks like we can move on the adoption of the boys next month, if you're ready?" Mr. Belton said as the door closed behind Flynn.

"I think that would be good. Until next month then."

"I'll begin the paper work and call you. Oh you don't have a phone. You need to get one."

"I don't need one of those things, I get along just fine without it. Maybe when I get old. Just come up to the house and get me."

"Ok, Norman, see you later," he said as he began to move some papers from one side of the desk to the other.

"Cathy, could you come in here, I need to get an adoption going?" Cathy came in and as Norman left everything seemed to be on track.

Chapter 11

The Fourth of July parade of 1962 marched down the street and we watched from our seats on the raised curb. The curbs in Tonopah were 18" to 24" high and made excellent seats. These curbs were high because of the flash floods that happened here. I couldn't believe they had floods; Tonopah is 6000ft above sea level and on the side of a mountain, but I've seen the water flow over these curbs. I've seen the water run into the drug store and stand 8 inches on the floor; I've seen it push cars down the street and flow so hard you couldn't walk across the street. The rain would come and last about an hour, wash everything down to the far end of town and then just as suddenly stop and the sun would shine and the water would be gone. I've seen it snowing on one block, raining on another and the sun shining on the rest of the town all at the same time. They have a saying here: if you don't like the weather wait a moment and it will change to suit you.

Someone tapped me on the shoulder, I turned, thinking it was one of my school friends, but it was Mom and Raul. It had been over two years since she had been deported, and almost the same length of time since I had last seen her. Many things had changed. Both Bill and I had been adopted and a Special Bill had been passed in the 86th Congress to allow me to stay in the United States indefinitely. The Bill S.1223 had been completed on May 31, 1960, so it seemed I was to become a citizen and settle down to a normal life.

"How you goin'?" she asked as she hugged me. "Where is your brother"?

"There he is, marching down the street with the miner's hat on. If he marches in the parade he gets a silver dollar." I answered with some excitement. Being older, my friends and I thought it was not cool to march in the parade. That was the tradition from the beginning of Tonopah, the miners donated the money for the kids and some local dignitary would hand out the dollars at the end of the parade.

Mom waved at Bill and he broke from the line and ran to her with Norman and Neva close behind, they hadn't seen Mom and they thought he was just running away.

"Mary, how are you?" Norman said as he caught up with Bill, just as he jumped into Mom's arms.

"I thought he was on his way to the house or something." Bill was always like that, he would just take off and run to wherever he was headed without looking in any direction, he would just run to the spot he had focused on.

I remember once we were at the parade in Carson City on Nevada Day. He was standing next to us and then he was under a float with his hand under the tire. He wasn't hurt but it scared him and he was crying because his fingernail was broken, and his hand was red from the blood rushing to it after the tire rolled over it. I usually got into trouble for not watching after him. It always seemed to be my fault when he would run off get into trouble. I took it in stride because he was my bother and I suppose he was my responsibility, at least it would always work out that way.

Mom and Raul had come from Reno the night before and were staying at one of the motels in town. They had arrived late and thought it would be better to see us the next day. I was glad to see them. It had been a long time and I did miss Mom. Something seemed different, I didn't see Joe anywhere. Joe was always with Raul. "Where is Joe?" I asked Mom as she released me from her death grip hug.

"Raul thought it would be better if Joe stayed in Jamaica and looked after things, besides we needed a vacation. Mark is here somewhere, you know how he is, never seen until needed," she said. That was true you would see Joe, sometimes, but never Mark. "How are you, my friend?" Raul asked as he took my hand. That was a strange greeting. He had always referred to me as 'Alan'. I felt something was up. He shook my hand as he would anyone else and I had the feeling that they were here for more than just a vacation. "You must be Neva and Norman, I've heard very much about you both."

"Nice to meet you, I hope it was all good," Norm answered with a laugh and they shook hands. Then they began to converse in the normal small talk that people seem to engage in when they first meet.

Bill hung onto Mom and she held him close to her with her hand as she stood next to Raul and held his hand with her other hand. I stood next to Bill and we tried to listen to what they were saying. The parade went on by and disappeared down the street to the end where the dollars would be handed out. A hand grasped Bill on the shoulder and he turned with a start. "You forgot to collect you dollar young man, and here it is," the District Attorney announced as he handed Bill a shiny silver Dollar. "I know you didn't march in the parade, Alan, but here's one for you too. Maybe you'll be able to miss the swimming contests today since your mother is here." I usually would race in the swimming at the pool and would win some of the races, but today I thought I would not go to the races.

"Nonsense, you need to defend the Aussies in the swimming," Mom said as she looked at the DA. They looked at each other with intensity, everything stopped for that moment. They had been on different but strangely enough same sides in the exchange of custody of us kids, and her deportation.

"It's good to see you again, Mary, how are you, and who is this?"

"This is Raul. He is a friend from Jamaica, where I am now." They exchanged greeting and began the small talk again.

We went to the pool and I swam very well that day. I won every race I entered which was unusual. It could have been the extra backing that day. Mom stood up and cheered after each race. It felt good to have her there. Raul and Norm even got into the excitement of the day. Bill sat in between Norm and Mom leaning against Norm to shade himself from the sun. It was obvious from where I stood that Bill was the favorite child of Norm. He had his arm around him and seemed to tend to his every whim. I realized from that day on I was to be only second in his eyes. Mom looked at Norm and I think she saw the same thing, then she looked at me and I knew they were here for something more than a visit. The swimming races were over and I had made about ten or twelve dollars. Norm said I should share with Bill because he was unable to race. I didn't mind sharing with him, after all he was my brother and that's what brothers did, more over that's what families did. He was grateful and I gave him a hug, because I had always cared for him. I could remember the time in Tungsten, a bigger kid was beating on him. I ran down and threw the kid onto the ground, then pulled Bill away. Then I proceeded to punch the other kid until an adult came and pulled me off. I don't remember the whole fight, because when I get that angry I lose all sense of my surroundings and tend to block out everything but my opponent.

We left the pool and went to one of the restaurants in town, the Northern, and sat down to a meal. The small talk continued as we ate with only an occasional interruption from people Norm knew coming over to congratulate me and say hello to Norm. Raul and Mom seemed comfortable with the visit and Mom said, "Let's go to the house. We need to discuss a proposal with you, Norm and Neva. It's about Alan and Bill."

"Okay, I thought it would come to this, but I want you to know I have a lot invested in these boys and their life here is better than anything you could provide," Norm snapped back as he picked up the tab to pay for the meal.

"Please allow me to get that," Raul said, trying to ease the tension that had began to build between Norm and Mom.

"Okay, we'll see you at the house," Norm said, as he got up and motioned us to the door.

"Can I go with Mom?" I asked.

"Sure, if they have enough room," he said as he kept moving to the door.

"I'm sure we have the room, actually for both of them if they want to ride with us," Mom answered back.

"I want to go with my Dad," squeaked out Bill as he grabbed Norm's hand, and off they went leaving the rest of us standing at the check out counter. Mom looked at Raul and he looked back at her with that cold blank stare that I would learn meant something was about to change. We got to the house just a little behind Norm. He was standing in the doorway waiting for us and stepped out to confront Mom when she got out of the car.

"I don't know what you think you're going to do, but I assure you I will not stand for anything that involves these kids, do you understand.?" he said as he approached her with his hand raised and his finger in her face. Raul moved between them and Norm stopped short looking at him with a surprised expression. I had not seen this side of Norman. He was usually calm and had the situation under control. He was a man that had no fear of anything and would never back down if he were in the right. Once he had broken another man's jaw in a fight over whether he could go to town from a mining camp. I thought at that moment there would be a fight, but Norman backed away and listened to Raul as he spoke. Maybe it was because Bill and I were standing there and he didn't want to cause us to hate him for confronting Mom.

"I don't know about your past relationship, but now I think we should be civilized and discuss the proposal, don't you?" Raul said as he took Norm's hand from Mom's face.

"Maybe you're right, let's talk."

"Why don't you and I go over here and talk, while Mary and the boys visit," Raul said as he motioned Norm to the car. I would never know until many years later what had transpired between them.

Raul told Norm they were there to take me back to Jamaica and I would live there, with Mom and him, and Bill would remain in

Tonopah. Raul was very persuasive. I think some money exchanged hands to cover the costs that Norm had put out to get the adoptions and all the other expenses. The adoption was to be nullified and I was to pass back to Mom. The legislation in Congress giving me American citizenship was to remain, because the entire transaction was between Raul, Mom, and Norm.

Chapter 12

Three Days later I was in the house on the hill above Kingston, Jamaica. Joe was there to greet us at the airport and drive us back. "How are you, little man, I haven't seen you for a while?" he said as he put the bags in the trunk. It was good to see him again; I had missed his stories and his constant presence. Mom, Raul, and Mark sat in the back and I sat with Joe in the front, the car speeding through the streets to the house. It was a long winding road up to the house, causing the car to slow to a crawl. From up on the hillside, it was good to see the rolling hills, the beaches, and the sea curling onto the sand. There is not a better view in all of Jamaica than the one from the house on the hill. I had really missed the island and wondered what would be in store for my life. Raul and Mom didn't say much on the trip back since they mostly slept, but I was wide-awake for the whole flight, looking down at the ocean and the occasional island that passed by. The plane we traveled in belonged to the organization that Raul managed and it was much nicer than flying commercial planes. The entire inside had been gutted and redesigned for only ten passengers. Instead of the rows of seats with no leg room there were lounge chairs, couches, and room to walk all around the cabin without bumping into anything. A steward brought food and anything else you wanted for the entire trip. I must have eaten ten pounds of candy and chocolate, and of course as my stomach knew too well, that was more than enough. When we arrived there were no customs or officials, just Joe.

Raul had tracked Mom after she was deported for the second time; she had been sent to Sydney, Australia. I didn't know at the time but it was all planned that she would be deported and he would go and bring her back to Jamaica. She was now a part of the organization, the courier.

She had a reason to go to States, Bill, and would most always be deported and not imprisoned. This was a good arrangement for New York, Chicago and Kingston. She had relayed the deal giving Kingston the control of the 'material' flow for all concerned. This put Raul in an excellent position to gain wealth and power, and be able to control their future.

I would soon be part of the network and take over the courier position from Mom. I was to graduate from high school the next year and then attend a university in New York. I was to learn business from the legitimate side and during the vacations the business of the organization. I would move between Chicago and New York, learning as much as I could from the 'family' members with which I would eventually be associated. Raul didn't have any children and now I was to be his son and heir to the business when he and Mom decided to retire. I liked the way I was accepted by the circle because I had never really had friends, except for 'Blue' and they trusted me and gave me respect. This arrangement went on through my senior year at the university, then, as with all perfect arrangements it came to an abrupt end.

I was studying for a final in my apartment in New York and there was a knock at the door. Joe stood at the partially open door with his hat down around his eyes and his collar on his coat up in the back to his cover the lower part of his ears. It was late fall and it had been raining, the water dripped down from his hat to his shoulders.

"Joe, come in, get out of those wet things, how are you?" I said, as he pushed his way in almost before the door was open all the way.

"No time, you need to come home now, I'll get your stuff," he said, looking around as if he were to pack everything that moment.

"What's wrong?"

"Mister M has been shot. You need to come now before they get here."

"Get here, who is going to be here?"

"The same people who shot Mister M. Now stop asking questions and pack up what you need now. I'll have someone get the rest later. Mark has a car downstairs and the plane is at La Guardia. Let's go!" With that, he took me by the arm and we were down the stairs, in the car, and before I realized it, I was in the plane roaring down the runway.

After I had a chance to catch my breath I asked Joe what had happened. At this juncture I had a choice, to really become part of what I had been slated for or back away and hide behind the pretense of the 'circles' protection. Raul had really wanted me to become an honest businessman with latent ties to the 'circle', but now I had to make the choice. I thought hard and long while the plane sped toward Kingston. "We don't know who hired the him, but we have a make on the hitter," Joe told me as we arrived in Kingston. It was thought that a Columbian had hired the hitter to kill Raul so he could take over the Jamaican organization. He didn't say if Raul was dead or if Mom had been hit.

The man from Arkansas or Mississippi had gotten away, but it was known who he was, and it wouldn't be long before Raul's associates would have him. His name was Tommy Lee Herbert. He was a low life, a small-time back wood assassin and was not well known in the 'Business,' but he would be easy to find. They had a description and a profile of where he would go after he thought he had completed the 'job'.

"We'll go to the house to see how Mister M is then we will discuss our plans. Are you in Alan?" Joe asked with the expectation of a yes answer.

"You don't need to ask. Raul is like a father to me and we will take care of this problem without the help of the circle," I answered with the slow steady voice I had seen Raul use when discussing business. That was the first time I had seen any expression in Joe's face since he had gathered me up in New York. It was as though he approved and it made me feel good inside but I would not show any emotion.

The car pulled up the road to the house and Joe told me that we would go to the house and see what had happened to Raul. If he was alive, he would be giving orders and the assassin, along with the man who hired him, would not be long for this world. I hoped and prayed Raul would be all right and that Mom had not been in the same place when he had been shot. The house was like an armed camp; there were armed men along the road below the house, armed men around the gate, and along the wall surrounding the house. Joe motioned to the guard at the gate and he opened it to allow the car to pass through to the circle drive. Mom was standing in the front door when we arrived. This gave me relief from worrying about her, but still I had concern for Raul. Mom ran to the car as it pulled into the drive behind a hedgerow protecting the front door from view.

"Alan, are you all right?" she asked as she hugged me.

"I'm fine, Mom, how are you and where is Raul?"

"He's in the house, up in the bedroom. He's been shot."

"Yes I know."

We went to his bedside. He was lying there with his eyes covered with bloodstained gauze and I thought the worst. He'd been shot in the head. The bullet had entered through his left eye and lodged in the left front part of his brain after glancing off the inside of his skull. The lucky part was that it was a small caliber bullet, and his skull slowed it down. But they were unable stop the bleeding and felt he would die, so they allowed us to see him.

"Alan, Mary, are you alright?" he asked. His voice was not as strong as usual, but he could still speak very clearly even though his mouth was muffled by the bandage. He motioned Joe to his side and Joe leaned down to hear his whisper. Then Joe motioned to me to come over. I went to them and Joe said, "Sit down here next to Mister M."

I sat down and leaned toward him so I could hear whatever he wanted to tell me. He took my hand in his and pulled me closer so I would be the only one to hear.

"Now, listen very carefully, don't interrupt, I might not make it, so I want you to take over with Joe to help you. We need to stop the Columbians from taking the organization. You have the blessing from both New York and Chicago, but if it goes bad they will go with the Columbians. It's just business, you understand?" I nodded and he went on. "The assassin needs to be eliminated and also the one who hired him. How you do this will be up to you, but don't forget you need to send a strong message that we will not be intimidated, do you understand?" I nodded again to show I understood. "Also, don't forget, trust no one! This is business." With that I looked at Joe and for the first time I could understand what loyalty meant. I peered into his eyes and there it was, that sense of loyalty to this 'family'. With that, Joe came over and put his hand on my shoulder, motioning me to come with him. At that moment I knew I would do as Raul had asked. I knew my destiny would be with the family that had taken Mom and me into their world and gave us a purpose, and I welcomed it. I had a chance to return something to Raul.

Raul released my hand and Mom came over to kneel beside him, holding his hand while the doctors tried to repair his wound. They let Mom stay next to him even though she was partially in the way. Joe and I went to the large office; I had often seen Raul lay out his orders from here. Joe led me behind the large desk in the back facing the door, then he closed the door.

"I want you to know that I am loyal to this family and you have my undying pledge to do whatever you need to maintain its place in the organization," Joe said. Then he took my hand and kissed it as I had seen others do to Raul. I didn't know how to take this at first, but apparently I was the new Mister "M". There was a knock at the door and Joe opened it to allow Mark to enter. He came over to me and performed the same gesture of loyalty as Joe had before. I had not felt such respect or dedication in my life; I knew I had to assume the role with the same power and fairness as Raul. I knew that both Joe and Mark would be my power and they would do as I asked.

"Joe, I will need you and Mark to find the assassin, alive, and bring him here to the island."

"Are you sure you want him alive?"

"Yes, we need to have the name of the man who hired him."

"Okay, give us a week, and he will be here."

"Not here, at the boat dock," I said, as I turned my head to look out the window that was covered with a shear drape. They nodded and left. I stood there behind the desk and wondered what I would do to with my new position in life; I knew I would need the loyalty and guidance from Raul, Joe, and Mark. I stood there for what seemed ages running over in my mind, was I strong enough to do this. I knew I would have to get all the understanding I could from Raul before he died. I didn't want that, but I had to prepare for the worst.

I went back to the bedroom where Raul and Mom were to see if he was going to survive.

"Alan! They have stopped the bleeding and they say he will be all right, only he will be in recovery for a long time," Mom said when I entered the room. I was relieved because I knew he would be back in charge soon and in the meantime I would have his consul. I looked over to where he was. His head was bandaged and I could hardly see any part of his face. He was asleep. They had to sedate him to allow his mind to rest since it had been racing from the time he was shot until we arrived. It was the only thing that had kept him alive, before he could be taken to the house.

He had been shot while he was down at the other house collecting. Tommy Lee ran into the large room and shot him from a distance. Camille returned fire from behind the bar and Justin came in from the rear of the house. Tommy Lee only fired once and then ran out to a waiting car that sped toward town. Camille and Justin saved Raul from being shot several times, which was the plan of Tommy Lee, but with them there, the plan went awry. Justin tried to pursue them, but they had a head start and they disappeared in the narrow streets of Kingston. He just disappeared along with the driver. Justin thought he recognized the driver but he wasn't sure, so Joe and Mark would need to use some local 'talent 'along with Justin to find him. Finding the driver was a priority for Justin and he would not rest until he was found. Raul had treated everyone in his employ well and they had grown to care deeply for him. Everyone was looking for the driver, and Joe and Mark would be in the States looking for Tommy Lee.

Joe and Mark had been gone for about a week and things were starting to get back to normal. I had been very close to Raul for that time, he was schooling me in the ways of the business, and lucky for me I was able pick up on what he had to say. I spent almost every waking moment with him as he passed on to me the total operation of the business. He was recovering from his wound and seemed to be very calm with all that had happened. I sat with him and was spell bound by all he told me. He told of how he had followed his father's footsteps, learned the business and how to read people, that was the most important lesson of all. He would know one's intentions before the person knew what he was going to do, and with only a few words knew if he could trust them or not. This was a valuable lesson I would never forget. This lesson helped me in learning the way of how people would attempt to deceive you. He taught me in that week more than I had learned most of my previous life, and he was very calming as he spoke, he made you feel as if you had been in his sphere all your life. You seemed to turn into a sponge and soaked in his words, and understood everything he said, more clearly than at any other time of your life. I sat there next to his bed in the low light of his room and listened to him as he schooled me about everything I would have to know about the business. We seemed to be in another part of the world away from the island and were the only ones in that space……. Then it happened, bringing us back to reality.

The phone on the desk in the office down the hall rang. The butler picked it up. I could hear the butler answer, "Hello, Medina residence."

He came down the hall and said, "It is for you, Master Alan," then he went to the side table near Raul's bed and picked up the phone and handed it to me.

"Yes," I said.

"We have him, see you tomorrow." Then all I heard was dial tone, the phone had hung up. I knew it was Joe and he had done better than the week he asked for, it only took two days. We had still not found the driver, but I knew that wouldn't be much longer either. I knew finding the driver would be hard because no one had really seen him, but Tommy Lee would help us with that, if Justin didn't find him before they came back. I felt it would only take a little persuasion for Tommy Lee to tell us who had hired him and we could proceed to send the message that Raul had suggested.

It was 8:00am and I could see Joe and Mark bringing Tommy Lee down the dock to the fishing boat where I was waiting. I was reminded of the days with Lonnie when I would be waiting, but now I was the one in control and I would use all the lessons I had learned as I watched him maintain control. The times I had watched Raul in his dealing would come into play also; always remain calm.

They had Tommy Lee between them with his hands tied behind his back, each one had an arm and they were semi-dragging him along. The others on the dock paid no attention to what was happening, because they were aware of what had happened to Raul and he was well liked on the fishing dock.

"Good morning, pleasant day for fishing," I said to Joe as he pushed Tommy Lee onto the swim platform and through the back gate into the cockpit against the fixed fishing chair. Mark climbed into the seat behind the wheel. I turned and signaled him, and the boat pulled out into the channel and headed for the breakwater, and from there to the sea. We were soon beyond the horizon, the engine stopped and we began to drift with the current. Joe tied Tommy Lee's hands to the hoist and swung him out onto the swim platform. I sat in the fishing chair and Joe and Mark stood on either side.

"I need to ask you a few questions and your well-being will be determined by the answers you give," I said, looking deep into his eyes with a blank cold stare. That stare I had learned by watching both Raul and Joe. It was also the same look I had inherited from Mom.

"Ya'll git nothing outa me!" he yelled.

"Maybe, maybe not, we will see. Joe did you bring the tools I told you to bring?"

"Yeah! Did you want to see?"

"No, but I think our quest would like to see them." With that Joe opened the case, showing a variety of knives.

"Ya'll think I scared?"

"I know you're not, but neither am I." I told Joe that for every wrong answer cut off a piece of his skin and throw it overboard. Joe took out one of the knives, cut off Tommy Lee's shirt and threw it overboard, then motioned to me he was ready to continue. I began with the name and location of the driver. Tommy Lee spit at me. Joe reached over, cut off a large piece of his left breast and threw it over the side. Tommy Lee looked at me and then at Joe with a look of disbelief. I again asked the same question. This time he first looked at Joe and then at his bleeding chest and blurted out a name and address. Mark wrote it down and I continued with the next question.

"How much were you paid?"

"I don't think that is any your business." Joe reached over and cut off another piece of flesh, and threw it over the side. I asked the question again.

"$10,000 plus expenses."

"That's not much to put your life at risk." This went on for an hour, then I asked the question we really wanted to know: who hired him?

"I can't tell. They will kill me and my family, please don't ask me that."

"It appears to me that your life is in my hands at this moment, so it would be wise for you to tell me, and don't worry about your family. We will protect them." He was now bleeding profusely and

I knew we would have to get the name soon or he would die. The offer to protect his family seemed to strike a nerve, but he wanted his safety to be included in the bargain. I agreed and he told the whole story including a name and location. Juan Carlos, a small time drug dealer from Chicago, who thought he could take over the trade route, and gain more respect with the Columbia connection. We had made an error in assuming it was orchestrated from Columbia, but now we knew all we needed to know and we could act accordingly. We still needed to send a message and I knew what that message would be. I drew back on my Scottish heritage and decided to send the same message that was sent to the old English Kings. I motioned to Joe to come to the cabin so I could tell him the plan out of earshot of Tommy Lee.

"We need to pick up the driver and then go to Chicago, find this Carlos, cut off their heads, put them on stakes in front of their houses, putting Tommy Lee's in front Carlos's house also. We need to send a message that we will not be intimidated or taken over. I want this message to be understood by all those who might think that since Raul has been attacked and may be out of the picture, we are still in charge of this organization. Do you understand?"

"Yes! I do, and it will be done," Joe assured me, and I knew from his conviction that it would be done very soon. We went back out to where Mark was standing, and I gave the gesture to finish the job, then I returned to the cabin. I could hear Tommy Lee pleading with Joe as Mark finished the job and threw the body into the sea for the waiting sharks. Mark packed the head into a leak-proof canvas bag. The engine started and we were on our way back to port. I had time to reflect on the events of the day, and how it had changed me.

I now had no compulsion about killing a rival in a business sense and I felt no remorse about Tommy Lee, Carlos, or the driver's fate. I felt they had chosen that path and whatever happened was more their fault than mine. I wondered if Raul would regain his health and I would be relieved of the position he had placed me in. I knew of the responsibility of the position and of the people who depended on the organization and now I was the organization.

Raul was asleep and Mom was sitting in the large room waiting to see if the operation on his head had been successful.

"How is he?" I asked as I came up to her from across the room.

"I don't know. They said it would be at least two to three days before we would know if the operation was a success. I fear he might not regain consciousness, and that would just kill me."

"I'm sure he will be all right, Mom, you know how strong he is," I assured her as I hugged her to show support for her grief. We stayed in that embrace until she felt she could believe he would be all right, and then I left her for the office where some of his minions were waiting for the same assurance. Camille was the first to greet me. "Now that yar' the new Mister "M", what are ya' goin' ta do?" she asked for the entire crowd that had assembled in the office. Justin was standing next to her along with most of the staff from the 'house'.

"I think the best for us to do is continue as before, and when Mister "M" recovers he will come back as if nothing had happened. In the mean time, Mark will come every Thursday and collect, the same as Mister "M". I know this is a little out of the ordinary, but I need to concentrate on the rest of the organization. "

"Okay! If tha's what ya' want, we'll take care and ya won' have to worry yar head about anythin'. Justin and I will watch da house for ya an' the others will do their jobs." That was all I needed to hear. I knew they would do what needed to be done and be loyal to the organization. After they left, Joe came in and told me they had found the driver and Mark had completed the job. The message would be sent at the same time as Carlos. He would be on the plane with Mark that evening and I would be hearing from them in a few days.

This is the hardest part of anything, waiting. Mom paced the floor outside the bedroom waiting for any sign Raul would awaken. Raul lay on the other side of the door, motionless with tubes in his arms, and under a plastic tent. She would pace the floor outside then go inside to check and see if he had moved. The strain was getting to her and I could see she might slip back to her dependence on alcohol. I sent for Justin to come and take her into town to the market to try and get her mind off Raul for a brief time.

"I don't need to go to the market! I need to be here, and I need to be near when Raul wakes up."

"Mom, it would be better if you gave yourself a rest. I will tell you when he wakes up."

"No! I need to be here just like your grandmother was when your grandfather was near death. You need to understand that." I put my hands on her shoulders and felt the strength of Grandmum as she spoke, and I knew it would be useless to try to send her to the market.

Suddenly the nurse appeared beside us and declared Raul had moved and could possibly be awake soon. We both went to his side and it was true, he had moved his arms and his eye was twitching as if he was in the REM stage of sleep. We stayed by his side in anticipation of his waking.

My thoughts drifted back to what Mom had said about my grandparents, and to the story of theft and betrayal. How they had worked hard and then had their life work stolen from them. I had often thought about the betrayal and the outright theft from my grandparents and if I had ever had an opportunity to right this wrong I would do it. Now I had the power, maybe only temporarily, to change that crime against my family. Raul always told me during my training that there was nothing more important than the family. I began to form a plan in my mind to avenge that wrong. As I drifted in and out of the plan, Mom suddenly grabbed my arm. "He's awake! Look he's awake." I looked at Raul as he tried to speak. I couldn't understand his words but it did seem he was going to be all right. He raised his hand and Mom knelt, took his hand and brought it to her tear-covered face. These were tears of joy and he responded with a tear in his eye. I touched his shoulder and he nodded to me in approval. I left them and returned to the office to formulate the plan to get the factory back for the family. I'm sure

Raul would approve. I would have a plan together by the time Joe and Mark completed their task in Chicago.

The phone rang and I answered. "We have the rest of the connection," said the voice on the phone, "and we will complete the message tonight. Tell Justin the other message needs to be done tonight as well." Then he hung up and I left to go the 'house' and tell Justin to complete his part of the message.

The next day in the Chicago paper the headlines read, "Headless body found in Grant Park." The story went on to say that two heads were on a stake in front of a known drug dealer's house and they thought one of the heads belonged to the body found in the park. The other head didn't appear to have any connection to the known dealers in the area. The Jamaican paper also had an article on a head on a stake in front of a local man's house, but there was no body to be found. I read the articles to Raul and he nodded in approval and looked at me with a new respect. I wanted to be sure he would approve so I took his hand and put it to my heart to show I was still his loyal servant. He looked at me and smiled. I thought I would tell him of my plan about Jack's grandson, Jason, to avenge my grandparents in Australia. I wanted his support and approval because I felt he was still the driving force in the organization. I had the plan pretty well worked, but I needed to find out what secret Jason had that I could use against him. This would be the prime factor of the plan. I needed some way to humiliate him and his family, then I would have him killed as a final insult. I would be there at the final insult, to show him who it was that brought his family down. I knew from the stories that I heard over the years, they had interest in many illegal activities throughout Australia and Japan. If this information were to come out, his position in Parliament would be ended. But I needed more, I needed their fortune to be eliminated along with their lives.

I was called into Raul's bedroom and he was lying there with his single eye staring at the ceiling. "What is it, Mister "M"? I asked.

"Come over next to the bed. I need to tell you something and I want you to understand every word. The rest of you leave us." Everyone went out of the room and closed the door. "Alan, I want you to take over permanently. That will mean you will be in charge of all operations and you will be the one everyone will depend on, do you understand?"

"I think so. Do you think I'm ready?"

"I have been grooming you for this since I brought you from Tonopah. Your mother and I will be retiring and we will be moving to the small house on the hill. I have had a lot of improvements done and as soon as I am on my feet we will be moving there. I have already contacted the rest of the circle and they agree. So what do you say?"

"I don't know what to say. Should I thank you or should I curse you?" He laughed; it was good to hear him laugh again. I thought it would be good to tell him more about what I had alluded to before when I was telling him about my grand parents, this time to get his final advice and if he thought I should continue with the plan.

"That would be up to you, what I think is not important."

"It is to me."

"If you think it would give closure to your family, then I would say go ahead."

"Thank you! That is all I need." He squeezed my hand, released it and I left to see Joe who was waiting for me. Joe had returned from Chicago and had a report on how it went with the message. I knew that the other small time dealers and any one else with designs on our organization would understand that we would not treat any aggression against us lightly. He was waiting in the office when I got there and after I went around the desk and faced him he began. "The message was well received and from the talk on the streets you are not one to cross. Mark is still in Chicago, and he will see the family connections in both Chicago and New York to ascertain their reaction. He should be back in two days. Is there anything else we need to do?"

"Yes, actually there is, but it will wait until Mark gets back. You should go and see Mister "M", he was asking about you." Joe excused himself. Mom came through the door just as Joe was leaving, they exchanged pleasantries and she came in.

"Alan, how you goin'?" she asked as she came over and hugged me.

"I'm okay, Mom, and you?"

"I'm better now that Raul in recovering, and should be up and about soon. I understand you are in charge now and Raul is going to retire."

"Yes, I just found out today. I hope I will be able to keep everything together."

"Raul would not have given this responsibility to you if he thought you couldn't handle it."

"I have something to tell you and I might need you advice, we are going to correct a wrong from along time ago."

"What do you mean 'a long time ago'?"

"The cheese factory." That's all I needed to say and Mom knew what I meant. We had often talked of this injustice and the revenge of it. I began to tell her of the plan I had put together in my mind and how I was going to humiliate the Carrigans. My only problem was what secret did Jason have that we could use against him. I would need to send Joe to Australia for research and that, I felt, would take time.

"Honey, you don't have to do that. Remember the cab driver in Brisbane? He would be happy to get what you need. I could call or better yet, I will go to Brisbane and find what you need."

I told her I didn't want her to go because it was too dangerous, and I was sure Joe could find out anything we needed. She put her hand up to my lips to stop me from talking and told me Joe would go with her for protection and she would get the information and that was all there was to it. She looked at me and felt she had made her point, then went off to tell Raul she would be away for a few days. Mom had a way of finalizing a conversation and getting her way. A week later she and Joe were on the plane to Australia. There was nothing for me to do but wait until they returned with the information.

They were greeted by the cab driver and he was soon on board with the assignment. He said he thought Jason sampled the girls at the waterfront brothel and could get the information from the madam. Mom and Joe set up house in one of the hotels as tourists so as not to attract attention. The cabbie would give them the information from the madam on when Jason would be at the brothel and which girl was his regular companion. There came an unexpected twist in his sexual preference, he was a switch hitter. We could not have been luckier, and this would be a big advantage. He would bring his male friend with him and they would go into the room with the girl. She would give Jason head and at the same time his friend would enter him from the back. This was pretty sick but it was just what we needed. Joe called me with the news and wanted to know how I wanted it handled. I told him we needed to film the act and then, we would have the first part of the scenario. Next we needed to look into his finances. I needed to contact New York because they had a connection in the worldwide banking industry and they would be able to provide the money trail. This would take some time, but after all these years a little more time wouldn't hurt. The madam agreed, along with the girl, that we could film the activity and no one would know because they both had no use for Jason or any of the Carrigans. Things were starting to fall into place and Mom could come home, but Joe would stay to collect the film and make sure all went well. Joe made contact with the Madam and told her the filming would have to be done within the next two weeks. Could she arrange it with the girl? Joe would install the camera and make sure it was not seen by Jason or anyone else. I called New York and was told the money trail would be uncovered and I would have all I needed, so I could proceed with the plan. I wanted to force him to give the 'Cheese Factory' back to the family or, at the bare minimum, pay for the forced take over by his father. I found at this time in my life it was good to be connected, connected to sources that could circumvent authority and had access to vital information that you needed.

The camera was in place, the trace placed on the money, the girl and Madam lined up and Joe was there to collect the tape. I knew it wouldn't be too long until Jason would request a session.

Mom came home and said, "I saw some of my old friends and I found I really don't miss that life. As soon as Raul gets on his feet we will retire, like he said, and let you run the business." Then she left to go to Raul's room.

I followed her out of the room and down the hall to check on Raul. She went into the room and I looked in to see him wave me on, and I knew he was okay.

I returned to the matter at hand, setting the stage for the family revenge. The telephone rang; answering it I heard what I had hoped.

Jason and his father had been transferring their finances through Japan, to the Bank of England, and back to Australia, to avoid the taxman. Now, with Jason in Parliament, this would be the perfect embarrassment, and with his sexual proclivities, it would destroy Jack's family for many years to come.

"Alan, I have the film. You should come down here and finish this."

"Good, I'll be down within the next two days. I need to go to New York first. Have Jason waiting for me in some convenient location so we can present our proposal to him."

"Okay, I'll have everything ready when you get here. Do we need a boat?"

"Not this time. I think we can handle this without a boat, but maybe it won't hurt to be ready to do a little "fishing". Line one up, just in case."

The trip to New York gave me time to reflect. Would it give closure to Grandmum and all she had suffered through Jack's action? I wondered if Graham would realize that we had revenge or if he had blocked out everything from that dreadful day when Millie was killed. These thoughts raced through my mind and I wondered if I would gain closure as well.

New York was cold and the wind whipped around the buildings as the cab dropped me at my destination. I met my contact and he gave me the package. I would be able to digest its contents over the next two days while on my way to Australia.

Joe was waiting at the Brisbane Airport, "Have a nice trip?"

"Just like any other, long and tiring."

"Everything is set and I have a boat chartered if we need it, for "fishing"."

"Good. Is our guest comfortable?"

"I think so, he hasn't complained."

"Does he know I'm coming and does he know the connection?"

"I'm not sure but you can explain it so he will understand the connection." With that we got into the cab Mom's friend was driving and headed to our destination. Jason had a puzzled look as I came into the room Joe had set up for him. He was sitting on a hard backed chair with his hands tied behind, facing the wall.

"Hello, Jason, I'm Winifred's grandson. Maybe your father mentioned Winifred and the 'Cheese Factory'? I'm here to show you a video you might like."

Joe started the video and we sat down to watch. I could only watch for a few moments. I stood up, went out onto porch and waited for it to end. "It's done. I think he wants to talk," Joe said as he stepped out.

"Okay, let's see what he has to say."

"You Yanks think you can come down here and dictate policy. Well, when my organization gets done with you, you'll wish you never heard of Australia...."

"I think you need to rethink that statement, you see I'm Australian and at this time in your life, I will be the one who will determine if my friend here ends your life or allows you to continue breathing. You see, I have other evidence you might be interested in," I said as I brought the papers showing the trail from Australia to England and back again. His eyes strained at the documents in the dim light of the room. He studied the trail and looked up saying, "You have nothing, all this could be a fabrication and with my press connections, I don't think it will get too far." I had thought about this and had already made a move to have everything printed. He thought he had connections, but with the help of New York and Chicago, the film and the story of the money transfers would be printed.

"Joe, is the boat ready?" I asked, looking at Jason with that stare I had learned from Joe, the one where you looked through someone while talking to him. "I think we need to go fishing."

"I can have it ready in fifteen minutes. Would you like to use the packaged 'chum' or will we be making our own?"

"I think we'll make our own. Bring him!"

The cabbie, Mom's friend, brought the cab around to the front of the building and Joe escorted Jason to the back seat. We drove to the dock where the boat was waiting and went on board. Joe pushed the throttle forward and we headed for the open ocean. We crossed over the horizon, just out of sight of land. Joe throttled back the engines and the boat began to drift with the current. The sea was calm and the only sounds were the seagulls diving at the surface fish off the port bow. The sea churned behind us and revealed a group of sharks heading to the surface fish to take their share from the gulls. Jason had no idea what was in store. He was still just as arrogant as before until Joe began to stroke the straight razor up and down on the leather strap.

"What are you going to do?"

"Well you see, we have a proposal for you. You will sign over the factory to the remaining family or pay for it at the fair market value in today's pounds and then increase Graham's allotment to what ever I determine, or this will be your last fishing trip."

"You must be crazy, do you know who I am? I'm in Parliament, a respected representative of the Australian people and you won't get away with this, whatever you think your going to do!" I nodded to Joe and he took Jason's arm and cut a small piece from it and threw it overboard, then held his bleeding arm over the stern. I will never forget the look of disbelief that came over Jason's face. He had never seen or experienced the brutality of organized crime. I nodded again and Joe reached for the razor to take another piece. Jason tried to pull away but the blade caught another piece of flesh and it was gone. The water behind the boat began to churn as the smell of blood spread to the olfactory senses of the waiting sharks.

"This is how we make our own chum, and we will continue until we come to an understanding on this matter before us. I have with me the papers to conclude this transaction, if you are in agreement."

"What guarantee do I have that I will get back from this trip?"

"Actually none, but if you sign the papers it will go much easier for you."

"Alright! Alright, I'll sign then you can kill me quickly."

I put the papers on the stern gunwale and handed him a pen. He signed and then stepped to edge of the swim platform expecting a small caliber shot to the back of his head. He was sobbing as he stood there expecting the sting of the hot bullet as it passed through his skull into his brain. I was looking at this pathetic excuse of a man when my attention was drawn to the sky. There, in all its glory, was a bright yellow Cessna airplane, circling around us several times and then back to the Mainland. I thought of the bright yellow model Cessna that my Grandmum and I had worked on together so many years before. I heard her voice, the familiar voice that I had not heard in so many years, saying to me, "Let it go, Luv! It's not worth tainting the family's honor!" I looked at Joe with the gun in his hand, the hammer back, waiting for my signal. I waved him away and pulled Jason back on board.

"Take us home, Joe, and get a bandage for this arm, so this scum doesn't dirty-up our boat."

WE HAD WHAT WE CAME FOR AND WITH THE HELP OF NEW YORK AND CHICAGO, JACK'S FAMILY NAME WAS SMEARED AND JASON'S CAREER WAS OVER...THAT WAS ENOUGH. WINIFRED'S FAMILY HONOR WAS SATISFIED AND I WAS SURE THAT SHE WOULD BE PROUD OF HER GRANDSON...THE "EXCESS BAGGAGE"... FOR MAKING THE RIGHT DECISION FOR THE FAMILY.